With thanks to Julie Huffer who painstakingly read through and edited this book. Thanks also to Christine Newman who encouraged me to start writing and supported me throughout.

Bed One. Kent

I think it would be fair to say that if you had used the phrase Grey Nomad a few years ago very few people outside of Australia would have had the faintest idea what you were talking about. Now however there is an ever increasing number of these restless retirees tramping around the globe in search of, actually I'm not sure what they are in search of and if I am totally honest I'm not entirely certain what my wife and I were in search of when we decided to join their ranks. I think it was probably just a change and a chance to see parts of the world that had simply been pictures in books and magazine and episodes in various television travel shows.

For us, and for me especially the years leading up to July 2015 had become a bit of a drudge. I was not coping well with the daily expectations of a senior member of the school common room. Small things were starting to get under my skin and I felt certain that it was only a matter of time before senior management caught the full fury of a tiring teacher and the resulting fall out was unlikely to end well. Colleagues were, I am certain, becoming blasé if not totally bored of the regular rants about how it used to be, and what should be done to change things. I am equally sure that some of these perhaps regret that my retirement came before the anticipated eruption as they would dearly have loved witness the old man of the staff room let rip at a management regime that was at best ill-informed and at worst verging on incompetent.

My wife and I retired on the same day after teaching for close to 60 years in all and over 40 at one school. We had seen our own children pass through our care and had the immense privilege to work alongside some truly inspirational men and women. Sadly, we had also worked with too many prats especially towards the end of our careers as the teaching profession moved from being education and pupil centred to administration and protocol centred.

We saw the end coming and it was not a gentle run in. Seldom if ever do two people have exactly the same ambitions for the future and we were no different to other mature couples. Countless hours were spent discussing, arguing, fighting and occasionally agreeing about the best way forward. Could we afford to stop working? Would I be bored with nothing to do all day? Where would we live? These questions when answered invariably gave rise to other difficult questions and more heated debate. One thing was, however, totally clear and indeed set in stone. Retirement was going to happen at the end of the summer term. I knew this as I had handed in my resignation prior to Christmas 2014. My wife was less sure and held out until almost the last day of the Easter term before finally handing in her resignation letter.

Anyway enough of the preamble, let me introduce ourselves. I am James, mostly called Jim, and I am a 59 years old recently retired PE teacher. I trained at Loughborough Colleges, as all good PE teachers did and spent 38 years in the profession. I did the hard yards in the early years working in North London at an all-boys comprehensive school. It was tough going and indeed quite brutal. The vast majority of the discipline at the school came via the sports department and students who fell foul of the PE staff generally regretted it. It was here that I started to develop a wanderlust and a desire to travel. Sports tours to France, Italy, Portugal and Germany along with alpine ski trips ignited a fire that has burned ever since. These trips in the late 70's and early 80's were very adventurous especially in tough London schools, but I loved planning and running them.

My wife of over 25 years is Andrea. After several years working in London for British Gas and then Decca Records she became a home economics teacher. She changed track mainly because she got fed up spending hours travelling into London every day. One of her claims to fame is that she taught at the school attended by one David Beckham although she never actually had him in her classes. Andrea is a home maker first and foremost and takes enormous pride in our house, the garden and the little things that generally go unnoticed by most men, sportsmen in particular. Had it not been for her I would have jumped ship two or three years earlier but her insistence that our pensions would be hammered and we would end up in the 21st century equivalent of a workhouse made me toil on. Andrea was still uncertain that retirement was the correct path when she handed in her letter of resignation.

My mind was made up and the only thing that troubled me was what should come next. I had a master plan and it was simple. Rent out our highly desirable house in a quiet Kentish village, and rent something cheaper in Spain, France or Italy and live on the balance. After a couple of years in the sun we could return home and none of the little buggers at school would even recognise us as we shopped or lunched in the village where we had taught and our children had grown up. I would even be able to watch the school 1st xv on Saturday mornings without too many conversations about the great teams of 1998 and 2003.

This master plan did not go down well with Andrea and I was faced with a barrage of questions every time the subject was raised. What's the point of doing that? What will we do all day? What shall we do with our stuff? (not an unreasonable question). How will we see our friends?

None of these things seemed particularly difficult to overcome but Andrea still had her knockout blow to land.

"I don't want to live abroad" she said; It will not be my house or my garden, so I'm not going. This was a real stumbling block and the only alternative was to reach a compromise.

After hours and hours of often heated debate and some very mature interventions from our children a compromise was achieved. We would not move abroad for a fixed period of time. Neither would we move directly from the school boarding house, where we were house parents, into our house in the village. We would travel for a few months, get away from it all, allow time to pass for the students and staff to forget us. This is how we became members of the Grey Nomads and how our adventure began.

Once this decision was made I clicked into organisational mode and there was a lot to be done. Much of it was stuff that I really enjoyed, booking flights, researching hotels and planning routes. Then there was the boring stuff like what would we do with our car and where would all of our belongings go and hardest of all who would look after Florence our slightly eccentric and very old cat. This side of the planning held no real interest to me but was the type of stuff Andrea kept on about most of the time. This did keep my enthusiasm in check a little bit and certainly kept my feet closer to the ground if not actually on it.

Friends played a key role during this planning period and mostly without even knowing that they were doing it. At the countless farewell bashes and leaving events the conversation inevitably turned to our plans. Andrea mostly replied in the same unenthusiastic manner, "Well that's really down to Jim" or "Actually Jims planning that side of things."

The plan was we were to buy a round the world flight and spend at least six months travelling to distant shores. The enthusiasm and envious comments from those listening gave me a great boost and made Andrea cower and cringe. Despite her agreeing to the plan she was still taking a massive amount of convincing that it would be a fantastic adventure and not be a punishment. Living out of a suitcase for over half a year was not something that filled her with enormous excitement. It did not seem that any of our friends shared her rather pessimistic outlook much to her dismay.

From this point on however there was no going back, and the actual point of no return was reached over supper one evening in January when I told Andrea that I had been researching around the world air tickets and it was time we booked one.

Students seemed to get good deals in the flight bucket shops dotted along Islington High Street and more importantly you didn't have to be a student to use these services. After a few phone calls and an exchange of emails with a nice man called Geoff I arranged an appointment during the February half term at the aptly named "Round the World Flights" office.

Andrea was in shock as we arrived at the door and although she had accepted the inevitable I think she still hoped that something or someone would change my mind. Geoff was certainly not going to try and do that as he enthusiastically ran through potential itineraries. I settled for seven stops in one direction with sufficient air miles included to make certain we could get back home. I did find it a little bizarre that some tickets knowingly sold as around the world actually had insufficient air miles and thus you could end up stuck in Argentina or the Azores. I had of course already spent time on the agency's web site and worked out that with seven stops and a bit of overland travel we should end up back in England.

Andrea's was stalling when she suggested that we go for coffee and have one last think before producing the magic plastic and paying for the flights. We sat nursing our coffee in a pub next to a rather inviting Brazilian restaurant at the end of Islington High Street. Andrea worried about, malaria, losing passports, snakes, spiders, pick pockets, and finally the quality of the airlines. "Surely" she said "at this price we must be flying with Air Afghan or Papua Airlines." I made no comment as this had already crossed my mind and agreed that if the airlines were not reputable we would go away and think again. Andrea smiled, hopeful her ace may might do the trick.

Geoff grinned broadly from behind his desk " Emirates followed by Qantas and finally BA." The die was cast Andrea's ace had been trumped and my credit card was placed on Geoff's desk. We discussed dates and decided to leave from Gatwick at the end of the first week in September, coincidentally the end of the first week of the 2015/16 school year. I did not choose this date to piss off my former colleagues although judging from the farewell emails we received it may well have had that effect.

The tickets cost just over £2000 each and allowed us to change the dates of flights once without incurring extra cost. Geoff explained that we could add extra flights with local airlines without this affecting our initial tickets. We chose our stops and set approximate dates and left the agency with the bare bones of our trip in place. The route was to be Dubai, Sri Lanka, Cambodia, Vietnam, Thailand, Malaysia, Indonesia, Australia, New Zealand, Chile, Uruguay, Brazil and Argentina. Our seven stops were Dubai, Colombo, Singapore, Siem Reap, Brisbane, Christchurch and Santiago. Our seven take offs points were of course different in order to manage the air miles. These were Dubai, Colombo, Singapore, Bali, Sydney, Auckland and Buenos Aires

I began planning in earnest and there was plenty to do. Andrea and I made the decision to rent out our house for the period of the trip. We calculated that with our pension money and the rental income we would be more or less in profit whilst in SE Asia and probably down a bit in the other countries. This would hopefully result in the trip breaking even. Any excess would be more than covered by our lump sum pension retirement payments. Andrea set about finding a well-respected local letting agent and a suitable tenant was contracted to move into our village house at the end of September.

I left Andrea in charge of putting our belongings into storage, not because I was uninterested but because everything I suggested was either wrong or very wrong. It wasn't straightforward as we needed to think about what to do when we got back so the contents of our containers needed to be carefully considered. It very quickly became clear that carefully thinking things out is not a great strength of removal men. At Andreas request I actually missed the first of two visits by the removal crew. She thought it better that I be on the golf course rather than " helping with the packing". I returned after a very fine round and a couple of beers to find that several of the items I had planned to personally take with me had been packed by the men. That left me without a kindle and my travel backgammon. I could think of no reasonable explanation as to why they would pack these things but they had. I also found that storage does not come cheap but we were still well in profit when the rent minus the storage cost was calculated.

I busied myself getting familiar with the places we were due to visit, visa requirements, inoculations and the like. It was an interesting process although in the initial stages it was very much my solo task as Andrea continued to ignore the fact we were going in the vain hope that it would go away.

I decided that I did not want anything left to chance in the first few weeks of our trip, the thought of turning up in Colombo or anywhere else for that matter with no accommodation booked was not something I wanted. I had this image in my head of two oldies standing on a street corner, having got off a bus, one with a back pack and the other a suitcase and having nowhere to stay and ending up sleeping in a park or by the railway line. I found booking.com a really user friendly site that allowed accommodation to be secured without a deposit and give me the freedom to make changes up to a pre advised date. I also spent hours reading reviews on TripAdvisor another very helpful site. I loved this process and as each hotel or home stay was booked my expectation and excitement increased.

I booked accommodation in Dubai, Colombo, Kandy, Mirissa Beach and Galle as well as a three-day package to the Sinharaja rainforest. Having done this, I felt certain that we were organised for the first few weeks and after this we would be confident enough to book as we moved along. Suddenly Andrea began to add her opinions, could we visit this place or that place? What are the beaches like in Mirissa? Will there be mosquitoes'. I seldom had an accurate answer but these were the first signs that Andrea was firstly accepting of the venture and secondly doing a bit of research herself. I also noticed the odd page from the Times or Telegraph travel supplements appearing on the bathroom reading shelf or the dining table.

Next on my "to do list" were the visas. These were pretty straightforward. None required for Dubai, Malaysia, New Zealand or South America. On-line visas for Sri Lanka and Australia. On entry visas for Cambodia and Indonesia (the latter were actually scrapped before we travelled). So only one visit to a London embassy to get a Vietnamese visa which I thought was pretty expensive. These were £55 each and in the end were not needed as the rules changed about a month after I bought them. So much for being ahead of the game.

The final weeks prior to take off were a bit of a blur. Sorting out what to take with us and how best to carry it. I opted for a backpack and took sound advice about which one to buy. I spent a happy couple of hours in Tunbridge Wells with a mate who was very knowledgeable and had a discount card for field and trek. The advice he gave me was invaluable as an ill-fitting backpack is so uncomfortable to carry around. Andrea decided on a suitcase on wheels. I opted for minimal extras while Andrea opted for lots of shampoo, sun creams etc. I strangely assumed that most of this stuff would be on sale in other countries while my wife assumed that it would not. I still find it hard to understand female thought processes.

Inoculations can be expensive but fortunately I did not need many as I was pretty much up to date. I opted out of rabies jabs as I felt it unlikely that I would be bitten by dogs and even less likely to receive a nip from a bat or a monkey. Japanese encephalitis was a potential issue in South East Asia but it is spread by mosquitoes which have been feeding on pigs and since a lot of the region is Muslim pig farms are not abundant. Andrea chose to be vaccinated against five of the more common diseases, Hep A and B, tetanus, polio and yellow fever. She left them all a little late and consequently had them close together. I do not recommend this to other travellers as sore arms and flu like headaches are not good bedfellows.

We took our cat Florence to our youngest daughter Sophie's home in the west country as she had agreed to look after her for the period of our trip. The journey was fraught as Florence is not a car cat and always gets very nervous. No relaxed sleeping in her warm carrying case for her. She simply sits and either meows, poos, pees or jumps around like a demented flea. Three hours later we were glad to drop her off at Sophie's and breathe some fresh air. We also said goodbye to Sophie during this visit even although she desperately wanted to see us off at the airport. I knew that Sophie and Andrea would not have coped well with an emotional airport goodbye.

To soften the blow of us leaving I had bought Sophie a return ticket to Australia so that she could meet up with us and spend a couple of weeks with our other daughter, India, who was living in Brisbane. Tactically this was one of my great moves and seemed to make everyone in the family a good deal more content. Despite Sophie being very capable 25-year-old nurse she was still very much the baby of the family and Andrea would miss her enormously.

The day of our departure finally arrived. Our taxi met us at 06.30 hrs and we set off for Gatwick initially, and the rest of the world ultimately. I pretended to be cool and in charge but I was nervous. There were so many things to be concerned about but if I am totally honest I was most concerned about how Andrea and I would get on with one and other with no real chance to spend time apart. Would we drive one another mad or would it help us to really start to understand each other in a way that working life simply does not permit. Only time would tell.

Bed 2 Its hot in the City

We landed in Dubai late afternoon and caught a cab into the city. I had booked us into an Airbnb apartment close to the Burj Kalifa building. Amazingly the taxi driver could not find the address despite its proximity to one of the world's most famous, and indeed tallest buildings. As we drove around with Ahmed asking us if we knew the way, the first potential crack in the Jim/Andrea travel plan began to widen. Andrea turned to me quietly said "why are we looking here? shouldn't we be at the Palm?"

I told her that she had insisted I book a room close to the Burj Kalifa. Her reply shocked me a little as she said that the building on the Palm shaped like a sail was the said building. I explained that that particularly building was in fact the Burj Al Arab. Andrea unperturbed by this, said "well you should have known that I wanted to stay there I just got the name wrong." Fortunately, at point the taxi driver hit on the idea of phoning our Airbnb to get directions and attention was temporarily deflected from debating the location of various Emirates buildings.

My conversation with Andrea in the taxi did however give me a great insight into how to manage tricky situations. Clearly being logical and right was insufficient, Andrea would simply use illogical arguments to strengthen her case. The fact that I had correctly identified the building and booked accordingly in no way helped me. I realised that she was still a long way out of her comfort zone and little things going wrong were going to impact more on Andrea than on me. I had to make the trip work. We were away too long for it to be a battle. I knew Andrea was going to test my patience and more importantly I was going to have to be more considerate and understanding in order to have any chance of travelling together comfortably for six months.

Upon arrival at our accommodation I noted it was really good, spacious, clean and very close to the metro rail link around the city. It was also considerably more convenient for everything than any places on the Palm would have been. We had never booked an Airbnb before so did not have any idea what to expect. I can say that the system of mutual reviews after a stay does seem to ensure that the host actually offers what they say they offer.

Our first bed was massive and certainly comfortable enough. It was slightly on the soft side but was king sized or possibly bigger. The sheets were good quality cotton and the duvet lightweight. Not a bad start all in all, although Andrea did get back ache because of the softness. I like a soft pillow rather than the modern trend for firm foam pillows. These pillows were foam but fortunately not to fat.

Dubai is an amazing place but it's not my scene. The main focus of the Emirate is the pursuit of luxury and wealth. The buildings are ostentatious with each tower or shopping mall trying to outdo the next. The decor is over the top and the opulence almost crude. Hotels provide a level of facilities unlike anything I have seen before. Anything Las Vegas has Dubai has but on a grander scale. Even the fountain show from the Bellagio has been copied and made bigger and better at the Dubai Mall.

I awoke on day one in the sure and certain knowledge that is was going to be a long day tramping around malls, souks and fancy buildings. I was not looking forward to it but it was going to be my first real test and one that I had to pass. This was Andreas day, she was so looking forward to exploring the shops, and although nothing about it made me feel good it was essential that I supported her and made her feel valued and important.

We started early and caught the metro to the Dubai Mall. The trains are driverless and provide a clean, quick and efficient way of travelling without frying in the blazing desert sun. Strangely for a city so obsessed with construction and perfection the Metro station was a good ten minutes' walk from the Mall. The walkway is of course covered and air conditioned. Dubai feels unbelievably safe. The only danger that I identified was the potential risk of hypothermia from the air conditioning in the stores.

Stepping into the entrance hall of the mall we saw the biggest aquarium we had ever seen. The external viewing area, set up to impress, is in fact so impressive that we felt it unnecessary to pay the extortionate entry fee to go inside. They actually have massive manta rays, sharks and turtles swimming in the foyer of the aquarium which is about three stories high and almost a block long.

Andrea was a little subdued in the Mall despite the magnificent array of shops. The reason was simple. She wanted to buy things but realised that anything purchased would have to be carried for the next six months, a prospect that did not thrill either of us.

Undaunted however she suggested we visit to the gold souk. My heart sunk at the prospect of no longer being able to use the excuse of added bulk in our luggage and the prospect of having to pay for some sort of gold bangle or ring. We jumped back on the metro and having reached the Dubai Creek we caught a river taxi along to the souk. The journey up river in a traditional Arab sailboat was enchanting and catching site of a magnificent pied kingfisher just added to the pleasure. Just for a few minutes it felt as if we were somehow transported back in time in the land of the Pharaohs.

Now like most men of my generation I hate shopping, I hate shopping even more when I am pestered by the shop keepers and expected to barter for goods. Why do sellers think it is a good idea to leap on you as soon as you even glance sideways at their stall. They then compound this by offering you trinkets at an exorbitant cost knowing full well that you will say no. Almost as soon as the polite "no thank you" leaves your mouth you are hit by a barrage of questions including;

" How much you want to pay? I give you good price" I feel like shouting at the top of my voice

"I don't want a fucking stuffed camel or a glass copy of the pyramids that twinkles when it's switched on"
English reserve dictates that my response is always a polite "no thank you" and a speedy escape. Thus even if there was actually something on the stall that I might have liked I have no chance to spot it let alone buy it.

Andrea however seemed immune to the annoying shopkeepers. She had switched to shopping mode. I had witnessed this many times before but still find it scary. She gets into the zone in the same way I used to before going out to bat. Eyes focused, oblivious to those around her, marching purposefully at a pace that defies belief. Questions are fired at the shopkeepers at such a rate that they feel as uneasy as I do. I am sure they sell her things at ridiculously low prices just to get rid of her.

Then it happened. In one of the numerous gold and jewellery outlets Andrea spotted a ring, actually a tray of rings that she liked. I knew in an instant that the next hour or two of my life would be spent rocking from leg to leg in the shop or sitting watching the world go by on a bench outside. The latter was by far the better option were it not for the street sellers who assumed that I would in some way be interested in, watches, sun glasses, gold chains, cold drinks, stuffed fucking camels, glass twinkling pyramids and anything else that they could carry or attempt to sell.

I sought the sanctuary of the interior of the jewellery shop and my worst fears were confirmed. Andrea was deep in a barter war with the Indian shop owner. He seemed like a nice enough chap, despite facing the full force of my shopping focused wife. We exchanged a few words about the state of Indian cricket and he rejoiced in the fact India had recently thumped their old enemy, Pakistan. I half expected him to say that he had sold Sachin Tendulkar a wedding ring in an attempt to curry favour but I think he had already realised Andrea was in for the long haul.

Andrea finally narrowed it down to three rings all of which seemed pretty much identical to me. Two of them fitted her perfectly while the third was too small. I knew in an instant which one she would choose and 30 minutes or so later I was proved right. This meant of course that we would have to wait for the ring to be adjusted. This task could not be performed in our shop. Oh no! The ring had to be sent out to another jeweller to be altered. I have to say I half expected this work to be completed only for Andrea to change her mind. The deal was finalised and I bought my wife a very nice but very expensive white gold half band ring inlaid with cubic zirconia. I would love to say that I know what cubic zirconia is but I haven't got a clue.

After the thrill of the hunt and the eventual capture of her intended prey Andrea drifted into a sedate state of mind that bordered on normality. She was rather like a lion relaxing after a successful hunt. The only difference was that she was not under a tree licking her lips. We caught the metro back to the Airbnb and got ready for the evening.

One of the subtle bonuses of working at a grammar school for more than 20 years is that a great many former pupils move into very good careers such as lawyers or doctors and the like. This often creates opportunities for them to work abroad and the Emirates are often the chosen destination for those trying to get rich quick. If any of these also happened to have been sporty while at school, the likelihood was that they would have reasonably fond memories of their old PE teacher. This certainly proved to be the case for me. Three former 1st xv rugby players were in the Dubai legal profession and a quick message on Facebook ensured that Andrea and I had company for drinks in the evening. This was especially useful as getting alcohol in Dubai is not as easy as at home unless you are staying in a big hotel. Plus, without a bit of local knowledge it could have been very damaging to our trip budget.

We met the lads at the oddly named Address Hotel Downtown and enjoyed a few happy hour beers while they reminisced about school days, boarding house pranks and 1st xv wins and losses. I am certain that most of it was lost on Andrea but I felt justified in my choice of evening having suffered for most of the day. At least she had a gin and tonic to keep her company. After drinks we ate a wonderful Lebanese restaurant called Calabar.

Calabar overlooked the Dubai fountains. The fountains are wonderfully pretty and a great drawcard for the tourists. Unlike Andrea I had not seen the fountains in Las Vegas so it was all very new to me. The whole evening was very enjoyable and meeting up with the lads made us both realise what excellent young men and women we had been teaching for the past two decades.

This inevitably led to Andrea and I discussing the sad state our school had been moving towards just prior to our retirement. The ridiculous league tables and incompetent inspections introduced by successive governments were bad enough. Add to this a new head teacher who had the man management skills of Pol Pot, a new deputy head who was about as popular as a pork pie at a Jewish wedding feast and a board of governors as gutless as lion in the Wizard of Oz. The net result was a common room who distrusted the management and a feeling of gloom that could not even be lifted by end of term beers, which indecently were banned. These conversations were really good fun and proved to me that both Andrea and I held similar views about the state of our former work place.

The following day, a Friday, began with a slightly fuzzy head and a plan to explore the touristy bits of the Emirate. We had planned to visit the Atlantis Hotel, the Burj al Arab and the bird sanctuary at the Creek. We had pretty much sorted out the timings and the planning and were ready to go by about 10am. But as Robbie Burns once said " The best laid plans of mice and men aft go awry".

It turned out that there were several obstacles in our way. Being a Muslim country nothing operated on a Friday as it is the holy day. Neither of us spotted this coming. So no public transport anywhere in the Emirate until early afternoon. Walking was clearly not an option as the temperature was well into the 90's and the distances were considerable.

No taxi drivers in Dubai appear to know how to get anywhere as none of them are from the Emirates. The good thing is that as most are non-Muslim they are working but the down side is most of them are totally clueless. Even a destination as prestigious as the Atlantis Hotel, one of the most famous resorts in the city (if not the world,) proved to be beyond our charming Nepalese driver. He was a lovely chap, very chatty and delighted to be able to practise his English. He had the sense of direction of a mole rat in the fog. My advice to anyone travelling by taxi in Dubai is to google directions before setting out and to print them in

Hindu, Urdu, Nepalese and Filipino. There is certainly no need to print a copy in Arabic.

We missed brunch at the Atlantis, (our Nepalese man made certain of that) but we did eventually pop along for a visit and it is spectacular. It oozes money. It also has another massive aquarium to wonder at. It's hardly surprising the earth's oceans are under stocked, as all of the fish are in aquariums in Dubai. By the time we had reached the Atlantis and marvelled at the splendour of the place the metro was almost ready to start operating. This made getting to the Creek and to the few malls we had not visited less of a lottery. We even popped back to the Dubai Mall to check out the indoor ski slope. It was bizarre to see people skiing on snow, while the temperatures outside reached the mid-forties.

Our short stopover in the UAE was all but over and as we set off for the airport to begin our adventure in earnest I had very mixed feelings about the place. It is an architectural wonder with so many spectacular high rise buildings. It is fantastic for shopping, at least that is what Andrea tells me but it is certainly not for the faint hearted or thin walleted. The food is good but pricy and not really Arabian. The hypocritical lifestyle of the local wealthy classes shocked me deeply.

The women folk dress in burkas while the men usually wear full-length white dish-dashas. This is to be expected in an Arab country and does not look in the least bit odd. From here however it is all downhill. The non-alcohol rule certainly does not apply in the posh hotel bars where westerners and locals drink and where prostitutes seem to outnumber non-working girls. Not only do local wives have to be subservient to the men but they are cheated on as a matter of course. So much for equality! The poorer classes are abused in every sense by the wealthy. To watch the rudeness displayed in shops, restaurants and public areas is hard. It beggars belief what must go on behind closed doors and I pity the household staff in many Arab homes.

It is also apparent that looking after Arab neighbours is not high on the agenda of the Emirati. They have taken no Syrian refugees during this current crisis. The local papers dispute these facts quoting large numbers of displaced peoples who have settled in Dubai, Sharjah and Abu Dhabi. They fail to say that only displaced people with massive wealth are welcome to live in the Emirates.

I would not return to Dubai although I can see why young go getters would want to spend a few years there earning the big bucks. I can also foresee at least one Andrea led shopping expedition in the future, with our children or friends

Beds 3 & 4. At the mercy of the tuk-tuk drivers

I think both Andrea and I were a little nervous as the plane circled Bandaranaike Airport preparing for landing. Dubai had been quite simple and although Arabic was the main language and it was clearly not a western style city in appearance it was most definitely first world. We had recognised the food and found transport easy, and been isolated from the extreme heat by icy air conditioning. It had been a gentle introduction.

Colombo would be different and despite plenty of prior reading and innumerable searches on TripAdvisor we were stepping, at least to a small degree, into the unknown. Sri Lanka is of course a regular holiday destination for many Brits of all ages. It is not however part of the usual gap year circuit and certainly not a common place for the older generation to explore without the help of Hayes and Jarvis or Thomas Cook.

Andrea was however not thinking beyond the luggage hall.

"What if my bag doesn't arrive. What will I do?"
I did understand her concern of course but I had other things on my mind.
Where was the nearest ATM? How do we get into the city? And most importantly was that guy walking past me Kumar Sangakara?

Our bags arrived and for the first time I put on my back pack like a real traveller. It was bloody uncomfortable, the waist band was nowhere near my waist, the shoulder straps were loose and this made the pack pull away from my back. I felt as though I would topple over backwards and end up on the arrivals hall floor looking and feeling like an upturned turtle. Fortunately, a couple of young Germans were on hand to show me how to adjust things and before long I was ready to go. Germans just seem to know everything and almost all seem to speak better English than most of the kids I taught in London.

We ventured into the arrivals lounge and were hit by the extreme heat and humidity. It felt as though a warm wet flannel had been draped over us. Andrea she was wearing her fleece which didn't help the situation.

"I told you that you wouldn't need it"
seemed, at the time, an appropriate thing for me to say.

" Fuck off" was probably the reply I deserved.

Almost at once we were bombarded by little men all offering wonderful deals on a ride into Colombo. As I politely turned down these unwanted approaches their replies were almost always the same.

" Ah! English. Lovely jubbly"
Bloody Del Boy has a lot to answer for.

We found an ATM and Andrea stepped forward. This was her domain. All matters relating to the money side of the trip had been down to her. We both were wearing our money belts stuffed with US dollars. Mine was an actual belt, holding up my shorts. Andrea wore one strapped around her middle but of course almost inaccessible under her fleece. We both carried various credit and debit cards each with a different use. We had a Halifax Clarity card that allowed us to spend abroad without incurring a fee and a Nationwide Flex Account debit card which could be used at ATM machines again without incurring a charge. I was not allowed one of these. We also had our Capitol one credit cards as backup, but these were for emergency only as they incurred a fee for oversees use.

So this was the acid test. Would the Nationwide card be free to use and would it work or be eaten by the first machine? I could feel the unease emanating from Andrea as she inserted the card.

I did my bit by carefully shielding the numbers from prying electronic eyes as she entered the pin code. We successfully withdrew 30,000. Sri Lankan rupees which was about £150, and the card was returned, Andreas relief was palpable. I resisted the urge to say "I told you it would work" as one "Fuck off" was enough for the time being.

Now armed with local currency we braved the maelstrom that was the transport area. I had checked and double checked the best way to get from Bandaranaike to Colombo district 1 and was not about to fall foul of the transport sharks.

I remembered the instructions from the web site almost to the word.

" The transport desk is at the far end of the arrivals hall and the cost of a taxi should be no more than 2000 rupees. Check carefully to make sure the price includes road tolls or you may end up paying those as well. Having purchased a ticket your driver will help you with the baggage and take you to his cab. Do not let anyone one else help you with baggage or you may never see it again"

At the transport desk a very scruffy guy quoted 3500 rupees, considerably more than the amount I was expecting to pay and in my best tough guy speak I responded,

" No thanks mate"

" How much do you want to pay"

" You missed your chance pal"

I was warming to task and my confidence was growing. The next quote was on the nose and I happily accepted and established that I could pay a little extra for tolls or travel by the old road without tolls. I opted for tolls as they seemed to be less than a couple of quid. We set off for Colombo District 1 and the Canes Boutique Hotel.

Andrea and I had been warned by a good friend that people in Sri Lanka who came across as super friendly and helpful almost always had an ulterior motive and almost without exception this was to make money out of the westerners.

This meant that we were somewhat on our guard when Kumar the hotel proprietor greeted us on our arrival. He was a charming man and offered us a cooling fruit punch and chilled towels as soon as we had checked in. In excellent English he explained that he would take us on a guided sightseeing tour of the locality after we had slept off the effects of the flight. He explained where breakfast would be served and showed us to the room.

As soon as he left Andrea and I simultaneously said,

" We'll the guided tour won't be free and I bet breakfast comes at an extra charge"

The room turned out to be very spacious and clean and most important of all the air conditioning worked, at least most of the time. The wi-fi was also intermittent but at least gave us the chance to let the girls know we were safe. The bathroom was massive and looked charming, decorated with painted white pebbles around the oval shaped bath tub and under the sink. These pebbles looked lovely in the light of day but they were so painful in the middle of the night when trodden on in bare feet whilst attempting to pee in the dark in order not to awaken Andrea. She confirmed the pain factor in the morning having also gone to the loo in the dark and trodden on the same pebbles. We agreed that in future lights could be turned on should either of us be caught short.

The bed was massive with cotton sheets, fluffy pillows but no mosquito net. Andrea almost panicked at this while I took a more phlegmatic line and assumed that no netting meant no mosquitoes. All in all, not a bad start to our Asian adventure.

When we finally surfaced in the morning the other guests had already breakfasted so we were the only ones in the room. Kumar served us fresh fruit, fried eggs, toast and tea breakfast it seemed was part of the deal. He then announced that if we could be ready in 30 minutes he and a driver would show us around. I enquired if we needed to pay or tip the driver and was told it was all part of the service.

We were ready as stipulated and were shown, amongst other things Independence Square, the test cricket venue at the Sri Lankan Cricket Club and the old colonial houses before being dropped at the Gangaramaya Buddhist temple. We were now on our own for the first time. On the plus side it was a Sunday so the traffic was not too manic and there were fewer people around than usual but it was 35 degrees Celsius with close to 100 per cent humidity and as Andrea said, it was a tad warm.

The temple was interesting from the outside, amazing from the inside and confusing to get into. We had to remove our footwear and give them to a little man to look after and then pay to get in. The cost was scaled with foreigners paying about five times what Sri Lankan's paid while the faithful obviously paid nothing. This was a pattern of charging we were to become familiar with over the coming weeks. I did contemplate writing to our House of Commons and suggesting we employed a similar payment structure at tourist sites in the UK.

Having negotiated the removal of shoes and the ticket price we entered the building. Sunday school was in sessions and dozens of children all dressed in immaculate white saris or robes thronged in the main hall. They looked wonderful and despite the supposed religious formality of the morning they were clearly having great fun. The smell of incense was all pervading but somehow not unpleasant as the rooms were large and airy. The religious statues, and paraphernalia were impressive, the monks were serene in orange robes and shaven heads but from this point the temple became bizarre in the extreme. It was like a cross between the old curiosity shop and something out of Hogwarts.

It appeared to us that everything that had ever been in the temple, given to the temple or indeed passed near the temple had been stored for posterity. There were wonderful knick-knacks from the British era, old radios, watches, photographs, pens, medals, crockery, cutlery and two vintage cars. Even a photo of the Queen and Prince Phillip who had clearly visited at some stage in the past. Pride of place was given to the temple elephant gloriously preserved by a high class taxidermist. Monkeys and chickens seemed to have free rein in the temple. We watched in amused amazement as offerings were left by the faithful at the feet of the Buddhist statues only to be raided by the cheeky monkeys or pecked at by the chickens.

After an hour at Gangaramaya we reclaimed our footwear and set off back to the Canes. The heat and humidity dictated that walking was not an option so for the first time in our lives we squeezed into a tuk-tuk. The driver was a cheery man with toothy grin stained red from chewing betel nuts. We made certain his vehicle was metred and set off. Fortunately, traffic at the weekends is lighter than in the week but the journey was still towards the white knuckle end of the riding spectrum. We dodged in and out between cars, buses and other tuk-tuks taking little notice of traffic lights, road signs or indeed generally accepted driving protocols like which side of the road should be used. Our man seemed to believe that if it was tarmac he could use it. This included the pavement.

This total disregard for road safety was one thing but what really concerned me was not the drivers attempts to become the first Sri Lankan grand prix rider but the small plastic bottle strapped to the inside of his cab. At first I thought it was a bottle of vodka or gin or more likely some illicitly home brewed grog that he used to shorten his long days on the road. Andrea was adamant that this was not the case and it was spare kerosene in case we ran out of fuel. This new information heightened my concern as the bottle was in a holder just to the side of the unprotected battery so we were to all intents and purposes riding at breakneck speed through the Colombo traffic in a Molotov cocktail. I had a vision of a small road shunt ending in a massive explosion with all vehicles involved engulfed in flames.

Colombo like many big cities hits you hard between the eyes. It was certainly not the easiest place for Andrea and I to find our travelling feet. I was worried that the rather break neck pace of the city would scare Andrea and make her even more certain that Asia was a bit too radical for us. I was wrong and despite the humidity and the near suicidal approach to road safety we enjoyed our short city stop.

The second evening was spent at Galle Front watching the sun set over the ocean. This large expanse of grass, worn almost bare by the constant traffic of locals and tourists alike was magnetic in its appeal. Children flew elaborate kites reminding me of the fabulous book by Khalid Hosseini. Snake charmers played haunting music while cobras swayed in the breeze like autumn branches at home. The aromas from the beach side food stalls carried across the grass and acted like a scented trail to be followed by all. Men with monkeys tried to encourage photos to be taken while others with brightly coloured parrots did the same.

This was Asia as I had pictured it, colourful, sensual, chaotic and enchanting. Andrea was ever busy with her camera and I was pleased to note that she had taken my warnings about opportunist thieves very seriously. She always secured the camera strap and kept her handbag across her body at all times. Things were indeed looking up.

We sat in a makeshift beach side eatery and ate street food for the first time. I have no idea what I ordered but it did not involve anything that had previously had a pulse. Andrea tried locally caught fish on the basis that it was likely to be safer than chicken. Men chopped onions and chillies whilst appearing to pay no attention to the razor sharp knives in their hands. Others turned wooden sticks laden with prawns, chicken and small fish over red-hot coals. Almost as soon as our food arrived the heavens opened, lightning lit up the sky and thunder crashed overhead. Within seconds our tent was packed with those sheltering from the storm. Despite this onions and chillies were still being chopped, skewers of food turned and meals still served. We ate as if nothing had happened. This is after all a totally different way of life.

We were gaining in confidence with every day. A currency app that gives us accurate conversion rates at the drop of a hat had made buying things much easier and reduced the chances of us getting ripped off. Our stomachs had stood up to the initial impact of the spicy food although I had remained steadfastly vegetarian for the first few days.

Prior to leaving the UK I had booked a three-day bird watching trip in the Sinharaja rainforest which occupies a small area of land south of Colombo and east of Galle. The forest is of great ecological importance being one of the very few pristine areas remaining in Sri Lanka. Birding is a great passion of mine and I have lugged various field guides in my back pack half way across the world.

Andrea does not quite share my passion but was interested enough and willing to join me on the bird safari. There were two provisos, no long walks in the sweltering heat, and no bugs. The walks could be avoided but I was far less confident about the bugs. I knew full well that Sinharaja had a reputation as one of the worst places in the world for leeches and as the monsoonal rains were only just over the mossies would be out in force.

Our guide Ashoka turned up at the Canes on time and in a lovely air conditioned 4x4. We set off for the forest some four hours away. The initial couple of hours on the newly opened Colombo to Galle toll road was very easy going but the last couple of hours were on country roads and lanes. This was far more interesting but much slower. We passed through tiny villages where local farmers sold vegetables and products on the road side. The larger towns buzzed with people going about their everyday lives. Sellers carrying goods stacked high on their heads pushed past cattle who moved slowly along as if they owned the place. The aromas of spices, garlic and other less savoury things drifted through our car as we journeyed past. As we reached more remote areas the sight of two white people in a car drew waves and shouts from local children who despite the heat, rain and mud were all immaculately dressed in white school uniforms.

We reached the Rock View Motel which would be our base for the next few days and quickly moved our gear into the room and changed ready for the first birding expedition. Ashoka explained that we would mostly be in a jeep and there would be little or no walking until tomorrow. We drove the couple of kilometres to the edge of the national park and met up with Aravinda, our local driver, and his jeep. The said vehicle appeared to be falling apart and was about as uncomfortable a ride as you could possibly imagine. The bench seats in the rear were unpadded and sides open to the elements. Luxury it was not but Aravinda was so proud of his jeep that Andrea and I simply smiled and climbed in.

    We did not go into the park rather we skirted the edge, as the light was fading. The rain made spotting birds difficult but I did have a few life ticks, the highlight being a yellow fronted barbet. Oh, a life tick in birding circles is a species you have never seen before. This means you can tick it off on your list.

    Back at the hotel we ate a fish curry drank a beer and settled in for a good night's sleep. The bed was big but hard. No mosquito net which once again I took as a good sign, but also no air conditioning, just a fan. We had a very early start the next morning to be in the park for daybreak or soon after. I slept well, Andrea on the other hand has had better nights. Hard beds are bad enough but the curry clearly was not to her taste and any deep or lengthy sleep was far too risky. It did cross my mind that this was all part of her master plan to avoid the early start and walks in the rainforest. However, the speed with which she moved from bed to bathroom on several occasions suggested otherwise. Needless to say I ate breakfast with Ashoka and set out without the company of my wife.

    The drive to the park was tortuous and if there was an award for the world's worst road the route into the Sinharaja rainforest reserve would have a reasonable shout. The rain was relentless. Indeed, the area was living up to its name. At the gates of the reserve we gave up the jeep and headed out on foot. Now those of you who have visited rain forests will know that you hear loads but see little. The forest is never quiet. Cicadas, birds, buzzy things and rain combine to make it an almost deafening place yet you see nothing but trees, mud and enormous ants.

Ashoka and Aravinda came into their own. The former detecting birds from the slightest movement while the latter darted into the undergrowth like a trained gun dog. The life ticks mounted: - scarlet minivet, red faced malkoha, and crested serpent eagle. Then it happened. Every birders magic moment. Now I had read that sometimes Sri Lankan forest birds fed in mixed flocks. Trust me this is unusual behaviour. Suddenly in a gap between storms the trees were full of brightly coloured birds in a feeding frenzy. It was hard to know where to look. To list all I saw seems like name dropping but within a few minutes I added, Malabar trogon, Sri Lankan blue magpie, velvet fronted nuthatch the list goes on. In all I had nearly fifty lifers in a morning and all without stepping off the path.

After an hour or so we returned to the jeep and were met by a very excited Aravinda who had left us a while back to check on his beloved jeep. He could barely contain his excitement and even although I knew no Sri Lankan it was clear he had found something a bit special. Askoka managed to translate even though he was clearly in an emotional state.

" He has found a beauty Jim sir. Serendib's Scops Owl. One of the newest birds on the world list. You will be one of a handful of Europeans who have seen it. It was only identified about ten years ago."

As you can imagine I was thrilled. There was however a but!
Askoka continued.

"The only problem Jim sir is that it is a way back in the jungle and a tough walk but not a long one."

I was up for it so long as my dodgy knees would cope. We set off over some reasonably accessible rocks and along a path by a stream. In the excitement I had forgotten about the leeches and by now it was too late.

We traversed the stream, at least the other two did, I clumsily fell in up to my knees. Now soaked to the skin with drenched feet and giving as much blood to the leeches as one would normally donate for transfusions we entered the forest proper. Thorny trees, spider's webs, and deep mud made the going tough but after fifteen minutes or so there it was. The Serendib's Scops Owl, tiny and brown huddled next to tree trunk like a drunk sheltering from the rain. Was it worth it? It was brilliant.

When we returned to the jeep Aravinda soaked a rag in petrol and began scrubbing every bit of my exposed skin along with my shoes and socks. Leeches hate petrol and seemed to fall off me from everywhere. They were no longer feeding but they were hard to get rid of. It reminded me of my childhood when noses could be picked and bogies flicked, I had not lost the knack. My ankles bore the marks of at least twenty leech attacks and Andrea later discovered as many more on the back of my arms my waist and my neck. How nothing got infected I have no idea I guess fortune favoured the brave.

Back at the Rock View Andrea was recovering. My advice of diorolyte and water and boiled rice seemed to be working. I really enjoyed my chick pea curry with naan bread and rice and a cold beer.

Beds 5/6 & 7. The Temple of the Tooth

Ashoka dropped us off at Colombo Fort Railway Station in good time for our train to the hill station of Kandy. I had already purchased first class tickets prior to setting off to the forest so now we could relax. The ticket office at Fort Station, with its sign stating foreigners only, would never be allowed in politically correct England. It made things so easy. The man behind the desk spoke English as if he was public school educated at Harrow or Eton. He was polite, well informed and very keen to please, just like our own British Rail. The tickets had cost me 1100 rupees each and we were assured seats in the observation car.

The train journey was amazing and the little extra payment to ensure a first class seat was money well spent. Andrea and I had a seat looking out of the back of the observation car as we slowly pulled away from the Fort. The soot stained buildings of the city gave way to ramshackle shacks in the shanty towns on the edge of Colombo. After thirty minutes or so the countryside began to roll past and the grime and hustle of the city drifted into memory.

The Colombo to Kandy rail route is an artery to the heart of Sri Lankan rural life. As we rumbled through the countryside the sides of the track were lined with laundry. It hung on the hedges, was draped over fences and laid on the ground. It added colour to the journey but we couldn't help wondering if the drying process rather negated the washing.

As we passed through small villages hordes of people parted to allow the train through and then re-formed behind the train to continue walking to work, or to school or to visit friends. The rail line being the most direct route was used by all.

After an hour the landscape changed and paddy fields lined the route. Women in brightly coloured sari's waded through deep water planting rice plants that would eventually provide the staple food for the community. The men folk in mud-stained dhotis controlled the sluice gates and patrolled the fields with wooden clubs. A local on the train said they were on cobra patrol. To be honest if I were on cobra patrol I would have wanted something more powerful than a stick.

We reached the edge of the escarpment marking the end of the lowlands and the train groaned to a halt. A second diesel engine was harnessed to the rear of the train totally blocking our view from the back facing observation car. The climb to Peradeniya Junction was painfully slow but gave us the chance to observe the changing flora and fauna as we gained height. Lowland palms gave way to jasmine and hibiscus. Flat featureless fields turned into rocky crags and impressive outcrops. Gradually the flat toped sacred Lion Rock came onto view and dominated the skyline.

Kandy gradually drew closer and Andrea and I prepared ourselves by going through our increasingly familiar routine. She made certain that our bags were secure and money belts were in place. I checked my notes which on this occasion were rather obviously entitled, "arrival in Kandy".

The notes contained information about our accommodation including address and phone number. I had the names of trusted cab companies gleaned from TripAdvisor and sometimes even a name of a local driver to look out for. Also had estimated cab fares to the various areas of the town. I discovered that almost any information was available on line with a little research. After all forewarned is forearmed.

The train pulled in to Kandy station and we were shocked by how few people there were on the platform. I assumed my worries about chaotic crowds were unfounded, but as I looked towards the station forecourt I realised it was indeed the calm before the storm.

Kandy was cooler than Colombo but only just and the change from air conditioned railway cab to humid railway platform saw both Andrea and I dissolve into pools of sweat. Nothing can really prepare you for tropical humidity and although we were slowly acclimatising there was clearly some way to go.

We walked through the ticket gates and into the mayhem. European backpackers with broken English were trying to negotiate with cabbies who had even more broken English. Tuk-tuk drivers tried desperately to attract customers while Andrea and I slipped through almost unnoticed.

" Hello sir and madam my name is Walter. Where are you going "

Now Walter is not a common Sri Lankan name and I figured very quickly that this guy could well be the man so warmly mentioned in despatches by so many travellers. Andrea boldly stepped forward and without even offering me a glance said

" Walter. We are staying a little out of town in a guest house on the hill called Kandy View. Do you know it?"
Walters reply came with a massive smile

" Of course memsahib I know everywhere around Kandy. It will cost 500 Rupees and you will arrive in comfort."

Andrea accepted the fare and we climbed into Walter's rather comfortable and very spacious minivan.

After the short drive to the Kandy View Guest House and Homestay Walter showed us his guest book and proudly told us that he had learned his near perfect English at school and kept it up to date whilst driving English tourists around the sites. If we would like him to drive us around his fee would be $50 for a day and he would plan a route to show us the best sites. He would the perfect guide. I was about to turn him down when Andrea said

" That would be wonderful. Please could you meet us the day after tomorrow and I will text you with the places we most want to see."

Inside I felt a mixture of smugness and relief at Andreas certainty. Firstly, it showed she was becoming more confident about our venture and secondly was embracing the idea that the trip was one we would probably never undertake again and therefore had to be enjoyed to the full.

We were met at the gate of Kandy View Guesthouse and Homestay by Chamindra and in the living area by Chaminda her husband. Andrea and I smiled at each other, at least we should be able to remember their names. We were served warm tea on the veranda overlooking the city along with delicious home baked ginger cake it felt like we were back at home save for 30 degrees of heat and the constant noise of cicadas.

I fully recommend homestays especially if you want to get a real feel for a place. Our two hosts were charming, very well educated and extremely knowledgeable about all things in Kandy. In essence we had the best possible opportunity to scratch beneath the surface of Sri Lanka's major inland city.

That evening we slept in a comfortable but slightly small bed. Clearly Sri Lankans are not as big as the British. The sheets were cotton but with no air conditioning and only a fan to keep us cool sleep did not come easy. I was all for an open window policy but Andreas fear of all bugs meant that this was never likely to be a popular option.

Kandy is a great place to explore. The hustle of Colombo is still apparent but less in one's face. The humidity is reduced but it is by no means the cool hill station so sought after by the British of the Raj.

Next morning over breakfast, which was wonderful, Chamindra gave us some tips for the day. After a plate of fresh mango and paw-paw she recommended the Temple of the Tooth. After our eggs served with pickled black pepper corns, she told us of a small British Garrison Cemetery that most tourists missed. After the small dish of dhal and ripe avocados we were regaled about the botanic gardens and after the toast and homemade jam, the best places to lunch in the city. Breakfast took well over an hour but time was already beginning to seem irrelevant.

Tuk-tuks in Kandy are not metered and therefore setting a price prior to embarking on a journey was essential. Sri Lankans are charming people but Europeans are potential targets for money making. I recommend a little bit of a barter but please remember that an extra saving of 10 pence is nothing to us but is a massive amount to a local. Barter with care and consideration.

We duly arrived at the Temple of the Tooth in our battered tuk-tuk and joined the queue to parade past the Tooth. Andrea was dressed in a fashion that did not arouse contempt from the temple authorities but I was not so fortunate and a rather brawny, hirsute, temple guard stepped across my path as I tried to enter the payment line. I was asked to don a rather unflattering, bedraggled, stained sarong provided at a charge by the staff. Fortunately, we had packed a bright clean one in our day pack so I was off the hook and the faithful never got to witness my knees.

Andrea and I queued in separate male and female lines and paid the now expected foreigner's entry fee. We paraded solemnly into the temple and after a few minutes wait we were in front of the tooth itself. Not that we or anyone else could actually see the fabled molar as it is kept behind closed doors in an elaborate shrine. None of this seemed to bother the faithful who knelt in prayer and offered a myriad of gifts to the closed shrine. All of this was a bit lost on me but there were some very mischievous monkeys living in the temple complex and I loved watching these little devils raid the offerings every time the faithful were caught off guard.

Andrea and I left the temple of the tooth and in blistering heat and humidity we walked the short distance to the British Garrison Cemetery. By the time we had walked the couple of hundred yards to the gates we were drenched in sweat and starting to flag. The water in our bottles was almost warm enough to make a cup of Dilmah tea and did nothing to cool us down. The cemetery however was cool, shaded by trees and provided a natural calm in the bustling city.

Each of the gravestones gave Andrea and I an insight into the trails and hardships faced by the British forces and their families while stationed in Kandy. We were reliably informed by curator Charles Carmichael that the cemetery was established in 1817. Charles was a charming Sri Lankan gent who also spoke impeccable English. He looked so old that he may actually have been at the opening ceremony. He took enormous pride in showing Andrea and I around and had an in depth knowledge of the cemetery. We hope that someone is being lined up to replace him as the years pass by.

In the cool shade of the palm trees Charles regaled us with stories of family tragedies, freak accidents and tropical diseases. His passion was infectious and we were drawn more and more into a world of English gentlemen soldiers and crinolined ladies. As we moved nearer to the back of the cemetery Charles ushered us towards a tombstone lying flat on the floor. The words on the stone had been eaten by time but Charles knew them by heart.

"Here lies Sargent James McGlashan' died in Kandy in 1817 of malaria, aged 24."

We looked at each other and then at Charles. So many had perished from malaria, so why was this was special? James had fought at the battle of Waterloo two years prior and midst the carnage of Wellington's great victory had escaped unscratched. Yet here, another world away, he had perished due to a tiny insect so far from his native Scotland and all while he was still younger than our children. This was a special place and one we felt privileged to have visited.

As we left Charles and the garrison cemetery behind us Andrea and I held hands. No words were necessary and none came for several minutes.

Time in Kandy passed so quickly while at the same time standing still. Walter met us the next morning with a massive smile and an itinerary for the day ahead. We set off for Dambulla and the cave temples, followed by the sacred hill known as Sigariya. Walter chatted to us about rice paddies, medicinal plants, coconuts and all things Sri Lankan. We loved him. Mid-morning brought an unscheduled stop at a spice garden.

Andrea tasted stuff, sniffed stuff, rubbed stuff in, applied stuff and generally got involved. I was less enthralled but did find one particular cream rather interesting. Our guide with the typical enthusiasm of a salesman rubbed the smelly gunk onto my lower leg and after a minute or two rubbed it off along with my leg hairs. Now I am somewhat hairy pretty much everywhere apart from my head, which Andrea says resembles a boiled egg. I was ready to give this stuff a go especially on my back, as it would be far less painful than waxing. The price, however, was more painful than waxing so we left after some ginger tea and with a hairy back.

The main purpose of our adventure was to see touristy things so Dambulla was high on the list. The usually preposterous entry fee was levied against us while the locals paid a few rupees. No political correctness in Sri Lanka, just the usual two price lists one headed "locals" and the other headed "foreigners". I was becoming even more certain that a letter to Number 10 was required.

As we ascended the hundreds of uneven steps up to the cave temples while the temperatures surged into the 90's Celsius. There was no shade and Andrea turned a worrying crimson. Had there been vultures in this part of Sri Lanka they would I am sure have begun to circle. The monkeys however thrived in the heat and in the discomfort of foreigners taking every opportunity to steal snacks and water bottles.

The temples themselves were gratifyingly cool in a very hot place and I did consider becoming a Buddhist just to avoid the walk down. Each temple housed elaborately carved Buddha's in every position known to man. The reclining ones were my favourites although the happy Buddha's did show a passing resemblance to me.

We overheard guides saying that it had taken many years for the faithful to carve the intricate patterns on the walls of the cave temples. I was becoming more and more aware of the importance of religion in the east. These temples were so impressive and the skills and patience of the ancient craftsmen must have been at a level that modern man can only dream of.

Walter had wisely decided to stay in the shade of the car park and sip tea with his fellow taxi drivers and guides. He was a wise man indeed.

Afterwards we drove into town for a local lunch of rice and curry. No choice, no menu just rice and curry. We sat in a cafe with Walter and discovered what busloads of tourists missed as they were shepherded from tourist site to western style eating house. At Walters beckoning the table filled with rice, dhal, vegetables, chicken, ladies' fingers and some dishes we did not recognise. Smiling, Walter informed us that he asked the staff to serve food with western rather than local heat.

The food was delicious washed down with chilled EGB (English ginger beer), the meal was magnificent. No foreigner's prices here. The magnificent meal cost less than a pound each.

We slumped into the minivan and snoozed a little as Walter drove us to the sacred rock Sigariya. Our hearts wanted to climb the rock but our bodies certainly did not and we made do with taking photos from ground level, or rather Andrea took photos. Firstly, with her phone then her camera then on a selfie stick and had she been carrying one I am sure she would have used a box brownie as well. Each photo took on average about five minutes which in sweltering heat seemed like an hour. I would be lying if I said my patience was not strained.

The afternoon light was fading into evening as we drove back into Kandy and up the hill to the Kandy View. Chamindra greeted us with a smile and a refreshing cup of Dilmah tea. Walter had been a total success. His calm manner, great personality and detailed local knowledge had made him the perfect guide for the day.

The next day we were due to set off for the beach resort of Mirissa en-route to Galle. Over supper we discussed methods of transport. Only two weeks earlier there would have been no discussion. It would have been a taxi or a driver for the day. Confidence was growing in both of us and the plan we came up with was that I would walk down to the station in the morning to buy tickets to Colombo on the first class train and from there we would catch the local train to Welligama the stop closest to Mirissa.

Everything went well with the first part of our plan and the journey from Kandy to the Capitol was spent in air conditioned comfort on the new Chinese built Blue train. At Colombo fort we crossed the platform and I popped into the ticket office to buy two second class tickets to Welligama via Galle. The tickets cost the equivalent of 17pence each. As Andrea and I sat and waited for the train to arrive we noted the platform was empty. We were relieved as getting on trains while heavily laden was not easy. Our mood changed quickly as the platform filled with school children, workers and just about everyone else in Colombo. The rush hour had clearly begun.

As the train pulled in the chaos erupted as hordes of suited businessmen, Sri Lankan ladies in brightly coloured saris and backpackers turned into rampaging animals in an attempt to board. To say we were taken by surprise would be the understatement of the century. When Andrea finally boarded the 2nd class carriage her suitcase remained on the platform. I hauled it on board only to discover that, the train was moving, and there was no space for me. By a miracle my plight was witnessed by a station worker who pushed me into the next open door in a manner similar to loading a horse into the starting stalls at Newmarket races.

Moving in the train was difficult in any circumstances but with a back pack on it was near impossible and it was at least half an hour before Andrea and I could exchange waves. Eventually we squeezed into a small space outside the somewhat pungent, and constantly in use bogs and Andrea began to calm down.

The carriage was stifling hot despite the windows and doors, where they existed, were wedged wide open. The ceiling was lined with 24 fans, I counted them all. Sadly, none of them were working. Despite this Sri Lankan Railways deemed it a good idea to employ a ticket inspector. The painfully thin little man seemed capable of squeezing through the smallest gaps in the hoard and was thorough, very thorough. Andrea showed her ticket but mine was in my back zipped pocket, and in order to retrieve it I must have made inappropriate physical contact with at least five unsuspecting businessmen who were squeezed in around me. Fortunately, the Sri Lankan response to most things is a smile and a nod. God knows what would have happened on the London Underground if a bald, sweaty man had reached behind himself and touched another man's arse!

The train rattled through the countryside stopping regularly at small town stations where it appeared that no one got off but even more people got on. Those already on the train, and clearly used to the cramped sweaty conditions seemed totally untroubled. One old lady who must have been in her eighties perched herself on my back pack which I had managed to place on the floor beside me. She seemed so comfortable I did not have the heart to ask her to move. Amazingly, when I though the train could get no fuller, women and children got on selling nuts and pasties and even more amazingly the passengers seemed delighted to see them. They made a roaring trade and with lithe thin bodies seemed to move along the carriage with little difficulty.

After three hours and forty minutes of total hell we reached Welligama and made a solemn vow as we left the train never again would we travel second class on Sri Lankan railways. Outside the station we piled into a tuk-tuk. Andrea, me and our bags in a space that was only just big enough for one. How we got in I do not know but I assume that the fact we were both melting helped us slide past each other into the seat.

Mirissa is a very cute little seaside village and is a haunt for ageing hippies. It is famous for two things. Blue whales are present close to shore for large parts of the year and for those able to cope with fairly choppy seas and scarily unsafe boats it is probably the best place in the world to view them. The other start attraction is the Number1 Dewani roti shop.

I missed the whales because it rained pretty much solidly during our stay in Mirissa and strange as it may seem the blue whales don't appear to like rain all that much. This did mean that we spent more time in the roti shop. For a few rupees we sampled savoury rotis and sweet rotis. We tried. chopped up roti called kottu. I can announce without fear of contradiction that they we delicious. My favourite was the mango and chocolate variety served with melting vanilla ice cream. Andrea being more sophisticated, preferred the chicken and prawn mixed roti. We both loved the Kottu which seem to be a speciality in the region.

When the rain did ease we started the long slow process of building a healthy tan. Once again our tactics were different. Andrea used sun screen with a different protection factor depending on the body part. I used my watch increasing the exposure carefully each session. Andrea missed a bit and managed to burn the sensitive area between her boobs, I donned my shirt after thirty minutes on each side and was fine. I did not however at any time say "I told you so."

The rain had a second downside and we really should have moved homestay but being staunch Brits and actually liking our hosts we stayed put. Our residence had a flat roof that had probably not been totally watertight at the best of times. This was definitely not the best of times. Going to the loo was an issue as the rainwater flooded through. We both on occasions sat on the throne under an umbrella. There are no photos to prove this but trust me it happened.

After five days of nonstop rain, (Thank God it was the dry season), we left Mirissa for Galle. I loved Mirissa and felt so sorry for the local restaurants and guest houses who depended totally on the ever decreasing numbers of tourists. Andrea, understandably, was glad to get away. Her idea of fun does not include going about her morning ablutions holding a toothbrush in one hand and a brolly in the other.

Galle is a wonderful city and the Fort area is well worth at least a day. The Fort walls give panoramic views of the city and the wonderful test cricket ground. The museum is excellent and the quaint white chapel gives an historical insight into the European inhabitants of a bygone age.

The usual chancers greeted us as we got off the bus on our first morning sightseeing, "hello sahib" or "hello memsahib"

"you remember me I work in your hotel"
I have learned to leave the responses to Andrea
" Very unlikely Sir as we are not in a hotel" or
" Excellent Sir. what hotel would that be"
When said with a polite but dismissive smile, we were seldom bothered for long.

As the afternoon heat grew stronger we ventured into a small cafe inside the fort and we uncovered a gem. The proprietor was a former journalist who had kept a wonderful photographic journal from the 2004 tsunami. He took us through the photos and explained the impact on Galle and Sri Lanka in wonderful detail as we sipped cold lemon squash. Sadly, I cannot remember the man's name but it was a truly wonderful and educational hour or so. For those following in our footsteps the café has a very small veranda area seating three or four people and has black and white photos of Galle on the wall. On the veranda are lovely English style patterned plates attached to the wall.

I found it increasingly hard to come to terms with the plight of the many beggars around the city. I am not sure if it was the knowledge that whatever I did would only be a drop in the ocean for these unfortunates this creating a feeling of hopelessness within me. I opted for not giving money but instead gave food or drink whenever I could. The toothless smiles from the recipients of these offerings suggested that they were at least very grateful for someone showing kindness. Sadly, the plight of beggars was something we would have to come to terms with throughout South East Asia.

The local buses in Galle are cheap and very easy to use. We visited local beaches, me with my watch and Andrea with a myriad of sun creams. We saw the local area and ate some wonderful sea food. We knew however that the time was upon us to move on and head for Cambodia and the great temples of Angkor Wat.

Bed 8 Glorious Angkor Wat

We did not have a direct flight to Cambodia and consequently had to spend a night in Singapore. We had decided not to make this a long stop over as we had been to the city state before plus it was bloody expensive. We were perfectly comfortable in Changi airport which I am happy to proclaim is the nicest airport I have been to. In fact, I have spent summer holidays in resorts that are less comfortable and less welcoming than Changi. Andrea and I booked into a temporary relax room and showered and rested up. We ate the complimentary food and even availed ourselves of a shoulder massage. All for the price of a round of drinks in our local at home. Heathrow could learn a lot from Changi.

The next morning, we caught our onward flight bright eyed and bushy tailed. We had left Colombo in a downpour and we circled over Siem Reap in an even more torrential downpour. I had spent hours prior to our trip looking at weather patterns, monsoon dates and general rainfall charts. Everything I had read and researched indicated that the rains should have been over in Sri Lanka and that Cambodia should be at the start of the drier season. As I looked out of our plane window I saw Cambodia was flooded. The rivers were raging torrents, the fields and villages were under water. Only the water buffalo seemed to be enjoying life. I felt deflated, guilty at having brought us half way across Asia only to be soaked day in and day out by rains that appeared to be a sign of impending disaster on a biblical scale.

I turned to Andrea sitting impassively next to me and admitted that if the rains continued we may have no alternative but to go home. I half expected an agreement but her mood was optimistic and encouraging. I smiled but my mood did not lift appreciably and I feared that another spell locked in less than luxurious accommodation would see a premature end to our adventure.

We queued at the visa on entry desk and expected the usual hour or so of pointless red tape that so often goes hand in hand with border crossings. No such delays here, the Cambodian machine was well oiled and we were in the arrivals hall in less than ten minutes. I was delighted that we had opted for the visa on arrival and not spent two days going to and from the embassy in London prior to our trip.

Andrea proudly produced her phone with the invaluable money conversion app from the Apple store. After a quick check of the exchange rate we withdrew money at an ATM and looked around for our man who was due to meet us.

I had contacted Patrick, the hotelier at the wonderfully named Avalon Boutique hotel and Spa and requested the free airport pick up and transfer never for one-minute expecting anyone to turn up to meet us.

"Jim look, over there" Andrea said.

In amongst the throng of people was a bedraggled drenched little man holding a soaked piece of paper with our names proudly written on it. Jim spelt correctly and Andreeada, which was close enough. Well there was no mistaking that this was our man so we introduced ourselves and followed him into the rain to the taxi!

The taxi turned out to be a Cambodian tuk-tuk. These vehicles bore a passing resemblance to those of Sri Lanka in that they looked likely to topple over in a strong wind and sounded like a lawn mower. Cambodian tuk-tuks are however grander affairs with wooden posts and facing seats. They look like a cross between a very small four poster bed and a rag and bone man's cart. This one was certainly not big enough for two largish Europeans and two sets of luggage.

After a brief game of tetras, we squeezed into the tuk-tuk and the plastic side panels were secured against the tempest. Tungay proudly set off towards the hotel in good spirits considering the state of the road, the torrential rain, and the fact that he sat totally exposed to the elements on the little moped that pulled our four-poster bed.

As we sped through the near flooded streets water sprayed innocent passers-by but no one seemed to care. It did appear that the only person in Siem Reap that was downcast due to the weather was me. Andrea pointed this out but it did little to raise my spirits.

We were met at the Avalon by Patrick and shown to our room on the third floor. No lifts in this establishment. I had as always booked with considerable care and only after as much research on TripAdvisor as one could reasonably do. I never booked the cheapest I could find and tended to restrict my choices to those scoring more than 7.5 out of 10. The Avalon ticked all of my boxes and at £58 for six nights excluding breakfast perhaps a lift was too much to expect.

The room was gloomy but spacious and the aircon worked. Sadly, it faced the main road and the open air cinema, so it would be fair to say it was not quiet. We slumped onto our bed and contemplated five days stuck in a Cambodian hotel with intermittent wi-fi and the prospect of not even getting out to see the temples that Siem Reap was so famous for. We decided to eat in the hotel and actually were served with a very acceptable dish of noodles and stir-fried vegetables. Then having checked the Google weather forecast decided on an early night.

Patrick as if sensing our mood did his best to cheer us up. In passable English for a French ex pat he explained that Cambodian weather was rather like a French woman, unpredictable, never boring, often sublime and occasionally totally frustrating. Then with a shrug of his shoulders and a loud expulsion of breath

"Pah! We will just have to wait and see"

As we entered our room we were greeted by a dripping sound and a thin film of water washing across the floor. It was not worthy of the name flood but did provoke a very loud "Oh my god my suitcase is on the floor" From Andrea. I panicked a good deal less as despite being told off more than once I had left my back pack on my bed.

Twenty minutes later and after much tutting, huffing and puffing we were in a new room. It was bigger with better aircon and did not face the road or the cinema. What a result. I was however a little puzzled by Andrea who seemed to be developing a series of noises that replaced words. Groans and aghs and oohs made her sound like Marge Simpson in a particularly frustrating episode of my favourite cartoon series.

I decided at this point to try and relax and take a shower. I was tired and fed up and hoped the effects of a good wash would lead to a sound night's sleep. Taking a shower proved to be another very different experience. Firstly, with specs on I checked the buttons and dials and was happy I knew what to do. I aimed the shower head and pushed the buttons. Nothing happened. After a second or two a dribble of water splashed onto the floor, and I removed the hand held shower head at the very second the water power returned. The piping hot water now gushed at the slatted door and soaked the bedroom. I dropped the shower head which then behaved like a cobra sitting up and soaking the whole bathroom, towels, toilet paper, my clothes, everything. Then, while, slipping all over the place on the tiled floor I regained control of the shower head just as the water ran out. As I left the bathroom I slipped on the water and crashed to the floor much to Andrea's amusement.

Breakfast came at an extra cost but the nasi goreng, which is simply fried rice with left overs, was both cheap and tasty. The coffee was foul but the tea was drinkable. I know it was the first morning but I was already assuming that Cambodia was not a place one visited for the cuisine.

The rain had stopped and as if by magic the previously flooded streets were now dry and rather than getting soaked by water splashed up by cars the passers-by were being engulfed in clouds of dust. I for one struggled to work out how this happened so quickly but my eyes definitely were not telling lies.

Andrea and I fell back on our fail-safe plan: day one, take it easy, plan carefully, and prepare for day two. We took advice from Patrick and headed off into town. It was a thirty-minute walk but we had all day. He had suggested lunch in Pub Street and some casual shopping in the central market. Andrea suggested we find the Hard Rock Cafe in order that she could buy a badge to add to her collection. I reluctantly agreed on the proviso that if it indeed existed, and we could find it that we would have lunch there.

Map in hand we set off into Siem Reap which thankfully is laid out in an American grid style with streets numbered in a logical manner. We passed the Angkor museum and despite the fact that there was no queue did not go in. That particular visit was scheduled for day two. As it turned out the Hard Rock was pretty straightforward to find and a burger was a welcome change from rice and vegetables.

We learned a number of very interesting facts about Cambodia on our stroll into town. Firstly, it became clear that tourists never walk anywhere and every tuk-tuk driver that passed us was shocked when we said we wanted to walk.

My explanation to these tuk-tuk men started with a very English "No thank you sir we would like to walk", but by about the sixtieth "You want tuk-tuk? Velly cheap I show you town" I struggled not to simple say " Fuck off".

Secondly, children in Cambodia do not appear to go to school, at least children of the poor do not go to school. Andrea and I both noticed that almost every woman we came across was accompanied by children most of whom were clearly of primary school age. Discussion with Patrick revealed that schools were available but the need to make money meant that children were kept away from school to help sell, beg and otherwise add to the family income. We became slightly depressed that the future of a country was being blighted by a lack of basic education. Especially a country that was so desperately trying to move forward after years of bitterness under Pol Pot.

The final and most amazing thing we discovered was that wi-fi is available almost everywhere in Cambodia. Even the road side stalls selling obscure types of street food advertised free wi-fi. Goodness knows how these grubby little street stalls managed this. We never established what they did partly because we spoke no Cambodian but mainly because we still hadn't plucked up enough courage to sample street food just yet.

Add to this other minor moments of enlightenment, like uneven pavement slabs always have muddy water under them and it always squirts right up your leg onto any clothing that has just been washed. It never rains when you are close to shelter but always pisses down when you are in the open. Also in Siem Reap a very large number of small round brown pebbles strewn across the path are in fact dog shit. Dog shit and open toed sandals are not a great mix. I was learning fast how to cope with the vagaries of life in Cambodia

After a burger lunch that cost more than a local would earn in a month we wandered over to the infamous Pub Street. Very aptly named and good fun. We looked around the market stalls where everything seemed to cost "wan dorror" and after an afternoon of aimless leisure we decided to have a beer. We followed Patrick's advice and did not sit at the tables adjacent to the road. This meant that the local teams of child beggars found it harder to get you. We learned pretty quickly that even although the poor little kids had a cheeky manner and looked in need of any help available, none of the money dished out by tourists went to them. The handlers, for want of a better word, hid in the shadows and like Fagin controlled their gang with what we feared was violence and cruelty. The police seemed to turn a blind eye.

After a couple of beers, we had a tricky decision to make: - settle in or head back to the Avalon. Without warning another storm hit Siem Reap. Thunder and lightning seemed to signal the end of the world. I have never in my life seen rain like it. Within minutes the streets were in full flood, water ran down the gutters and spilled over into the restaurants and shops. Water ran shin deep down the street and still the locals seemed to carry on. Cambodians are a people who cope with adversity in a way that the west could follow, they set a great example.

We jumped into a tuk-tuk and almost sailed back home to shelter and the sanctuary of our room. The lights flickered on and off as the storm raged. Rain hammered onto the roof and the thunder roared around the city like a raging bull elephant. Once again my dream of seeing a sun rise over the temples of Angkor seemed to be fading. As the light of the day finally disappeared and night engulfed the city I sunk into the bed in the vain hope that it would engulf me and keep me safe until summer came.

Unusually Andrea was up before me the next morning and was keen to get moving. She had already met with Patrick and purchased entry tickets to the Angkor Museum. I knew at once that her upbeat approach was a brave attempt to cheer me up and I was pleased. The rain hammering on the windows soon dulled my mood and like a sulky schoolchild I rolled over and started to grumble. After some persuading I joined her for breakfast and over a plate of toast and bouncy scrambled eggs we made plans for the day, or rather Andrea made plans for the day while I checked my I-pad only to find that rain was forecast for the next couple of days.

Now I clearly remember Michael Fish's infamous announcement on the BBC back in 1987." No hurricane was approaching the UK", just hours before it struck causing devastation across the country. Fortunately, the weathermen in Siem Reap appear to have gone to the same school as Mr Fish. Over the next few hours the clouds cleared and the sun shone. Just maybe things were on the up.

We walked to the museum and spent a couple of hours discovering the ancient secrets of the Temple complex and the civilisations that built it. The numerous statues of multi-armed and animal-headed gods and goddesses did get boring. The video rooms were however great for learning the stories associated with the temples. I had done some research and knew that there were several temples but the scale of the place shocked me. We faced the choice of racing around as many of these as possible or doing a few but with more time to spend at each.

After considering the facts Andrea and I decided that we would go for the small inner circuit rather than the much longer outer circuit. My desire to see the temples by push bicycle was crushed when Andrea announced that she could not ride a bike and under no circumstances was she going to try. We duly booked a tuk-tuk for the following morning and arranged for our driver to meet us at 05.30am if it was a clear morning or 09.00am if it was cloudy. The idea of two potential meet times was the brain child of our driver Bili.

"I am Bili Nugal sir. I know the temples well and will be very good driver, you can rely on me sir! Better to have two plans as sunrise over the temples is not worth seeing if the sun is hidden, only the Chinese go to the temple to see the sun when the sun is hidden"

As I had no reason to doubt Bili's wisdom we agreed a price for the day of $20, shook hands and went our different ways.

In bright sunshine we continued to explore Siem Reap. Patrick had told us that the town had its own killing field memorial site. We were of course planning to visit the infamous School 21 in Phnom Penh and were fascinated to discover how the brutality of Pol Pot and the Khmer Rouge had extended to points far away from the nation's capital.

The memorial grounds were just around the corner from the Avalon. We walked through the colourful local market with stalls selling all manner of things. No tourist trinkets or tacky T-shirts but an array of vegetables, fruits, herbs and spices alongside cages full of forlorn chickens and ducks who seemed to realise that their days were numbered.

Women surrounded by bare bottomed toddlers struggled to make sales whilst controlling their enthusiastic offspring. Older children, fascinated by the sight of western tourists clamoured for sweets or anything else that might be on offer. The children were happy and smiling but had already started to see westerners as a potential cash cow. The ex-teacher in me came to the fore and I could not help but fear for these innocents who would undoubtedly forsake education in order to try and make a quick buck from the ever growing numbers of visitors. The longer I spent in Cambodia the more I realised that the aftermath of genocide was not that of rediscovery or a drive to develop and educate. More it was the need to survive and the poor as always were bottom of the pile. The prospect of a long education with no family income or no education but some tourist dollars left families with little or no choice. Only the very far-sighted were likely to break this mould.

The smells from the food stalls drew Andrea and I like moths to a flame but despite our growing experience as travellers we were yet to sample real street food for fear of the dreaded shits. This was not helped by the fact that toilets were few and far between and the thought of squatting over a small hole while every fly in Cambodia tried to fly up your nose, into your mouth or far worse made it too great a risk. Indeed, squatting itself presented enough problems not so much the getting down but the risk of not being able to get up again. Getting old certainly has its drawbacks.

We both knew however that at some stage we had to embrace all aspects of life on the road and any trip to South East Asia was not the genuine article without sampling the local delights. Andrea, who generally has a cast iron constitution, went first and I decided to await the results. I figured at least one of us needed to be fit to meet Bili Nugal the next morning.

After Andrea had eaten a quick snack of an indeterminate meat on a skewer we set off to find the memorial garden and museum. The site was understated and serene. A large courtyard flanked a small temple and two rather shabby out buildings. In front of the temple was a statue of Buddha and a small ossuary. On either side of the courtyard hawkers sold cold drinks and snacks. A group of students had erected a small gazebo and were handing out leaflets with a political massage that was totally lost on us due to the language barrier. A tall tree rose majestically from the middle of the courtyard and dwarfed around it. It seemed to bow its branches in sorrow for what it had witnessed in the past.

I have always loved old trees, the cracked bark mirroring the wrinkles of the old and wise. The shade from the branches providing relief from the scorching sun or shelter from the rain. This sanctuary is often a meeting place for the young or for family picnics or for village elders to discuss anything of importance. Yet here, this aging giant had borne witness to acts of such horror that forever its branches would bow in remembrance of the fallen.

Andrea and I approached the larger of the two out buildings unsure of what to expect. The classy polished floors of the Angkor Museum were not replicated here. This place was not for tourists it was for the Cambodians and it bore witness to the horrors that their people had suffered. The room housed a dozen or so paintings depicting scenes of torture, executions and brutality. The text told the story of a one person's experience at the hands of the Khmer Rouge.

We looked at the child-like paintings in silence, the innocence of the artistic style belying the gruesome nature of the story that was depicted. I'm not sure if Andrea cried because I could not look at her. I think men find it hard to shed tears in public and I wanted mine to go unwitnessed.

We left the memorial grounds soon after, still in silence but holding hands. Somehow that helped. There was an acknowledgment between us that our forthcoming visit to S21 would be even more difficult to come to terms with.

Over a leisurely supper we discussed the events of the day and prepared for the highlight of the trip to date. I had seen images of the Temple at Angkor Wat in countless magazines and on TV travel shows on television. I had seen photos on mobile phones and on Facebook as numerous former students had trudged the gap year route through South East Asia and then returned to school to show the next generation in assemblies and tutor group meetings. This was a place I had waited years to see and my excitement was palpably building.

Despite the fact that beer was under 20 pence a glass and it was Happy Hour I resisted the temptation. If the day dawned fine I was certainly not going to be hung-over, not for this special day.

Andrea's alarm went off at 05.00am and I was already wide awake listening to the rain patter against the windows. She awoke and rolled over,

"Is it raining Jim?"

"It's bloody tipping down"

"Have you looked out of the window to see if the sky is clearing?"

"It's pitch bloody dark outside. What use would that be"

She quickly realised that my mood was not going to improve by optimistic chat and started to explore other ways of cheering me up. Morning sex is often the best and despite still being in a bit of a sulk it did make me feel better. As we lay in each other's arms I am sure the rain started to ease.

Bili was early and stood smiling outside of the Avalon as we came downstairs.

"Rain stopping, Chinese already wet and see nothing. Velly funny"

Bili was right and the sky was clearing, blue patches were appearing and thin shafts of sunlight were piercing though and reflecting off the massive puddles that covered the road.

We climbed into Bili's tuk-tuk and set off for the temples. The queue at the ticket office was long but once again the efficiency of the locals meant that it moved at a great speed. Andrea and I were in possession of our $20 photo identity tickets with ten minutes.

The road into the temple complex was heaving. Tuk-tuks, cycles, mini busses, coaches and walkers. Monkeys played by the roadside and begged for food from anyone silly enough to stop. The puddles shrank as blue became the dominant colour in the sky overhead.

Angkor Wat is surrounded by a moat and protected by the remnants of a once great forest. Tourism is taking its toll and as we approached I wished I could have visited thirty years earlier. A massive car park, food stalls, trinket stands and children selling everything from postcards to t-shirts, fridge magnets and small carvings make it very clear that this is one of the biggest tourist attraction globally let alone in Cambodia.

The causeway leading to the main temple was a seething mass of humanity and, it did detract from the majesty of the buildings. Photos or TV documentaries never show thousands of people clamouring to get into the temple. Andrea kept stopping to take photos and made me pose or worse making me take photos while all the time I just wanted to watch in silence and take it all in.

There was a reflection in the lake but nothing like as impressive as I had hoped it would be and I was beginning to feel that my expectations had far exceeded the reality of the place. Inside the massive temple it was possible to find nooks and crannies where no other tourists were but they were few and far between. The building was impressive but the mystical aura that I had created for Angkor Was was not there and I was bitterly disappointed.

We trudged around the temple for around an hour and spotted carvings and statues that we had learned about in the museum. The intricacies of the stone work were mind boggling and the painstaking detail created by workers with only basic tools way back in the 12th century showed how advanced the Khmer civilization must have been.

As we walked back across the causeway towards Bili and our tuk-tuk I was left with a feeling that maybe I should never have come, maybe my own imagination was better than the reality.

Bili loaded us up and on we went to the next temple Angkor Thom. Massive statues lined the approach to the temple and enormous faces stared down at us from the towers. The tales of the Hindu deities and the creation of the world are depicted on the walls of the temple with snake's heads and demons terrorising the carved people.

By the time we had walked around this temple we were beginning to flag, we had run out of water and the temperature was now well into the thirties.

We opted to miss a couple of ruins and go directly to Ta Prohn the temple made famous by Lara Croft and the Tomb Raider film. This place was awesome the jungle had already started to reclaim the temple and tree roots fell over the walls of the tumble down ruins like giant strands of candle wax. Invisible birds called in the trees while shafts of sunlight pierced the ruins and the canopy to create dancing shadows on the walls and the floor. I started to feel that the magic of my imaginary Angkor was returning.

We joined a queue to get the quintessential photo where the most impressive tree roots poured over the walls of the Temple like a waxy waterfall. We were standing with a group of young English backpackers who, like all well raised Brits were chatting and awaiting their turn. Without warning a Chinese man pushed us aside and promptly stood in front of the photo spot while another man took a series of photos. They then swapped over. The youngsters looked at each other, bemused by the rudeness but too polite to say anything. I lost the plot in a matter of seconds. Not being the violent type I resorted to a teacher's best friend: - "sarcasm".

"No seriously that's fine. If I could just stand here waiting in 90 degrees of heat while you push in that would be just perfect. Perhaps I could clean your shoes while you are here or maybe give you a piggy back if you are tired? Please go get the rest of your family as we are happy to stand and wait after all its not hot or anything. Maybe I could kneel on the floor and you could sit on me for a different pose I would love to do that. You selfish, inconsiderate, ill-mannered bastard!"

I am sure they understood little of my rant but I felt so much better and did get a round of applause from those who understood English. Andrea had heard it all before and sighed saying. "Oh Jim."

As we left the ruins we managed to either lose Bili or simply get lost but in the sweltering heat we took a good hour to find the tuk-tuk. I thought we would both overheat and pass out. In desperation we purchased two chilled coconuts from a stall and sipped the coconut water through a straw. Never has anything tasted so good. We eventually found Bili and drove back to the Avalon.

As we cooled off in our room I tried to explain how the day had left me feeling but found it very difficult to put into words. I did say that the taking of photos at Angkor Wat had made me impatient because I had wanted to experience the place without interference. My explanation was at best garbled and I was not sure whether Andrea understood me.

As evening approached there was a knock at the door and there stood Bili.

"It is time to go Madam Andrea. Are you ready"
I had wondered why Andrea had woken me from my snooze and wondered still more as we left the room to retrace the morning route back to Angkor Wat.

"It will be perfect madam. No Chinese. They only come in the morning. The sun is setting. You see. It is beautiful"

Well beautiful does not come close to describing the sunset at Angkor. The subtle changes in light, the reflection of the majestic temple in the lakes in front of the buildings. Almost by the minute the vista changes. Angkor one second sunlit the next an eerie silhouette framed against the jungle. The children selling tat and the smells from tiny barbeques so invasive that morning, added to the evening experience.

We stood on the edge of the lake until the light had completely gone and the Temple of Angkor Wat had disappeared as if devoured by the jungle. It was one of the greatest experiences of my life and one that I will never forget. My imaginary visons of this sacred place could never match the reality of this sunset. I even bought a t-shirt from a tiny little girl "asking for "wan dorror". It actually cost me five. I ripped off by a five-year-old and I didn't care a bit. Andrea had understood my afternoon ramblings and had with a little help from Bili made everything right again.

The next day I started planning the next leg of the trip. The overland journey from Siem Reap to Phnom Penh did not appear to be especially arduous and the choice of bus companies meant, at least in my mind, that healthy competition would ensure a good service. I duly booked two seats on the day bus at the right royal price of $15 each. Giant Ibis, the bus company, promised a packed breakfast, free wi-fi and comfort break half way. The seats were advertised as reclining and super comfortable, I was, to say the least, optimistic. Andrea was less certain and her general dislike of buses meant that it was with a fair degree of trepidation that we said goodbye to Patrick and climbed into Bili's tuk-tuk for the short journey to the bus station.

We were one of the first to arrive at the Giant Ibis station and we were certainly the first westerners. We were greeted by the now familiar smiling Cambodian workers. This country has very little but my goodness the people are cheerful and generous and always willing to help, even more so when a dollar bill is pushed in their direction. Mind you such a small amount of money for us is a massive help to them. As we waited more and more people arrived and luggage was checked in in a very ordered fashion, I felt rather smug that my choice of bus company was clearly a good one. Several other westerners joined us and we exchanged stories of adventures so far and of those yet to come. Most of these adventurers were considerably younger than us and I could see from Andreas face that she was very proud of what we were undertaking and really enjoyed telling stories about Sri Lanka, the monkeys and even the leeches from the rainforest.

Bed 9 The Killing Fields

The bus left on time, a packed breakfast was served, the wi-fi worked and we duly stopped half way for a snack and a break. The seats were fine, not super comfortable but plenty big enough and with lots of leg room. All in all, $15 well spent.

We arrived in Phnom Penh and as always caught a taxi to our hotel. I am sure that the younger bus travellers thought us extravagant but the security of getting sorted quickly and without fuss was the best way for us. We only used taxis on arrival in a new place and after that did our best on busses and local tuk-tuks.

We checked in at the rather elegant Asian Tea House resort on number 32 street. The room was spacious and very clean with brilliant air conditioning. The views over the city were frankly a little disappointing but sitting on the balcony watching the masses go about their daily business was rather like looking down on a busy ant's nest. People scurried along pushing carts laden with fruits and vegetables. Women swept pavements in a frenetic manner that would give any time and motion man a heart attack. Children dodged the cars and motor bikes kicking footballs or peddling feverishly on tiny tricycles and push bikes. My first impression of Phnom Penh was that it was very much alive and bursting with life.

Andrea and I were both tired after a near seven-hour coach trip but we were excited to explore. Nonetheless a nap seemed like the best idea and we passed the late afternoon and early evening in a peaceful slumber.

We ate mid evening and in all honesty I cannot recommend Cambodian wine to anyone but the beer was cold and the food although hardly ethnic was fine. Andrea who loves to experiment with local food stuffs was disappointed by the lack of genuine Cambodian fare. In our experience European meals are generally best left to European chefs. The highlight of our supper was the discovery of red dragon fruit.

At a table just over from ours an Aussie man was eating what looked like a giant beetroot. Andrea was curious but as always was very reluctant to let me ask him what the hell he was eating. I love talking to fellow travellers but Andrea fears I may pick a weirdo. I have to say this seldom stops me. The Aussie like most in his nation was keen for a chat.

"Mate this is real proper, you should try one. We can't get them at home but they are everywhere over here"

Only after much more celebration of the said fruit was I able to get a word in and finally discover what they were.

"Red dragon fruits mate, bloody marvellous"
Once again in true blue Aussie fashion my new mate proved to be very generous.

"Here mate take this one over to your missus and have a try. I've got another in my room and the rest of the family don't really do fruit"

We chatted for a couple of minutes me asking question about things to do in the city and him telling me the best place for beer and which bars had the sports channels.

I returned to Andrea with a massive red dragon fruit in my hands and we skulked off back to our room to give it a go. Well it was a treat, juicy, and tasty just so much better than the white ones. There was one major issue however. Actually there were two major issues but one only became apparent the next morning. The fruits colour was a vivid dark red almost purple. It stained everything it came into contact with. Now Andrea is a pretty careful eater but I can be a little clumsy and suffice to say that one previously white t-shirt ended up soaking in the sink with the last of our Vanish powder.

The next morning, I went to the loo for my normal morning ablutions. The shock when I looked down nearly made me scream. I was haemorrhaging and although feeling fine I felt that a trip to hospital was only minutes away. Through the door I shouted to Andrea that something was very wrong and that I might need a doctor. I explained that the toilet was bright red and I was in trouble, I was shocked, and a little hurt at her almost uncontrollable laughter. Remember the after effect of red dragon fruit should you ever discover them.

Andrea and I were not exactly on a whistle stop tour of Cambodia but our time was limited as I had for reasons best known to myself already booked our next Giant Ibis bus from Phnom Penh to Saigon. I can't bring myself to call it Ho Chi Minh city. So bright and early the next morning we were up and ready to go. It was a Saturday so the streets were less busy than on a working day and getting around on foot was straightforward. Most of what we wanted to see was within walking distance and I planned a route taking in the central market, the Royal Palace a few Wats and the riverfront.

The market was heaving and Andrea was in her element. Stalls are set out in a pattern with each area of the market specialising in a specific thing. Watches and jewels in one area, material and clothes in another and of course food in another. Khmer street food stalls selling everything from hot dogs of the American variety to hot dogs of the South East Asian variety. We both had a cooling freshly made fruit juice made from a selection of tropical fruits. Nothing in the food market cost more than a couple of dollars and every stall holder far preferred dollars to Cambodian Riels. It was odd to be in a country where the local currency was hardly ever used. It was also confusing when change was given in a mixture of dollars and Riels especially as there were over 4000 Riels to the green back.

Our main purchases or rather Andreas main purchases were a couple of pashminas and a purse for each of our girls. Strangely, it took over two hours just to do this.

We walked on to the Royal Palace and the Silver Pagoda and joined the queue to have a look around. The Pagoda was jaw dropping and quite simply took my breath away. The walls are tiled in silver, the marble columns are majestic and the bejewelled statues simply stunning. The centre piece was the Emerald Buddha hewn out of baccarat crystal. The Royal Palace, the home of Khmer Kings for a century and a half was in my view far less impressive. From here we strolled alongside the Tonle Sap river where it merged with the mighty Mekong. Small boats and ferries crossed the brown water as they would have done for centuries. People washed clothes in the water and the poverty stricken huddled by riverside fires beside crude shelters that appeared to be their only comforts. On the river side walkway, the wealthy ate ice cream and paraded in their weekend best clothes. Children played with balls or rode on cycles. The inequality that plagues all countries was more apparent here than in any place we had visited to date.

I was struck by the dignity of the destitute, no one begged, some sold trinkets they had crafted from discarded rubbish, others cleaned shoes. Some with more enterprise were cooking over open fires and selling to those who had any money to spare.

The sun set over the Mekong and we returned to the Tea House Resort for gin and tonics in the happy hour. Time spent in Asia was changing us, Andrea and I spoke at length about this strange country and the charming people. How could it have moved on from the carnage of the mid 70's. yet the city seemed to be thriving.

We ate supper that evening in a reflective silence not because we had nothing to say but because we were deep in our own thoughts. It wasn't the silence that followed pointless arguments about bills or control of the TV remote or who didn't tidy up what, those mundane tiffs that come after 25 years of marriage. This was altogether different. This was a profound and meaningful silence as we started to come to terms with our own feelings and began to realise how we were growing as people as we travelled. We were closer than we had been for many years and I really liked it.

Cambodia was making us think in a way that we had not for many years if ever. The magnificent temples, the jungle, the newfound technology the mad dash to get the dollar and the spectre of the Khmer Rouge that hung over the country like a dark blanket obscuring the light. To understand Cambodia, we had to understand the past and that meant digging into the genocide of the Pol Pot regime.

I was not fully prepared for the day that lay ahead of us as it is impossible to prepare yourself for the horrors that overwhelmed this beautiful nation. We took a tour bus to Tuoi Seing Genocide Museum better known as S-21, or school 21. Until 1975 this school in a quiet suburb of the capitol had been the daily home to happy school children eager to learn to play their part in the nation's future.

Pol Pot rode triumphant into Phnom Penh on the 17th April 1975. The people rejoiced but the joy was short lived and the evacuation of the city began almost at once. The Death March saw the city cleared as people under pain of death were forced into the rural areas. Four months later, Tuoi Seing was transformed from a place of learning to a place of nightmares.

Monks, Christians, the educated, the disabled, those with contacts in the west or in Vietnam, Laotians, and the wealthy were targeted and executed. Some 1.5 million people were exterminated 21per cent of the population. Around 20,000 of these spent their last days in the hell that was S-21. Only seven people are known to have entered the camp and survived. The murder squads were grotesquely efficient.

The school has been preserved and has to be witnessed to be truly understood. There are places on our planet that are pure evil, and that feeling remains even although the atrocities have long since ceased.

The cold silent rooms hold rusty iron beds often with the original shackles still attached. Stains that discolour the floors and walls provide lasting evidence of the torture that took place. Expressionless photos of innocent victims line the walls. People without names just numbers often pinned directly onto the flesh stare into the distance, a distance that hopefully held peace and relief for the innocents.

Some of the classrooms are divided into small cells little bigger than dog kennels where up to 1500 prisoners were held at any one time. No frills, no comforts just the most effective use of space to enable maximum efficiency for Pol Pot's murderous gang. It was impossible not to draw parallels with Hitler's Nazis and the Holocaust from WWii.

On the day we visited S-21 one of the three remaining survivors was signing books for the school children who had visited the museum. I would have loved to talk to this diminutive little man who had seen and experienced so much horror in his life. He looked just like any other old man wrinkled and weak smiling under his American style baseball cap. He was a link to the past but with no translator available I had to content myself with a smile and a nod of admiration and respect. I hope he understood the meaning of my simple actions.

Andrea and I slowly made our way back to the minivan and tried to prepare ourselves for the second part of the trip. Two young Italians seated in front of us were close to tears while the other two couples simply sat in reverent silence. We moved off through the traffic towards Choeung Ek and the killing fields.

The sun shone as we arrived but dark clouds both physical and metaphorical gathered over our heads. We each collected a head set to guide us through the horrific but somehow magnetically fascinating and macabre site. We passed into the killing field as so many had done before us, the present day visitors guaranteed a safe passage. Rising from the centre of the fields stood the ossuary containing the skulls of countless victims. Tourists squeezed through the narrow doorway to see close up the shattered bones bleached white by time. This was not for me and I walked away to learn of the horrors that faced those who entered with no hope of ever leaving.

Mounds dot the fields where each of the mass graves are situated. After heavy rains bones and strips of clothing still surface as if their owners are struggling to escape this most evil of places. The headset recording continued with, numbers of dead, the means of execution, the stench of decay the methods of keeping the area secret. Finally, I reached a place that will stay with me as long as I live.

A large tree stands in the back corner of Choeung Ek, next to one of the larger mass graves. There is a simple sign beside the tree written in Khmer and English. The words read "killing tree against which executioners beat children".

Nothing more, no elaboration, no grotesque descriptions, just those simple words. Coloured bracelets and ribbons act as reminders of those long gone.

This great tree is the lasting memorial to the dead. It reminds everyone who sees it of the fragility of life. There are thousands of these trees in Cambodia but you need see only one. I walked away slowly tears running down my cheeks seeking my own solace. Andrea and I hugged each other and held hands. The killing field at Choeung Ek is forever etched in my memory.

Cambodia is a beautiful country and Andrea and I saw just a tiny part of it. I think to truly understand the place would take years. The people are friendly and welcoming and remarkably adept at making the best out of a bad situation. Tourists flood in to experience the real South East Asia but what is real? Certainly not the clamour for the Yankee dollar. This is just a by-product of the people's survival instinct. Children can earn more than their parents because westerners swoon at their tiny smiling faces with deep brown eyes and their learned phrases;

"Velly cheap wan dorror"

"You buy two good luck"

"Beautiful lady buy wan for heem"

In both places we visited there were orphanages encouraging volunteers to help and donate money. They seemed so genuine and it was tempting to help. We discovered that many of these places were simply money making scams and often the children were bought in and not orphans at all. Quick fix money making may well work in the short term but ultimately it will be education that moves Cambodia forward and until a way can be found to get all children into school the future will not be particularly rosy.

Bed 10 Saigon the city of motor cycles.

As the weak morning sun rose over Phnom Penh the sleek grey Giant Ibis bus pulled away en-route to Saigon. Unlike the journey from Siem Reap most of the roads were tarmac and the journey was easy.

The bus was packed with locals heading towards the border town. All manner of goods had been stowed in the luggage hold. Khmer people do not travel light. To us it appeared that some may even have been moving house. On the bus homemade packed breakfasts were being devoured with gusto by the locals and the smell was horrendous. Dried fish seemed to be a local favourite even overpowering the smell of the eggs and other mysterious foods. What a relief it was when breakfast seemed to be over. The smell however remained and it took us a while to figure out why. I spotted it first but fortunately I always store my day pack overhead. Andrea keeps hers at her feet not trusting anyone. Well, fish oil stinks and day packs standing in fish oil stink and as it turned out they stink for a good few days. As always I resisted the urge to say "I told you so."

For the first few hours the journey was not remotely eventful and the scenery was the now familiar patch work of ramshackle peasant houses and rice paddies. We drove through countless small villages creating a minor dust storm and encouraging cheerful waves from the children playing by the road side. I had a window seat and consequently was able to bird watch as we progressed towards the border crossing. The coach slowed and I assumed that the comfort break was approaching, the locals began to gather things together but the coach didn't stop. I tried to look forward to see what the holdup was and noticed a dust cloud kicked up by a slow moving farm vehicle. I hesitate to say tractor as it was more like a large lawn mower towing a flatbed trailer. On the trailer appeared to be two large greeny brown rolled up lumps of something that were very difficult to make out from behind. As we pulled alongside the trailer it was clear that the objects were not rolled up anything, but two 10-foot-long crocodiles, trussed and secured to the flat bad. Andrea struggled to get her camera from her backpack forgetting it was fish oil soaked. Still at least she reacted well to the damp patch the oil created on her travelling dungarees. The crocs were tied at the feet and taped at the mouth but were massive. I assume that they will be now have provided a good few meals for the owners and probably a pair of shoes or a handbag for some wealthy Parisian or New Yorker.

I was bobbing up and down pointing and trying to get everyone else to look out of the window. The Cambodians around me looked at me as if I was mad and ignored what to me, was something akin to seeing the Loch Ness Monster. I love South East Asia and the sights, sounds and smells that invade your senses every day.

The Giant Ibis bus pulled up at the border crossing and our driver explained exactly what we were to do. Well that's what Andrea and I assumed he did, but as it was in Cambodian we understood nothing.

I quickly switched into control mode which was somewhat timely as Andrea was approaching mild panic mode, not helped by the all-pervading fish smell that seemed to be getting stronger as the air conditioning was turned off and the temperature began to rise.

"Don't worry Andrea. All we have to do is watch what the others do and follow them."

"What if they don't fucking know what to do? We could end up stuck at the border or miss the coach or lose our luggage or have our passports stolen or be robbed?"

I looked over at her and said,

"Or we could just follow the others, breeze through passport control, and be in Vietnam in no time at all"

Well, Andrea's panic was unnecessary and my optimism was a little misplaced. The border between Vietnam and Cambodia at Macobai-Bavet is chaotic to say the least. Worryingly all passports were collected by the bus conductor and taken to the border post. We had to gather our belongings and queue for no apparent reason in the blistering sun. Slowly the line moved forward until we were inside the building where all humanity seemed to jostle to get to the front of the queue only to be met by Cambodian border guards who, despite being diminutive, were rather fierce looking. Of course without a passport we could not cross but at least everyone else seemed to be in the same predicament. So stalemate ensued, people pushing forward all sweating and carrying luggage but unable to cross into Vietnam.

Then I spotted how the system worked. The coach conductors were at the front talking to the border guards and eventually our man seemed to have persuaded an official to make a gate available to our bus load. There then ensued a second wave of pushing very reminiscent of England Scrum driving the Scots for a push over try at Twickenham. Our coach passengers drove through the melee to the correct gate and we waited until our name was called and crossed out of Cambodia. Mind you recognising our names being softly spoken in a Cambodian accent against the din of some 500 other travellers was not so simple. I suggested that Andrea and I push to the front and wait until our passports could be handed to us, it worked and we were on our way again.

Getting into Vietnam was simple in comparison to getting out of Cambodia. We had visas already even though by October 2016 they were no longer needed. A grim faced little Vietnamese soldier sat at a small desk and hardly looked at us as he stamped our passports and waved us through. We walked back into the sunlight and into a country that had fascinated me since I was a child.

I could vividly recall news bulletins about the Vietnam war. I had seen so many films: - Platoon, Apocalypse Now, Full Metal Jacket and Rambo. I recalled the music that had provided a sound track to the conflict. Paint it Black by the Stones, the ride of the Valkyrie, Credence and the Animals. Now I had a real chance to learn about the conflict and legacy of war in this intriguing country.

Our big silver bus rolled through the outskirts of Saigon and as it did so pedestrians, dogs and motor cyclists seemed to leap for cover. At out final destination the normal mayhem of arriving in a strange city greeted us. A quick $5 taxi ride and we were safe in our downtown hotel ready for a snooze. The Xavier hotel in District 1 was clean, welcoming and right in the middle of everything. Perfect for exploring the city.

An evening stroll around the block taught us quite a few things about Saigon. Firstly, the roads are almost impossible to cross Andrea and I stood and stared at the road and had it not been for a tiny little Vietnamese woman who took my hand we may well never have ventured to the other side. Literally hundreds of motor bikes crowd the streets and they seem to obey none of the normal road rules of the road. Indeed, there appears to be almost as much chance of being hit by one on the pavement. It was frightening. Well this dear little lady took my hand and just walked out into the traffic. I held onto Andrea and it was a bit like Moses at the Red Sea the motor bikes parted and we walked safely across. On the other side she simply smiled and nodded and went on her way.

Later our hotel receptionist explained that the key was to walk at an even pace allowing the bikes to avoid you rather than you trying to avoid the bikes. She explained that you should never stop or run as this made it impossible for the riders to assess where you would be on the road when they reached you. I am not sure if this gave us confidence but at least it meant that we could potentially see more of the city than just the block we were staying on.

Secondly, Saigon is an incredibly cheap place to have manicures, massages and by the look of some of the establishments any other type of personal service. Andrea leapt at the chance to have a manicure and nails polished for just under $5. I, whilst searching for my feminine side, settled for the manicure and skipped the polish.

Finally eating out in the city was going to be a mystery ride. Most of the menus were not in English and where they were it was very hard to fully understand what the dishes consisted of. The food was inexpensive and tasty but in all honesty half the time we had no idea what we were eating. We found the best thing to do was to look up typical Vietnamese dishes on the internet and order them. Pho was really excellent and appeared to be eaten for breakfast lunch and dinner but at under $2 who cared.

As we slumped onto our bed after a day of travelling, queuing at the border and risking life and limb on the roads, the communist propaganda concert started. We had noticed the outdoor stage in the park at the end of the road while out walking but had no idea what was in store. The rousing triumphal music, the singing of patriotic songs and the crowds of excited party members did not augur well for a good night's sleep. However much to our surprise and delight at exactly 10pm the music stopped and the crowd in a quiet, orderly fashion dispersed. This was the pattern for our whole stay in Saigon. We couldn't help but wonder what would have been the situation at home after say the Notting Hill Carnival or Hyde Park Calling.

For me the main reason for visiting Saigon was to see the War Museum and the Cu Chi tunnels. For Andrea it seemed to be to go to the Hard Rock Café and get another badge, to have as many parts of her body pampered as possible and to get the material she had purchased in Sri Lanka turned into custom made garments. So we made a plan for the next few days. Andrea took charge, as she was now keen to do, especially when shopping was possible. Our time was limited as we had a flight to catch out of Hanoi to Bangkok in ten days and overland travel was at best slow and occasionally stationary.

I had wanted to travel by rail on the Re-unification Express from Saigon northwards but when I looked into timings I quickly realised the term express may not mean the same in Vietnam as it does at home.

Thus we allowed ourselves four days in Saigon and then planned to travel to Hoi An for a further five days and finally onto Hanoi to catch our onward flight. This made the Re-unification Express an impossibility as it took over a day. I checked flights and was delighted to find that Jet Star Vietnam flew any number of daily flights to Da Nang and from there it was a short bus journey to Hoi An. I booked us flights at the astronomical cost of £14 each.

Our first day exploring was Andrea's day and I suppose it was very successful. We managed to find the Hard Rock and buy a badge. She was fitted for various tops all to be made to order and be ready by the next afternoon. The tailors seemed very enthusiastic to make up the garments and were totally confident that everything would be fine. This, however, did not stop Andrea asking the same questions twenty times over and changing her mind about the patterns almost as many times. It was very clear to me that the Vietnamese had boundless patience.

We found the Saigon Post Office building which was a masterpiece of Colonial architecture and well worth a visit. It nestled behind the Cathedral and most certainly was a product of a by-gone age. The inside of the building had not changed for decades. Polished wooden benches dotted the large waiting gallery and overheating tourists took refuge here. Several old phone booths stood on one side of the entrance hall, each with a clock mounted above. These showed the times in New York, Paris, London and Moscow. Postcards were on sale and the great and good from all parts of the world sat writing home to mothers, lovers and grandparents. It was a place of calm in a city where calm is at a premium. We could have sat there for hours just watching the comings and goings it was fascinating, but while the shops were open Andrea has a purpose and we moved, on a little too quickly for my liking.

From there we walked to the Central Market but by the time we reached it we were far too hot and tired to cope with the enthusiasm of the market sellers. Even Andrea had to admit that the thought of bartering or even trying on clothes in 90-degree heat was too much. We skirted the edge of the covered market place and looked in at the masses inside. It seemed to me that the inside of an ant's nest would look very similar. Even on the outside we were offered sunglasses, fans, lighters, watches and just about anything else that could be mounted on a board and carried by a smiling Vietnamese seller.

We settled for afternoon tea in a French style bakery close to the Xavier before returning to our room for the now obligatory late afternoon siesta. Actually the French style bakeries in Saigon are well worthy of mention as they serve delicious pastries and cakes at a fraction of the cost in

Europe and what's more the people working in the shops seem genuinely pleased to serve you.

In the early evening we walked out into district 1 to find a suitable place to have supper. We had barely left the Xavier when we were beckoned over by a rather large Australian gent who seemed to be holding court in a small café.

"Mate you look like a couple of poms how about sitting down and having a beer with the two of us?"

He pointed sideways to a homely looking women who appeared very embarrassed by his forwardness.

"I need to chat to some white folks, just about had enough trying to make myself understood by these little fellas. Plus, mate the beer is cold and bloody cheap and the tucker pretty good too"

I checked with boss and we decided that a chat and a beer would be good and we could slip off to eat any time we wanted.

"I'm Dave and this is Regina we're from Perth"

"Andrea and Jim from Kent in the UK. Good to meet you both"

Well a quick beer turned into a few beers and slipping off to eat became ordering something in the café. It wasn't that we necessarily planned the evening but Dave was hilarious and his endless anecdotes and stories kept us amused for the rest of the night.

Dave had every ailment known to man or so it appeared, most however seemed to stem from the fact that he weighed in at well over 25 stone, ate too much, drank too much and smoked too much. He seemed to be the only person that failed to make a connection between his lifestyle and his health.

"I can't understand it mate, the bloody knees are giving out and in this heat well you can see I'm sweating like a fat lady in a cake shop. Regina, you tell them. Can't even put my socks on in the morning can I?"

"No Dave really struggles"

Dave cut in.

"Tell em about my shortage of breath and the bloody lift not working in the hotel. And the bloody bog keeps bunging up"

"Dave they won't want to hear about you bunging up the dunny."

After an extensive medical report, we widened the scope of the conversation and it turned out that Dave and Regina were in Saigon for two main reasons. They were on a shopping spree to buy as much art and craft stuff as they could carry back to Perth in order to furnish their little cottage industry at home. Dave promised to show us some of their work the following evening if we fancied another beer or two. It appeared that Dave sat in the same seat in the same bar every night he was in Saigon.

Dave then sat proudly bolt upright and said

"Now I'll show you the other reason we are here." Andrea and I were not sure if he was going to roll up his trousers and show us a wooden leg or lift his shirt to show us in detail where the surgeons were going to begin liposuction. We were thankfully wrong on both counts.

Dave smiled a beaming smile and then said after clicking his teeth together for show.

"What do you think of those beauties? All cleaned crowned, and polished by a brilliant little dentist around the corner. Even taking into account the airfare and hotel price I'm still in bloody profit mate."

He continued,

"We're gonna tell everyone when we get home, these little yellow buggers are bloody good dentists and they love working on Aussies. They reckon we've got bigger mouths so it's much easier."

It was true his teeth were white and straight and it appeared as if these little yellow buggers had indeed done a very good job. Nonetheless I declined his offer of an introduction to the said dentist.

"Yeh, well mate you got a pretty good set of choppers there anyway. Probably don't need to see him just yet"

I was flattered.

We ate Vietnamese spring rolls and a bowl of pho, and drank another chilled beer sitting at a pavement table. Regina was interested in our adventures in Cambodia and Sri Lanka and Dave had plenty of other body parts to show us that were either non-functioning or in need of urgent repair. The sounds of the city and the communist propaganda from the end of the street accompanied us until bedtime and we agreed to join our new pals for beer the following evening.

After breakfast in a bakery Andrea and I set off for the Saigon war museum. We had no idea what to expect but we assumed it would reveal in depth the Vietnam conflict from the Vietnamese viewpoint.

The museum is set in a residential area and is very easy to find. As always we walked and my God it was a hot day. By the time we arrived at the gates we were dripping and longing for the air conditioning. No such luck as the first part of the museum is outside in full sunlight. Tanks, military trucks and even a couple of aeroplanes were displayed outside the main building. French made detention cells had been recreated to ensure that the brutal French rule period did not go unforgotten. In the cells were metal cages used to detain political dissidents as well as grotesque implements of torture that would not have gone amiss during the Spanish Inquisition. Somehow popular history seems to have allowed

France to get away with many atrocities against Vietnam at least if it hasn't we are certainly not taught about it in school.

Andrea and I eventually entered the cool of the museum building and we were surprised to find that it was not a collection of old uniforms and weapons but a photographic memorial to the conflict. Magnificently reproduced photos from war correspondents and photographers led us through the conflict. Punches were certainly not pulled and the graphic images were not for the faint hearted. The written text that accompanied the images was anti American' but to be honest I expected nothing less.

There was none of the Apocalyptic: -

"I love the smell of napalm in the morning, it reminds me of victory"

No all American heroes, no John Rambo. Only young men thousands of miles from home or fighting to preserve their homes. Mere boys from the Bronx or Chicago, beach bums from California and Florida thrown into a conflict that was impossible to understand and impossible to win.

The horrors of My Lai, of napalm attacks and of jungle warfare were depicted and explained. When Andrea and I left we felt deep sorrow for both sides. The young GI's, confused and terrified, committed unimaginable atrocities in the name of freedom or on the orders of unhinged military leaders. However, we felt for them in such an alien environment against an often unseen enemy. To face death so far from home was not something Andrea and I could imagine.

The Vietnamese fought like cornered tigers to preserve their freedom. Their losses were astronomical and they developed military tactics that left a generation of American young men unable to return to normal life. The scars of this ill thought out conflict have blighted a generation on both sides of the globe.

Andrea and I had experienced more in a couple of weeks than in our lifetimes. We had both visited the battle fields of France and Belgium. We had learned about the carnage of Passchendaele and the Somme. We had studied the Holocaust and seen stories from Nagasaki and Hiroshima, but all of these event had taken place before we were born. The crimes against humanity committed by Pol Pot and the pointless bloodshed of Vietnam had played out in our young lives and had remained with us to this time.

Somehow visiting the Killing Fields and the War Museum had been like a purge. It did not make it easier but it provided colour, turning opaque memories into pictures that could be sorted, analysed and categorised under the heading "This happened in my lifetime."

We spent a second evening with Dave and Regina in the same bar at the same tables. It turned out they had quite a little cottage industry back in rural Western Australia. They sold all manner of home-made goods at farmer's markets and town sales and what they made looked really good. They cut and designed plywood figurines that were meticulously painted. These ranged from Disney characters, to exotic animals and birds and famous people from history. While Regina showed us photos on her phone, Dave regaled us with stories of his many new injuries and he drank. In fact, he drank about three times as much as me. Not bad for someone trying to shed a stone or ten.

As they evening drew to a close Dave rose to wish us farewell and toppled over the table. This in itself was funny. We humans always laugh at other's misfortunes. It was made more amusing by the shock on the faces of the tiny Vietnamese staff as this mountain of a man rolled down the few steps of the open fronted café. As he rolled he nearly demolished several other tables. Bowls of Pho were thrown in the air, beer bottles crashed onto the floor and one particularly petite waitress was almost steam rolled into the floor. Big Dave ended up looking like an upended hippo on the Saigon pavement.

"Geez Dave way to make an exit, you bloody mongrel."

Several locals tried to help Dave back to his feet, but it was not an easy task, Regina simple finished her G&T, bid us a cheery "Bye youse two" and walked across the road to her hotel.

"You'd better bloody sober up before you get back here or you'll be sleeping in the corridor"
were her parting words to her rather forlorn husband.

Andrea and I bade fare well to the two Aussies They had been great company and we both felt we knew a great deal more about the ailments that effect the Aussie male. We strolled slowly back to the Xavier listening to the triumphal music coming from the communist gathering at the end of the street.

Our final day in Saigon continued the war theme but was altogether less harrowing than the day before. Indeed, it was very light hearted, made even more so by the excellent people who joined us on our tourist minivan to visit the Cu Chi Tunnels.

We joined up with Raj and Anna, a newlywed couple from North London, honeymooning in Vietnam. Raj, of Indian descent and Anna returning to the country that her parents had fled from, as boat people in the early 1980's. Our other van mates were Ramon and Mercedes from Madrid who had taken a break from work to travel in Asia for six weeks. From the moment we boarded the van until the end of the day we got on well. Even Andrea let her guard down and chatted away to strangers.

"Three monkeys sitting in a tree looking down and three chickens under the tree looking up. How many eyes looking down and how many looking up?"

A Vietnamese puzzle set by our guide as we began the hour or so drive to the tunnels.

"A free beer to the person that gets the correct answer"

Well we tried to the obvious six up and six down, along with variations on blind monkeys and beheaded chickens but even with a scatter gun of answers we failed to guess correctly. Ramon assumed it was a trick and said that chickens were afraid of monkeys and ran away so none was looking up.

No answer was forthcoming from the guide, inscrutable lot these Vietnamese, so we moved on. We were all a bit jealous of the luxury that the newlyweds were being so brave to endure as they honeymooned. Spa treatments, star-lit roof top dinners and most important of all no bloody communist rallies at the end of the street. Ramon and Mercedes made the odd playful comment in Spanish, usually at Raj's expense until they heard me laugh in back seat.

"Jim, hablas espanol?"

"Si Ramon jo hablo y jo intiendo, Andrea tambien"

"Oh! mierda" was the reply

More laughter and bemused looks from our two love birds.

As we reached the countryside we passed the now familiar motorbike with a family and all its belongings on the back and then several with cages attached to the back seats. These held ducks, chickens and very occasionally dogs. These mutts sat in their cages mouths open and tongues lolling out looking very excited to be going to their new homes. We all sighed a very European agh! as we passed. Our illusions were shattered when our guide said that few Vietnamese kept dogs as pets and these poor unfortunates were more likely to be Sunday dinner than kid's companions. This revelation rather pissed on our bonfire as they say in high rolling society.

We stopped en-route to Cu Chi at a craft village to do some tourist shopping. The workers inside were creating beautiful art using egg shells to make elaborate mosaics. Each individually painted in minute detail. All of the workers were severely handicapped as a result of Agent Orange. This vile chemical was sprayed onto the forest to clear the land in order that war could be fought on more equal terms. The poisons still effect thousands of people in hot spots across the country. The widespread use of this toxin by the US is probably the single most shameful legacy of the Vietnam conflict and one that is seldom if ever mentioned in the films.

These very dignified people with missing or incompletely formed limbs are adept and skilful at manufacturing artwork. What they produce is spectacular and well worth buying. Some of the workers are so badly handicapped that they work using their mouths or with paint brushes wedged between misshapen toes. The after effects of conflict all too often fade from the memory of the powerful western nations which are so keen to engage in foreign wars. I fear that the devastations in Syria and other parts of the Middle East will long haunt the locals after the super powers have left. In Vietnam the legacy of war is certainly felt in rural areas as Agent Orange still creates disfigurement and heartache for innocent families.

Cu Chi itself is very interesting and well worth a visit. Our group threw themselves into everything. The experience was a cross between a history lesson and visiting a mini theme park. After the prior harrowing experiences, I certainly found this more enjoyable, than thought provoking. Fortunately, Ramon was very much on my wave length and Raj wanted to join in but was worried about offending Anna.

He needn't have worried as she saw the funny side in pretty much everything.

We all watched the black and white propaganda film, that had been created, showing the tunnels during the war period. The sound track crackled and the pictures flickered. My offhand comment enquiring if Charlie Chaplin was in the film did not go down well with the stuffy Brits in front but Ramon nearly wet himself. Andrea thumped me hard in the ribs with her elbow but could not conceal a broad smile.

Next was a tunnel walk with our guide. After about five minutes it became apparent why the yanks had lost: - the Viet Cong may well have been the most crafty, ingenious and bravest people on earth.

We saw hideous booby traps made from sharpened bamboo, fortunately they were pointed out to us because we never would have spotted them in the jungle. We saw workshops, living quarters, food stores and medical rooms that were all direct copies of those built underground by the Viet Cong. There were shoes made from the tyres of captured US vehicles. These had been made backwards to create the impression the soldiers had moved in the opposite direction.

Finally, we reached the underground tunnels themselves. Raj and I could not even fit into the entrance of the real tunnel. Anna and Mercedes could and did but it was a squeeze even for these slight lassies. Andrea may well have fitted but refused on the grounds that spiders might lurk in the depths. At the modified, tunnels we awaited the chance to experience the real thing, or at least the enlarged European sized thing. A tunnel 100 metres long had been opened up. The first 20 metres was big enough for pretty much everyone, probably not Dave had he ventured this far. Each subsequent 20 meters got smaller until the last 20 meters was the size the Viet Cong used.

I made it through the first leg and then in a state of mild panic cut out, closely followed by Raj, Anna and Mercedes. We were greeted at the surface by Andrea, her fear of spiders had prevented her from entering the tunnel. Ramon braved the next section and the next before emerging looking like a startled mole.

"Es horrible, oops sorry, its bloody horrible down there and it stinks. I think that German bloke in front of me must have farted"

Amazing how everyone speaks English so well these days.

It was onto the fire range and for $10 you could buy a clip of ten bullets and use one of the authentic ex-war rifles under the careful gaze of a former soldier. I chose an M16 and Ramon an AK47, Raj, was banned from taking part by Anna, but after a pleading look and much grovelling he got his way and selected an M60.

Well if these were authentic rifles I'm surprised anyone was killed I couldn't have hit a cow's arse with a banjo and the other two were no better. Andrea and I were undecided whether this particular type of tourism was a good idea. Did it glorify war and past horrors? I decided no and simply put it down as a bit of fun.

On the journey home we were told that six eyes looked down but only three up as chickens have eyes on the side of their heads so to look up with one eye the other must look down. No free beer but mystery solved.

Bed 11. Learning to cook Viet style.

Our taxi driver from DaNang airport to Hoi An was a lovely chap and spoke excellent English. He gave us lots of information about the American wartime landings in and around the area and showed us various sites of bombing raids and former military sites. He also explained that he had been a university lecturer until it was discovered that his parents had sided with the South during the war and not the Viet Cong. He had been removed from his job at the university and was now allowed only menial jobs. It seemed such a shame to be punished for the sins of his fathers if indeed they were sins at all.

Our hotel was on the outskirts of Hoi An old town close to the river and away from the hustle and bustle. It was a wonderful little place called the Nova Villa. The staff were friendly and helpful and we could not fault standard of service and cleanliness. We arrived in the early afternoon and spent the last few hours of daylight by the small pool. In order to top up our tans we had to move around the sun beds as the sun dipped between buildings, but as we were the only ones by the pool this was pretty straightforward. If any of the hotel staff were watching these operations, they must have thought we were mad. The vast majority of Vietnamese people try to avoid the sun as here a deep brown skin signifies lack of wealth and only those who work on the land have tans.

The next day we gathered all of the local information from Han the girl behind the reception desk. She explained the entry fee to the old town, gave us tips about food to order and where to eat. She also warned us against paying marked prices in some of the clothing stores and insisted we barter, immediately ruling out me buying anything but heightening

Andreas shopping senses. We left the Nova Villa with a town map ready and fully armed for a day in Hoi An.

We walked along the river in the morning sunshine. Women in typical conical Vietnamese hats were setting up small stalls selling fruits and vegetables. Cafes and bars were preparing for the day, with staff moving small tables and chairs on to the pavements and smoothing out brightly coloured tablecloths. Small boats were already operating on the river offering rides to tourists and transporting workers and goods as they had done for centuries. The slow pace of life in Hoi An was a marked change to that of Saigon.

We reached the main bridge into the old city and paid our $6 entry fee (the money going towards preserving the wonderful buildings of this world heritage site). The fee covered entrance to the old town and admission to any five of the many temples, family houses and famous buildings.

I did find it amusing to hear well-heeled European and Australian tourists complaining about the entrance fee, especially as the ticket vendors spoke very little English and therefore understood none of the complaints just smiling their Vietnamese smile. Personally I would have paid a good deal more and still felt it worthwhile, What a place!

Hoi An developed as a small trading post in the 15th century and has remained such until the present day. Every country that has set up a base here has influenced the architecture of the town. Rather like modern cookery it is a fusion of ideas and styles. The temples are Chinese and Japanese while the shops boast intricate carvings of dragons and other beasts. The backs of the houses are on the river to allow for the loading and unloading of supplies but most of these are now restaurants or shops in their own right. The fronts of the building face the narrow streets in a jumbled but somehow orderly manner. At the far end of the town, alongside the river is a daily market selling all manner of goods to locals and tourist alike. To stand for five minutes in the market is to immerse yourself in the timeless life of Hoi An. It is easy to drift back to the 17th century with the calls of the traders and the high pitched almost argumentative conversation of the local shoppers as the try to bargain for their daily requirements.

Pride of place amongst the towns 1000 or so wooden buildings is the Japanese covered bridge dating from the 1590s. It is guarded by statues of monkeys at one end and dogs at the other. Originally it linked the Japanese part of the town with the Chinese sector. Now it is a major tourist attraction and Andrea and I did what everyone else was doing and posed for photographs to post on Facebook and to send home to the girls.

By now I had become a bit of a fan of Facebook and was regularly updating my profile picture as we moved from place to place. When I say I was regularly updating my photo what I mean is Andrea was doing it for me. This was not only because I do not own a camera and therefore relied totally on her photography. Also my I-Pad was so ancient that I could not get it to do much other than play solitaire and hold my blogs. To publish my blogs, I had to send them to Andrea and get her to upload them onto WordPress. My attempts to move into the technological age seemed to provide great amusement to Andrea but fortunately I could take the ribbing, and actually had no choice if I wished to continue getting this on line.

Food plays a massive part in the life of the people of Hoi An. Enormous numbers are employed cooking it, serving it and indeed teaching westerners how to cook it. Andrea and I decided that we were pretty good at eating it and maybe we would like to cook it and serve it to our friends when we eventually got back to the UK.

The local speciality is Cao Lau a dish of braised and spiced pork with noodles and greens. The water for the dish traditionally comes from one well just outside the town. Cao Lau is fragrant and filling, and when accompanied by a chilled beer is about as good as it gets. Other traditional Viet dishes are served in all the local restaurants and the quality is wonderful. The restaurants within the old town are more expensive than those outside and tourists tend to flock to the old town. Andrea I tended to eat our evening meal away from the tourists either at riverside or street stalls and we were never disappointed.

Han had told us not to sit too close to the road as child beggars often pestered those in the cheap seats. We had received the same advice in Siem Reap so we understood. We did not worry too much about this as a few dong handed over to a smiling child gave us pleasure. As we sat eating sipping a happy hour beer watching the floating lanterns drift lazily down the river a pretty little teenage girl approached us trying to sell fridge magnets.

She greeted us in broken English with a massive smile and said

"Where you from?"

"We are from England"

"Why you have no hair"

She pointed at my shaven bonce which with the sun long gone was now exposed.

"I shave it off"

"Why you do that?"

She then patted my stomach

"Happy Buddha, when baby due"

With this Andrea nearly fell off her stool and the little girl went on her way.

I was well used to being greeted as "happy Buddha" and since I had lost at least two stone in South East Asia I wondered if she would have called for the midwife had she seen me a month or so earlier.

The next morning, we were up early for the next part of our foody adventure. Andrea had booked us both on a cookery course, of which there are many in Hoi An. She had chosen carefully not opting for the hotel based courses that proliferated the river side. The one she chose involved a forty-minute river-boat ride to a small island and was called Grandma's home cooking.

We walked the short distance from the Villa Nova to the meeting place where we were met by the charming Ang Su who was our hostess for the day. We were soon joined by three Australian couples and made our way down to the jetty.

Our boat looked sturdy enough and as we chugged out into the centre of the river we passed tiny little crafts loaded to the brim with bales of cloth, grain and of course fishermen. We continued downstream passing small houses and countless river bank fishermen. On our way we got to know our companions for the day. Doug and Mary from Sydney, Alan and Sue from just outside Sydney and Bruce and Yvonne from Brisbane. Ang Su, in near perfect, self-taught English chatted to us all and explained the day in detail.

We asked questions about grandma as well as the dishes to be prepared. Grandma it turned out was 90 years of age and had lived on the tiny island for all of her life. She had survived floods and more amazingly a stray US bomb that had fallen on the island and killed several of the islanders. The crater was still clearly visible and only a matter of yards from the bottom of her garden.

Ang Su had grown up in Hoi An and attended the local school. She had spotted the opportunity to work with tourists and taught herself English. She had worked for other tourist enterprises but realising she could do it herself set up the cookery school. This little entrepreneur was a smart cookie indeed. She stood no more than five feet tall and was stunningly pretty. She wore a black traditional Viet costume of baggie trousers and a black, round necked button up jacket. She wore gloves and socks to protect her from the effects of the sun and a quintessential Viet conical hat. Her bright red lipstick accentuated a smile that seldom left her lips.

Andrea chatted nonstop to Ang Su, while I took the opportunity to do a bit of river bank birding. I managed to spot several cinnamon bitterns and a pied kingfisher during the journey.

When we reached the island we walked past the shrimp pools and the bomb crater from the war, before entering Grandmas family home and meeting the great lady. The house was wooden and simple, but very welcoming. In the back Ang Su had constructed a thatch-covered veranda style cooking area. It was kitted out with four large work surfaces and on each were two small gas burners, chopping boards and a selection of knives, spoons and condiments. These work areas surrounded a similar central unit at which Ang Su demonstrated.

After a cooling glass of fresh fruit juice, which I guess was passion fruit and mango, and the distribution of aprons etc., we were introduced to the staff and to the traditional tools found in a Viet kitchen.

Grandma popped in to see us and in a crouched position so typical of those in far East proceeded to use a massive rice shaker to produce rice flour. It was amazing to see a lady of such great age and so little size, handle a very large sifting tray. Grandma looked every bit of her 90 years and I guessed she had done so for many years. Clearly life had not been easy for Grandma but the dignity she displayed was heart-warming. I suspect she may not have too many years left but hopefully the cookery school will stand as a lasting memory to her.

Over the next few hours we had a wonderful time, cooking, chatting, laughing and of course eating. We ground rice flour, made Vietnamese crepes and cooked four tasty dishes. Andrea as a former food teacher was a pretty good cook, whereas I being a klutz was fairly ordinary. However, the fact that my dishes looked very unlike those prepared by Ang Su was irrelevant because they tasted great and only I had to eat them. The green papaya salad we prepared was to die for and assuming we can get green papayas in the UK it will be a regular feature on our dinner party menus.

Our Aussie mates had varying degrees of success with the dishes. When a naked flame was involved in the cooking process they excelled especially the men folk I guess it reminded them of barbecues back home. When more delicate skills were needed the ladies excelled. I did feel sorry for Bruce when he took a great chunk out of his finger whilst chopping carrot batons but in true Aussie style he battled on to the end.

Throughout the day the ribbing and joking continued in a way that only Aussies and POMs can manage. I took great delight when Bruce, bad finger and all, dropped his pork skewers on the floor
.   "Another one dropped mate just like you blokes in the Ashes tests"

"Bloody POM. If you'd nearly sliced off your finger you'd be running home to mummy"
Actually, he might have been right on that one.

The boat journey back to town was uneventful for everyone except me. I missed my opportunity to use the loo before we left the island and half way back desperately needed to go. The boat had no facilities and seemed to be going much slower than on the outward journey. By the time the jetty came into view I had gone silent and was perched on the edge of the boat with my buttocks clenched ready to sprint to the nearest bar. There was no nearest bar, so I ran to the first house I could see and using my best mime skills indicated my predicament. By a stroke of good fortune, the house had a facility which resembled a loo and a messy emergency was avoided. Andrea was as always very sympathetic to my plight and the local family no doubt still talks about the day happy Buddha rushed in to use their toilet.

Grandmas cookery school cost $30 and it was one of the best $30 we spent on our whole adventure. The way that the Vietnamese people have recovered and prospered since the dark days of the conflict is in total contrast its near neighbours in Cambodia. Andrea and I loved this place and we both vowed to return as soon as we could.

Sadly, we were not in a position to take advantage of the numerous excellent tailors who ply their trade in Hoi An simple logistics made this an impossibility. We did however get to see several well-crafted suits and dresses purchased by other residents of the Nova Villa. On couple had actually had all of the bridesmaid's dresses along with a wedding suit made up at a fraction of the cost in the west. Andrea and I both noted this excellent idea away in our heads, not that we would need an excuse to revisit Hoi An.

Our journey to Bangkok via Da Nang and Hanoi was uneventful. Jet star Vietnam offer services that really are very inexpensive. They do have a knack of changing flight times without too much notice but once they say they are going they go on time. By now both Andrea and I were seasoned travellers and a delay even of a few hours really didn't bother us too much. We sat in the departure lounge at Hanoi airport catching up on emails and reading our kindles and simply watching the world go by. Looking back, it is amazing how a month or so on the road changes one's outlook on travel.

I wonder if it will be the same when we get home or if we will revert to the nervous agitation that tends to accompany almost all flights to holiday destinations.

Bed 11 & 12 British rail it isn't

We arrived in Bangkok and once again found our hotel without mishap. We were staying a couple of blocks from the infamous Khao San Road in a modern, city centre hotel, the Tara Place. Andrea and I had both visited Bangkok when our girls were in their teens so we were at least familiar with the money and the sprawling layout of the city. It is a city I do not warm to, as it is simply too big and too crowded but does have a vibrancy that is exciting in small doses. Andrea and I saw Bangkok as little more than a stopping off point from where we would catch the train south to Surat Thani and on to Phuket.

An evening spent on the Khao San Road is an experience and one that suits all ages and all bank balances. Backpackers mix with older, wealthier, tourists who in turn rub shoulders with sleazy overweight men looking and sadly often finding beautiful young Thai girls.

Middle aged couples come to shop at the multitude of stalls that line the street in front of the ostentatious bars blasting out rock music. Each stall sells varieties on the same theme. T Shirts, tailored clothing, tacky souvenirs and electronic goods.

Between the two lines of stalls is the road itself although in the evenings few vehicles travel down it. Hawkers sell food, children try to sell trinkets and local police wander around hoping that no trouble will break out as the drunks spill onto the streets. The food stalls fascinated us both. We tried sticky rice with fresh mango, barbecue chicken and pork on sticks and chilled pineapple sold in small plastic bags. We shied away from the charred tarantulas and scorpions on sticks. They looked like the sort of delicacy you see on an episode of "I'm a celebrity get me out of here."

I tried to persuade Andrea to experiment with one of these local delicacies, her being the adventurous eater but to no avail.

Behind the stalls, and in front of the bars and restaurants, scantily clad girls gyrated and posed to the music. Most wore tiny shorts, which in my day we called hot pants and flimsy bra tops that left very little to the imagination. Old men who seemed to be mostly British or German drooled and tried to encourage the girls to be even more explicit but we assumed that only took place inside these establishments.

The restaurants competed with each other for the tourist trade, selling king size burgers, hot dogs, pizza and pastas. Basically anything that appeared European. More authentic Thai food could be purchased on the street and for less than a dollar we ate a delicious pad thai cooked in front of us in a searing wok. It was as much fun to watch the chef cook it as it was to eat.

As the evening wore on and as we sat drinking chilled Chang beer, people watching became more interesting. The older couples, like ourselves seemed to be the most at ease. We had nothing to prove and no ulterior motive for being on the Road, it was all just good fun. We smiled at the street sellers, showed an interest if we had one, and politely declined if we did not.

The girl hunters were altogether different and seemed to fall into three main categories. Those who had already captured their prize seemed to parade up and down the street almost as if they were on show. The diminutive Thai girls, looking stunning but somehow sad at the same time, walked hand in hand with sweaty 50 and 60-year-old resembling Henry viii. Andrea and I both felt sorry for the girls. Even though the financial rewards might have been great and security for the family important, it seemed a high price to pay.

Next there were older men who had quite clearly come to Bangkok on holiday in order to experience all of the delights on offer locally. They ranged in age from early thirties through to fifty plus. I guessed they were mostly single but this could easily have been me putting a moralistic spin on things. They approached the girls confidently and engaged in conversation before disappearing into the alleyways alongside the bars to no doubt find some sort of satisfaction. Andrea and I had a very different view about these working arrangements and I could not fully establish who was taking advantage of who. Prostitution may indeed be the oldest profession but I suppose we were just not used to seeing it so obviously exposed to the outside world.

The final group were the young men who were clearly very excited by being in the proximity of so many beautiful girls and desperately wanted to sample their wares but lacked the confidence of the older more experienced men. It was rather like watching young males in a David Attenborough nature documentary. Sex was the only thing on their mind but they were not quite sure how to go about getting it.

They watched the older males with admiration and gathered in groups to plan and discuss tactics but were not quite assured enough to close the deal. Often one would break from the group and walk towards the chosen girl only to veer off into a t-shirt stall at the vital moment. Now and again if a girl took the lead and made an approach one of the one men would become separated from the group and would disappear whilst waving to his mates and soaking up the cheers. We suspected that his enjoyment may not have been of the lasting kind.

After several beers and plenty of Pad Thai Andrea and I wandered back to the Tara Place Hotel. The street stalls showed no signs of closing despite it being well past midnight, the restaurants were still busy and the bars heaving. The dark underbelly of a giant third world city was gradually emerging from the gloom. People had set up night camps in doorways, children slept huddled close to poverty stricken mothers who held out grubby hands for change. The foul stenches associated with down and outs of all great cities pervaded the night air and caught in our throats. We did not feel threatened but we did feel in some way immune to the sights. We were gradually becoming accepting of poverty and hardship and this was not a nice feeling.

Exploring big cities is fun and exploring them on foot is even more revealing. We were by now fitter and even Andrea's great reluctance to walks was becoming a thing of the past. We jumped on the hotel shuttle to the Royal Grand Palace and joined the throng to visit the temple of the Emerald Buddha one of the country's most sacred sites. The Buddha was impressive, shrouded in a golden cape, worn because it was officially the cold season. The Buddha has different golden outfits depending on the season.

The faithful paid respect while the westerners like ourselves took photos and marvelled at the beauty of the temple and the elaborate carvings and decorations. Andrea turned to me and said

"I still find it odd that in countries where so many, like those on the street last night, live in abject poverty that the churches contain so much wealth".

It is hard to comprehend and having no real faith myself, I found it a little offensive.

We then set off across the city to explore. Our goal was to reach the main train station at Hualamphong in order to buy tickets for our journey south. We walked for over six hours in total and probably lost about a stone each in sweat. Stopping occasionally for a beer or a coffee we passed through residential areas and into Chinatown.

As we entered this quarter, the streets narrowed and traders spilled out onto the street or into gaps between buildings. No usable space was wasted and everything imaginable was on sale. The smell of garlic and charred meats filled the air and the shouts of the traders made me think of Fools and Horses, Del boy would have loved this place.

We stopped at a stall and bought two fresh chilled pomegranate juices and they were the nicest thing I have ever drank. Even the tourist tip that we should not drink iced drinks on the street was forgotten. We were baking and dehydrating and these were just perfect.

As we moved through the back streets of the city, each area seemed to specialise in different goods. We passed the obvious retailers of clothing, electric goods car parts and shoes and then moved into the exotic areas of pets, antiques and religious icons etc. Then into the darn right weird world of wigs, prosthetic limbs, glass eyes second hand spectacles. Everything you could possible imagine is available for purchase in Bangkok if you look hard enough.

By the time we reached Hualamphong Andrea was a woman barely alive and the air conditioned ticket office was a life saver. I removed my day-pack and as I squeezed the back of my shirt sweat literally dripped onto the floor. Our pre-ordered tickets for the Bangkok to Surat Thani night train were ready for collection although the young Thai girl did apologise that we had top bunk rather than lower bunks, but this did not bother us at the time.

Two days later, after visiting more Buddhist Wats each containing a different type of Buddha, some reclining others meditating or happy. After lots more pad thai, chilled Chang beer and sticky rice with mango we arrived at the station for our epic train journey.

As we boarded the train we began to realise why the girl in the ticket office had apologised for the fact we had been allocated top bunks. The carriage was narrow and cramped but the seating areas were comfortable enough. The aircon worked and the first couple of hours of the journey were spent in relative peace. Sellers plied their wares up and down the gangways selling cool drinks, pre-packed food, crisps and the like.

Andrea after spending a couple of months being very careful about what she ate then suddenly ordered a meal from a random woman on a train. Not to be outdone I did the same. The meal was served wrapped in banana leaf and contained an unspecified meat but was really tasty and not too fiery hot.

Soon after that, the carriage guard started to move through the carriage turning the seating into bunks and making up the bunks with sheets and blankets. From this point we had nowhere to sit and had no option but to clamber into the top bunks.

The lower bunks were wide having previously been the width of two seats. The top bunk, however, was narrowed by the curvature of the train roof. Thus we had two tiny Thai's in the massive lower bunks and two pretty big Europeans on the top bunks.

The size of the bunks was not the only hurdle we had to overcome. We had to find a way of clambering into them. I threw my back pack up and scaled the rather sharp metal ladder to the bunk. After storing my pack in the luggage area and getting out my kindle, biscuits and water. I settled down for the journey. Andrea however was still down below. She passed her bags up and stared up the five-rung ladder.

Now Andrea has never been especially agile and in the tight space of the gangway, on a narrow ladder she failed miserably to reach the bunk. Her first couple of attempts drew the attention of other travellers. Some gave what I assumed was valuable advice on how to climb the ladder, but as they were not speaking English it was of little use. I did fear the onset of overtired tears but instead somewhat manic laughter accompanied her third failed attempt.

I climbed back down from my side and came up with a master plan. By now most of those in the carriage were looking and giving as much encouragement as they possible. Andrea climbed the first two steps whereupon I crouched down and placed my shoulder under her backside. She steadied herself and on a count of three took one more step. At this point I straightened my legs and heaved her upwards. This propelled her unceremoniously onto her bunk to the applause of the gathering crowd. I received a couple of pats on the back for my efforts and smiles and laughter were all cautious but genuine.

Once up there was no going back, I only hoped the banana wrapped evening meal did not work its magic during the journey as getting out of the bunk would have proved immensely tricky for Andrea especially if she was in a rush. I slept pretty well, the rolling of the train was soporific and I awoke early the next morning when the breakfast sellers started their rounds. I fully expected when I pulled back the curtains to welcome the day to see Andrea well rested, but there was no such luck.

My bunk although tight had been comfortable enough and the air nicely cool thus enabling me to get to sleep. Andrea had for some reason not trusted the luggage rack so had kept her bags on her bunk, thus reducing the size even more. The air conditioning unit that had cooled me nicely had been directly over Andreas middle and had chilled her all night. With no space on the bunk to open her bags she could not get extra clothes and had been so cold she could not sleep. This added to a desperate need to pee and an unwillingness to wake me saw morning arrive with her in a foul mood.

We started the new day by Andrea climbing onto the ladder and then half sitting on my shoulders lowering herself down. The loo on an inter-city train in the UK is a pretty gross thing especially on the Saturday late night special. Well, image a tropical train bog that has been in use all night. No sit down toilet, just a hole in the floor through to the tracks. No working light and of course no toilet paper. The train tracks seemed to ensure that the train itself shook in all directions as it rumbled towards its destination. Andrea's mood had improved little when she returned from the bog and in case I was unsure she made it very clear that over night train journeys would not be repeated on our trip.

We arrived in Surat Thani in the early morning and piled out of the train. The remainder of the journey was to be by coach. Almost as soon as we set foot on the platform we were surrounded by people trying to sell us tickets for the rest of the journey. In normal circumstances we would almost certainly have paid up but I, as always had done my homework. I knew our train tickets were not valid for the bus journey but I also knew where to buy the bus tickets and how much they should cost. Some of the arguments that raged on the train platform clearly indicated that other passengers were not so well prepared. We strolled purposefully to a small café in the station car park and purchased our cheap onward tickets while sipping a coffees and eating a tasty pastry.

The buses ran on time, they were comfortable, our luggage was not lost and we arrived on time. Just like public transport at home!

Bed 13 Lady boys and hotel days.

We were booked for fun in the sun at the Seven Seas hotel in Patong Beach. It was a clean and quiet hotel well along the beach away from the main street of the Bangla Road. Unfortunately, the hotel was surrounded by other tall building so no view of the beach was possible and the small pool was in the shade for all but about 40 minutes each day. Still such things are meant to try us.

I am not a great beach lover and much prefer a sunlit pool. Andrea is happier on the beach but if a nice pool is available will often opt for that. Thus we had a problem: no pool to speak of and the alternative would be days on the beach being pestered by sellers and sand not to mention getting sand stuck everywhere. In my opinion, there are few things more uncomfortable than walking along a beach front path with sand in your flip flops or even worse in your swimmers. It's rather like sandpapering your private parts.

Andrea can up with a wonderful solution: -

"Why don't we just use the pool at one of the big hotels. They will never suspect a couple of old codgers."

"Hmm good idea but it will be really embarrassing if we get flung out."

"Doesn't matter no-one knows us and they will never see us again."

I was beginning to see the rebelliousness of old re-emerging in my wife.

Andrea hatched a plan. That evening as we strolled into town for supper we would carefully scrutinise the posh hotels and try to establish which would be the easiest to gate crash. After careful consideration we opted for the Graceland Resort which seemed busy, but not heaving with guests and it had several entrances. Andrea's master plan involved walking into the hotel beach front restaurant as if we were resident's intent on breakfast, and then leaving through the side door as if we had just taken breakfast. From there it was a very short walk to the sun loungers and the pool. She had checked carefully to see if any of the guests were wearing tell-tale wrist bands indicating an all-inclusive resort. Content that this was not the case we were set for a day at the pool.

Getting in was easy and having chosen excellent sun beds we spotted problem number one. Every towel around the massive pool was green and emblazoned with the Graceland logo. Mine however was decorated with Disney's Little Mermaid and Andrea's with the Lion King. Both towels had been purchased for our girls when they were younger. I was concerned, but Andrea was not. She walked slowly around the pool and quickly spied two unoccupied, but claimed, isolated sun beds. In no time at all she returned with two Graceland towels. No doubt the holiday makers, probably Germans, who had staked an early morning claim to their place in the sun would be complaining to the reception desk in due course.

"Shouldn't bloody put towels on sun beds and then bugger off should they."

It wasn't until mid-afternoon that things started to go wrong. We had brought with us a supply of water and a few biscuits but in the blazing sun the water did not last that long and we were getting parched. I suggested I pop out for a walk and buy more from a local stall. Andrea now totally confident of her subterfuge simply ordered drinks from the pool waiter. On his return he requested our room number in order to bill us for the drinks. I offered to pay but he said that all pool drinks must be charged to the room. Andrea unflinchingly gave him our room number but unbeknown to us the room she chose didn't exist.

As the waiter walked away I saw him stop and chat to a security guard and then point in our direction. The guard did nothing at first, his error, as it gave Andrea and I a minute of time to get organised. Before he could walk around the pool we calmly set off in the other direction. After a second or two he clearly saw we had gone and set off after us. We were out on the street when he spotted us and gave chase albeit rather half-heartedly. We scuttled away like two naughty school kids and found a bar for a beer and a giggle. Andrea smiled and said "Guess I'd better chose another hotel for tomorrow then."

We spent seven days in Phuket and tried several new hotels. We got braver as the week went on even using roof top pools. One day we managed to spend several hours at a private roof top pool with no other guests around. It was idyllic. In the Bangla Suites off the Bangla road we were even served complimentary afternoon tea: - top result I thought.

Phuket itself reveals the best and worst of Thailand. The choice of restaurants is endless and the quality of the food can be quite stunning. Competition is manic between the restaurants so good deals are always available. As a rule of thumb if a place is busy it's generally good, beach front places are slightly more expensive than those a few streets back and if it looks pretentious it probably is.

The streets throng with tourists and the buzz is quite intoxicating. Souvenirs are on sale everywhere and there are certainly bargains around. As night falls the atmosphere changes and if you are not prepared it can most definitely come as a bit of a shock. We lost count of the number of ping-pong shows we were encouraged to visit and the prostitution on the streets and in the bars and massage parlours is very in your face.

In the Bangla Rd the Lady Boys parade and strut their stuff making money from posing for photographs with the tourists. These men range from stunningly beautiful, through odd, too downright unattractive. Andrea and I love Thailand but we are not fans of Phuket and will not be visiting it again. This is a shame as the natural beauty of the island and the friendliness of the people is wonderful. Maybe it's just Patong but the endless cries of "You want massaaage! Sir?" can get you down and when some of the massage parlours actually have signs in the windows saying.
"No Sex" it makes it pretty clear what is on offer in other establishments.

Bed 14. Kuala Lumpur.

After her experience on the Bangkok to Surat Thani express Andrea flatly refused to travel to Kuala Lumpur by train so we booked a cheap flight with Air Asia and made the short trip south. The airport is miles from the city but the fast train is really efficient and the journey into the city was easy.

As a former geography teacher I was shocked by how much natural forest had been cut down and replaced by palms for palm oil production. The palm forests seemed never ending. I was very clear that ecological concerns were put well on the back burner in order to plant cash crops.

I had booked us into the Pacific Central Hotel and once in our room we set about our normal routine of planning what to see and do. We were staying really close to Chinatown and almost on the mono rail route. This meant that food was sorted and travelling around was simple.

Any visit to KL must include the iconic Petronas Towers which stand as giant guardians of the city. The journey to the top cost around £15 but the views were stunning. I would have loved to see the city at night but we settled for a morning trip and booked early having been warned that the towers can get very busy. Unsurprisingly we went to the towers via the KL Hard Rock Café so that Andrea could add another badge to her collection.

After viewing the city from the towers we spent an hour or so in the park next door and saw the towers form the city. We did our best to get wonderfully aesthetic pictures of one and other with the towers in the background and pretty much failed miserably.

From there we strolled to the Buket Nanas Rainforest Reserve, which is a small oasis of rainforest preserved in the centre of the city. The heat was oppressive and even though the trees provided shade there was no escape from the near 100 per cent humidity. Andrea and I must have looked a sight as we slowly walked wandered around. Nothing in the reserve is flat, the uphill stretches were so tough our faces went from healthy and well-tanned too bright red and flushed. Sweat poured from every pore and I would be lying if I said it was a nice experience.

However, I did see some excellent new birds so it was all worth it. The stars were oriental magpie robin, black napped oriole and a hornbill, although I could not get a good enough view to be certain of the species. We also saw plenty of monkeys who seemed intent on crapping on our heads. The mischievous little buggers seemed to stay high in the trees but follow us around. I am convinced they knew what they were doing as they aimed their arses at us. Fortunately, they were not as good at aiming as they were at crapping.

The next day we walked to the Merdeka Square where Malaysia proclaimed its independence from Britain on the 31 August 1957. The square is home to the tallest flag pole in the world standing 95 meters tall. The buildings around the square are quite simply magnificent. On one side is the Royal Selangor Club, which was once a cricket club. The old pavilion and adjacent building are so English in style it was easy to imagine the Lords and Ladies sipping tea while the cricketers bowled and batted in the blazing Malay heat.

The Tudor style buildings once known as the "Spotted Dog" reminded us of some of the quaint cottages back home in the Kent.

The cricket ground was immaculate but sadly no longer used for cricket. It now hosts parades and rock concerts and built beneath it is the new Plaza Putra shopping centre.

On the other side are the administrative buildings built in a Moorish style. The arched balconies are typical of this style the domed copulas are copper covered and shine in the morning sun. The building was used by the British during its rule but now are occupied by government ministries.

Behind the giant flagpole is a tiny museum that we decided to visit. There was a small entrance fee which could be recovered by presenting our tickets at the café afterwards. The museum had an exhibition of local dresses throughout the ages and I have to say was not that interesting for me. Andrea with her background in textiles loved it.

The café however was a different matter and the food looked excellent. Andrea cashed in her entry fee in and ordered nasi lamak, a local speciality. I did not fancy curry for breakfast so chose with great care.

The menu was in Malay but the pictures made choosing pretty easy. I went for a dish of two poached eggs and a toasted cheese sandwich. I was so excited as meals recognisable from home were a rarity on the trip. Andrea's nasi lamak arrived first and did look fantastic with everything arranged on the plate with great care. A small portion of chicken with vegetables and potato curry and of course a serving of rice.

Mine arrived a minute or so later.

Two eggs in a dish with the whites showing some sign of having at least been near heat. The eggs had been cooked for less than a minute and were all but raw. My face dropped but then I had a fantastic idea. The dish could be saved if I added soy sauce, which was on the table. I splashed the sauce over the eggs and mixed it all together. My first taste almost initiated a spontaneous vomit, as the sauce was actually a strong fish sauce not soy. Andrea by this stage was almost on the floor with laughter. It got worse. My toasted cheese sandwich which turned out to be toast all right but with butter about a centimetre thick and no cheese at all. It was inedible.

After she recovered her composure Andrea did offer me some curry but with the taste of raw eggs and fish sauce combined with butter still in my mouth I could not accept.

From here we jumped on the free shuttle train to visit the bird park and the orchid gardens in the Perdana Botanic Gardens. The little train was the type often seen at seaside resorts in the UK and was great fun to ride.

We saw our first venomous snake as a black krait slithered across the path in front of us. It was not a big snake but our driver said that many Malays died every year from krait bites.

Chinatown in KL is a maze of tightly packed stalls selling the usual market goods. It was very easy to get disorientated and lose track of our way. Like many Chinatowns around the world this one was packed with tourists and locals all looking for a bargain and for something to eat. We bought nothing but did eat supper there a couple of times and the food was excellent.

Bed 15 In the footsteps of the tea planters

From KL we caught a bus to the hill station known as the Cameron Highlands. We had read that this area of the country had been developed by tea planters as a resort to escape the heat and humidity of the lowlands. The architecture was very British influenced and there was a feel of a bygone era about the place. We stayed in a homestay in Brinchang from where we explored what the highlands had to offer.

We were expecting so much from the Highlands as everyone we had encountered had told us just how beautiful the region was. Perhaps it was this expectation that led to a feeling of disappointment when we actually arrived. Certainly the scenery was spectacular with tea plantations and market gardens, Tudor style hotels, quaint tea rooms and lush vegetation. the near incessant rain put a damper on the experience for us.

Brinchang itself is scruffy, the buildings are shabby and generally the place feels unclean. The restaurants too are unappealing. We tried the main dish of the town, food cooked at the table in a steamboat. It was pretty unsuccessful and not altogether pleasant. The steamboat contain broth and was served with a variety of goodies to drop into mix and cook. The steamer didn't look great and half of the food we tried stuck to the metal parts of the dish and became impossible to pry off. I ended up with more broth on the front of my shirt than in my mouth. Some of the meat pieces were recognisable (the prawns and bits of chicken) but others were aa mystery that I have no wish to solve.

Strawberry farms, were everywhere but I didn't find then particularly interesting. Sure you can buy, strawberry juice, strawberry ice cream and jam, inflatable strawberries, strawberry shaped erasers and just about everything else strawberry you can imagine but the novelty wore off quickly, especially as I am allergic to the bloody things.

The Old Smokehouse tea room, tucked away behind the golf course, was an altogether different experience. Sitting at a table it is easy to imagine you are in a Thames side village and not the middle of Asia. The Tudor style building complete with red phone box, garden roses and hanging baskets has changed little since it was built to serve the social elite escaping the KL heat back in the 1940's. Afternoon tea was served by an impeccably dressed waiter with grace and manners so typical of that bygone age.

We ate scones and jam, along with dainty sandwiches and drank superb local tea. It was a wonderful way to pass a rainy afternoon. While we wiled away the afternoon various coach loads of Chinese tourists arrived in the car park. They unloaded, took, photos and climbed back into the coach. Not a scone or a finger sandwich was eaten. The more I see of the Chinese tourists the more puzzled I become. There appears to be no enjoyment or time to stand and stare it's just a simple. "Been there, done that, got the photo and move on."

Aside from strawberry farms the Cameron Highlands is a market garden of epic size growing just about everything. The carefully maintained plots of land produce salad crops as well as fruits and of course honey. Bees are needed a plenty to pollinate the crops. The most famous produce of all is tea and the plantations around the town are spectacular. Andrea and I walked to the Boh Tea Plantation just to the north of Brinchang.

Actually it was a bloody long walk and had a cheerful Malay family not offered us a lift half way we may well not have made it. Mr Ng seemed very proud to have a couple of Brits in his small family saloon. We were also delighted, if a little cramped, with Mr and Mrs Ng, four little Ng's and a dog along with what seemed to be a month's supply of groceries some of which were still alive and clucking.

They dropped us at the entrance to the Boh Tea plantation and we walked the last mile into the tourist centre. The view from the veranda of the modern visitor centre was spectacular. Rolling fields of tea plants covered the hill sides in a mosaic that would have made the world's most difficult jigsaw puzzle. The fields stretched as far as the eye could see. The green expanse was broken up by the paths used by the pickers. It was as if someone had pencilled lines on the field to create an elaborate pattern. Overhead eagles wheeled in the sky and swifts screeched and dived around the visitor centre. It was magical and well worth the walk. The tea itself was fresh and delicious and very welcome after our long trek.

The walk back into Brinchang took a couple of hours and the Ng's were long gone. About half way the rains returned and I discovered that no matter how I held my umbrella I could only keep half of myself dry. Andrea was fine as she had a big golf style brolly, but mine however, was tiny, having been purchased in haste, and totally ineffective in the face of such a deluge. When we got back I was drenched, Andrea was dry and in excellent humour at my discomfort.

"Told you, should have taken more time and chosen a good brolly and not that crappy one."

Not for the first time on the trip the only suitable reply appeared to be

"Fuck off."

Our home stay in Brinchang was interesting. We were in a nice apartment just off the main town square and staying with an Englishman and his Malay wife. She was charming and so easy to chat too. She was a teacher so we had plenty in common and she was very keen to talk about the differences between the two education systems. She was very keen to talk, unless her husband was around. When he was there he would hardly let her finish a sentence and continually cut in with; "Lillian means this or Lillian means that"

She was a very bright woman who was clearly capable of expressing her own feelings if given half a chance. We found this very awkward and hugely annoying. He was also something of a Walter Mitty type and we were regaled by his triumphs in the field of commerce and business. Strange he was living tucked away in a small mountain village in Malaysia. His tales grew longer and more elaborate as the days passed. He would appear to have cycled around most of Malaysia, and was supposedly the most important man in town, and claimed to have restructured many schools in country. We half expected him to say he was the President elect or had indeed been the first person on the moon.

Travelling in Malaysia is so simple. The buses are cheap and reliable and very comfortable. They seem to cover the country well and Andrea and I had no problems getting about. We caught the bus from the local station out of the Highlands and on to Penang. There were several bus companies to choose from but I chose the Unititti express just because I liked the name. It certainly wasn't an express particularly driving around the hairpin turns of the highlands but once on the flat we soon reached our next destination.

Bed 16. Frog Porridge in Penang

Penang was made famous by the highly acclaimed TV series Indian Summers. Personally I think the show is overrated but Andrea loves it. I already knew that much of the next few days would be spent finding and then photographing various sites relating to the show. Filming was over when we were there so at least we wouldn't have to spend hours trying to hunt down Julie Walters.

The Chulia Mansion Hotel in Georgetown is one I would recommend to anyone. Modern and clean it serves an excellent breakfast, with the eggs benedict being the highlight. In the afternoon the café opens for tea and coffee with snacks and ice cream provided free of charge. The ice cream was so welcome in the heat.

The Chulia is within walking distance of most of the sights and there is so much to see and do in Penang. The Island is famous for its street food markets and the quality and variety of dishes on offer is mind boggling. The Red Garden hawker centre was around the corner from our hotel so we headed there as soon as it was dark.

The food court heaves in the evening Tourists and locals alike mill around the covered area comparing menus and selecting dishes. The smartly dressed waiters rush between tables delivering fragrant and tasty dishes at breakneck speed. Chilled beers are served and if you are really lucky. The live music will not have started.

Sadly, we arrived a few minutes too late and a cover band was already in full voice. Cover bands are not great at the best of times, unless you happen to be listening to the Australian Pink Floyd, and this was most certainly not the best of times. The musicians were OK and mostly played in tune but listening to old Beatles numbers sung by a girl who could neither pronounce her W's or her R's and had only a vague notion of the actual words was irritating. Why they don't stick to local music and their own language is beyond me. Still at least the speakers seemed to work really well so it was not all bad!

Andrea was in her element choosing several small dishes from a selection of outlets. Chilli prawns from one, pork dumplings from another and so on. I tended to panic and order the first thing I recognised and had often finished before her dishes arrived. I really couldn't get the hang of hawker centres. I did however, start a list of the most bizarre dishes I have ever seen on a menu. The highlights are disturbing and would not be amiss in a horror movie. How would you fancy oyster porridge, clay pot frog porridge, fish stomach soup or pork trotter rice? Why would anyone want to eat these dishes when Nasi goring, beef rendang and Malay chicken curries were available?

There is a treasure trove of delights to see in Penang and we made every effort to see as much as possible. We rode the funicular railway up Penang hill to get spectacular views across the island. We sat in a tea-room overlooking the city and had an overpriced but delicious cream tea.

The railway was constructed in the 1920's by the British, who thought the oppressive heat could be tempered by spending time at a higher altitude. The homes built on the hill originally housed the Colonial Governors and the like. They perch precariously overlooking Georgetown. There is a Hindu temple at the summit along with a Buddhist temple and a mosque.

It was comforting to see that in some place religions can live together in some sort of harmony. The various pathways made it easy to wander around and look at the old buildings. Andrea very quickly established where the main house from Indian Summers was located. I was not in least surprised that it was the one furthest way from the main hill station and it was not open to the public even after we had slogged for half an hour in the blazing sun, to reach it.

Back in Georgetown murals adorn the city buildings and with the help of a very detailed map we located almost all of them. Our favourite was a massive ginger cat sprawled along the length of a garden wall. The mural of a steam engine and of children on bikes were also impressive. Everywhere we turned in Georgetown we found curios to amuse us. Short poems or historic facts are located on the walls of buildings. We found the house where Jimmy Choo, he of shoes fame, started out. Any antiques dealer worth their salt would I am sure have a wonderful time exploring the back street shops and dimly lit alleys of the town.

We passed the afternoon exploring the waterfront piers, which each home a different Chinese clan. It is a wonder that these rickety old wooden piers can support the buildings let alone the huge numbers of tourists visiting. As we walked to the end of the piers looking into the houses it was clear that a traditional way of life was still alive. Each house contained a small shrine and elaborately carved wooden idols and furniture. Some were simply family homes while others served as shops selling Chinese lanterns and carvings or cool drinks and ice creams. Andrea and I both found the Chew Clan Jetty to be the most accessible and interesting but we were willing to bet that at Chinese New Year the whole place would be rocking.

Our time in Penang came to an end all too soon and we readied ourselves for the next, and most adventurous phase of the journey. We would miss the delicious food, the reminders of a bygone age, the architecture and of course afternoon teas at the Chulia Mansion. Despite all of this we set off back to KL by express bus, Unititti of course, and then to the airport by fast train. We arrived at KL international airport to find that our flight to Bali was likely to be delayed due to volcanic activity on the Island of Lombok. Mount Rinjani had decided to awaken and the ash cloud meant that Jet Star was not flying. This was going to be a tester.

Fortunately, from a financial point of view we had not booked accommodation on Bali so we did not have to reach there on any particular date. So I put on my planning hat, actually this is probably my favourite hat of all, and set to work devising an alternative.

There were one or two options available to us and we discussed them over copious cups of tea and the odd meal. We were after all in no rush to get anywhere. Jet Star informed us they would not honour our ticket at a later date or give us a refund which was about as useful as a one-legged man in an arse kicking contest. They did say we could fly to Singapore free of charge which was also not a huge amount of use to us.

The over indulgence of tea did help to highlight a massive issue: - the toilets at KL airport are just about the worst I have every come across. The smell in the gents was appalling and Andrea said the same about the ladies' loo. I have often wondered why people find it so hard to piss into a bloody great bog but here it was not just piss. Either travellers through KL all suffer from some ghastly stomach complaint or they must be in such a rush that aiming takes too much time. Whatever the cause, the end result was a bog that was totally unusable by anyone with either a functioning nose or not wearing wellington boots.

Bed 17 Jungle life.

To this point our trip had been exciting, but hardly right out there. I decided that since Bali was on hold we should really try and experience some of the real Indonesia. Thus I got in touch with a mate from my teaching days who was working for Operation Wallacea on the island of Sulawesi. Opwal as they are known, do significant scientific research towards the ultimate goal of attaining funding to preserve some of the planets most endangered habitats and ecosystems.

Alan was delighted to hear from us and said that providing we could be in Jakarta in three days' time the rest would be easy. With part one of my plan in place all I had to do was break the news to Andrea that the easy part of the trip was over for a couple of weeks and that we were going bush.

If I remove the expletives from her reply, there would be very few words left but after several hours of negotiation she finally agreed to give it a go. I knew this was going to push us both well out of our comfort zones but was reasonably confident I could cope; I was less sure about Andrea but decided to keep this to myself.

I popped into see the friendly Jet Star man and tried to exchange our two tickets to Bali for two tickets to Jakarta and on to Makassar in Sulawesi. The Jet Star man smiled and, said "No." I had to purchase new tickets but thankfully they were not massively expensive. From Makassar we would need an onward flight to Bau Bau but I left this to Alan. We spent the night trying, for the most part unsuccessfully, to get some sleep in the airport. The combination of foul smelling bogs, noisy Indonesians, disgruntled Jet Star passengers, and a bloody hard floor made it a night to forget.

By the time we reached Alan in Jakarta we were frazzled. Andrea turned to me and in all innocence said

"Well the jungle can't be worse than last night can it Jim?"

I didn't have the heart to answer honestly, so said

"Of course not pet if you can survive that you can survive anything."

It was a couple of years since I'd last crossed paths with Alan and his cheerful face and boundless enthusiasm for his new life style was infectious. We drove to his apartment and settled down for a leisurely breakfast followed by a welcome shower and quick nap. When we resurfaced Alan ran through what we could expect from the next ten days. I just loved listening to him. When a person is totally captivated by what they do they describe things with a childish enthusiasm. They gloss over the bad bits, or simply do not recognised them, and get excited about everything else.

"Jim we operate out of a small village in the rainforest area a few hours north of Bau-Bau and our aim is to complete a pretty thorough census of all flora and fauna in the area." Alan said. "There are scientists in situ all of the time and the school and university groups that visit help out the experts"

He said that the aim was to submit a paper a paper to the UN at the end of the survey and hopefully get funding to protect the forest.

"This type of stuff is going on in other parts of the world so we have got to outbid them."

So far so good.

"You and Andrea will join one of the groups and work in the rainforest for six days"

Andrea asked about the jungle accommodation.

"What are the jungle huts like Alan?

"They are like hammocks between trees covered by a large tarpaulin."

Andreas face dropped and the daggers aimed in my direction could have killed.

"Dare I ask about the toilets, showers and cooking" Andrea said.

"Probably best to wait until you get there. It's not as bad as it sounds and most people take to it very quickly."

I could see from my wife's face that Alans tactful but non-committal answer did nothing to allay her fears, indeed it may well have made things worse.

Andrea went to bed early that night probably hoping all of this would go away while at least taking full advantage of the last real bed she would see for a while.

Alan and I reminisced and drank whisky until the wee small hours.

"Jim. This couple of weeks will be bloody tough. Are you sure Andrea's up to it?"

"Bit bloody late now, we are here and anyway she is tougher than she thinks."

"She's gonna need to be mate. Alan replied, "and for that matter so are you. None of us are as fit as we used to be"

The next morning silence we set off for the airport in relative silence and took two flights into increasingly remote areas of Indonesia. Makassar airport was modern and well equipped but, Bau Bau was altogether different. We landed in our 30-seat propeller plane and had to unload our own bags before walking to the single airport building which acted as a terminal, check in, café and general meeting place.

There was an old ex-army jeep waiting to collect Alan and we joined him in the vehicle after throwing our bags in the back. The journey into town was uneventful, but it was already clear that we were in the remote back country. We met up with a few other Opwal operatives and a group of students from a school in Sydney before joining a convoy of jeeps heading inland to Labundo Bundo, our final destination. The journey took around four hours and before very long we had left the built up areas behind and were driving through fields and jungle.

Rice paddies lined the road for the first couple of hours and small towns came and went as we headed inland. The standard of driving in this part of Indonesia was interesting and now and then we were actually on our own side of the road. The odd rural bus flew past at breakneck speed carrying mothers and children along with what seemed like everyone's worldly goods.

There were hundreds of dogs walking purposefully along the road side. Every dog looked the same. They were a light tan colour with short sturdy legs an erect tail and quite a long snout. They all seemed to know exactly where they were going but never seemed to get there. They looked in good health although they seemed ownerless so I assumed finding food was not too much of an issue. During the whole four-hour journey, I saw no dog corpses on the edge of the road. They certainly had a better road sense than many pedestrians in London and a greater sense of self-preservation than English foxes and badgers.

Heavy logging lorries roared along roads that were clearly designed for mopeds and carts not massive vehicles. As they passed dogs and chickens dived for cover into the forest and pedestrians were covered in thick clouds of dust and fumes. It quickly became clear why Opwal had chosen this area of forest to protect and it did seem as if speed was of the essence. We saw dozens of logging lorries over the course of our journey and Alan explained that almost all of the de-forestation in the area was illegal but the Indonesian government seemed powerless to stop it.

We arrived in Labundo in the late afternoon and we were exhausted, filthy and ready for a rest. The village was located along a single half-mud half-stone road. The locals seemed well used to the influx of foreigners and were well prepared. Small house front stalls sold recognisable western snacks like Pringles and Coke and it was even possible to buy a Magnum ice cream. Other house front stalls sold local souvenirs but all were very much eco-friendly, there were no ornaments adorned with butterflies or giant beetles or scorpions encased in Perspex as there so often are on Asian market stalls. Clearly, the Opwal message of conservation was getting through.

Throughout the journey Andrea had hardly spoken and I was worried. Whatever happened we could net get back to Bau-Bau until the next convoy set off and that was not going to happen for over a week. I was beginning to doubt the wisdom of this particular trip.

Alan also sensing Andreas fragile state, brought us both a cup of tea and then left us to come to terms with the situation. Before I could say a word Andrea burst into tears and for several minutes was totally inconsolable.

A tiny Indonesian girl aged no more than four tapped her on the leg and smiled, saying

"You Ok lady? Come see, come with me"

This tiny little urchin dressed in shorts and flip flops took Andreas hand and led her a few steps to show her a litter of kittens. The connection was immediate and although language was an issue and conversation minimal, the ice was broken and I could see a way forward.

That night, like everyone else in the Opwal groups, we stayed in the house of a local family. The sleeping arrangements were the most basic I had ever encountered. We had a mattress each. It was stuffed with straw and placed on the floor of a raised platform at the back of the house.

There was a mosquito net and a sheet and the windows were open to the world. The roof was corrugated metal, which played a sleep breaking tune every time the rain started. The bamboo that made up the walls and the floor was held together with twine and shook even in lightest of winds but is was home for the next few days while we acclimatised and learned about the tasks to be performed in the jungle.

Our host family were so kind and welcoming even though we couldn't understand a word they said. It was hard to look accepting of their hospitality because it was so alien to us. We both realised however that this situation was their everyday reality and to look too worried or fussed would be unacceptably rude.

Andrea however, was still worried and cuddled up close despite the humidity I tried hard to make out that everything was fine but inside I was a little scared about the coming days.

For two days we attended talks from the scientists in charge of; flora, insects, bats, birds, reptiles and larger mammals. We went on short forays into the rainforest mostly at dawn or dusk when things including bugs like I had never seen before are most active.

They tended to fly directly at our head torches making us dodge and weave as if we were fighting a world class featherweight boxer. Trust me when you get hit by a low flying atlas beetle straight between the eyes it is a bloody shock. These beasties can grow to over 10 centimetres in size. Although I would never have admitted it to Andrea, just watching her provided me with some wonderful amusement.

We ate and drank with the scientists and students in a central eating area but slept in our own little hut. The washing facilities was nothing more than a tank of cool water and a scoop and the loo was a hole in the ground with water and another scoop. The washing area was known as the mandi and after a day in the jungle cool water and a scoop seemed like the height of luxury.

Andrea was settling in and of course keeping a close eye on the kittens with the help of her little minder Melati. Melati was a bright little thing who was already picking up a few words of English, and she was also a little older that the four years we had estimated. Each morning she set off to school in her maroon skirt and white blouse, and goodness knows how her mother kept them clean. Andrea walked Melati down the road on the second morning and met her class teacher. My wife did not reappear until well after lunch after a morning back in the classroom. Old habits die hard. Melati was in the seven-year-old class along with thirty-four others. No sign of a falling birth rate in this part of Indonesia.

Labundo is a place that operates to the rhythm of the day. The village springs into life as the sun rises and slowly drifts to sleep as the sun sets. Clocks and the hours of the day become almost irrelevant. Our meet time for the following morning was day break and although that was around 5am, it did not seem an issue.

We packed the night before, transferring our jungle gear, or rather our clothes that seemed most suitable to the jungle, into my pack and our normal gear into Andreas suitcase which was to be left in the village. Neither of us had walking boots but our strong trainers would suffice and as advised, we also packed two sets of clothes each. One set would certainly get pretty wet and was for the day time, the other had to be kept dry and was for night. Alan advised us to buy talc in the local store as we would need it in the jungle camp and, he turned out to be right of course.

We boarded a rather unsafe looking minivan with several scientists and set off from Labundo. The van had no doors and the windows were permanently stuck open. The bench style seats on the sides of the van were such that every time we changed gradient we would slide towards the driver or the space where the rear door had been. At least the back packs on the floor in the middle of the van stopped us flying across the void when we turned corners. The spare tyres were stored in the floor of the minivan making it almost impossible to get out feet comfortably.

After fifteen minutes or so the van stopped at a small hut and we unloaded the gear. Shortly after a second van containing villagers arrived and I hoped that these guys would be our Sherpas. No such luck as they unloaded bags of rice, animal traps and various other bits and pieces to be transferred to the jungle camp. There was so much that I could not imagine how so few tiny little men would be able to carry it all, but they did.

The students, who would be our companions in the jungle, were already waiting and were excitedly chattering about the week ahead. They looked very young and very fit and I did wonder how we could possibly keep up with them on the trek to camp. I made a snap decision that the best way to keep up was to go first, that way no matter how slow we were everybody else would be behind us.

We set off into the jungle with the aim of being in camp by around noon. The first part of the walk was easy, the terrain was flat and the ground underfoot, although muddy, was solid. The trees however were altogether different. They seemed to be leaning in against us and were covered with all manner of weapons.

The rattan tree with inch long thorns made any wobble from the chosen path a painful experience. Spider webs hung menacingly from the branches of almost every tree and multi coloured orb spiders looked down on us from the centre of their traps. Leeches sensed the passing of fresh blood and made rapid nose to tail progress onto any exposed flesh. There was another menace, so small yet so painful. Biting ants were using the trees as super highways and they got really pissed off when a hand interrupted their progress up or down the tree.

The only thing in our favour was that the rain held off but with the rising humidity it was clear that the thunder storms so typical of this area were building and although the giant cumulonimbus clouds could not be seen through the forest canopy I knew they were menacingly overhead.

After an hour or so the ground became steeper and the path less well defined. Andrea was coping pretty well, but she did not have a pack to carry, I was beginning to struggle. My litre of water had long gone and my pack seemed to get heavier with every step. Thunder crashed overhead and a patter of raindrops signalled the onset of the storm. Much of the rain was trapped by the canopy and dripped onto us from giant leaves acting as mini reservoirs until the weight became too great. The path became a slimy, sticky, mud bath and walking straight became almost impossible. The rattan trees claimed victims especially a few young enthusiastic Aussie students.

Andrea and I found a fallen tree and after checking for creepy crawlies rested, she turned to me a whispered "What the bloody hell had we let ourselves in for, and we hadn't even reached camp." We ate our snack in silence and having re-fuelled we felt able to press on. The young ones were well ahead, but the local guides and porters were taking it steady so we walked with them. Two of the Aussies, both looking like timid academic types asked if they could walk with us as they were finding the pace up ahead too much and we were glad of the company. They also had extra water supplies which was a real result.

The next couple of hours passed in a mindless slog. It was mostly uphill and always painful. With each step forward I seemed to slide at least half a step backwards. In places the land fell away on one side or the other and the prospect of sliding down a jungle slope into who knows what, certainly focused my mind. Jenny, one of the Aussies slipped and fell grabbing the nearest support to steady herself. It took Andrea a good five minutes to remove the rattan thorns form her hand and put on a temporary protective bandage to stop the bleeding.

The storm raged on and tiny streams no more than a foot or so wide crossed the path with a fury that one day they would want to grow into big stream. The forest was quiet except for the rain The insects, birds and monkeys had all sheltered from the deluge. As suddenly as it had started, the storm abated Such is the way in the rain-forest. Almost at once steam started to rise and the heat began to build. It was like walking through a green, dark and oppressive Chinese laundry. It was impossible to keep my specs clear and each wipe from my hand smeared mud over the lenses and made vison almost impossible.

At last we reached the top of the slope and looked down into a jungle clearing that would be our home for the next few days. At first sight it seemed very organised and had clearly been in place for a good few weeks, if not longer. A stream marked the border of the camp and beyond this the ground rose slightly to a large open-sided tent that housed trestle tables and chairs. To the left was a longer canvas construction, again open-sided, containing two long rows of hammocks. The cooking area was nearer to the stream and a large camp fire was surrounded by makeshift tarpaulin shelters occupied by the local guides and staff. A little further away from the camp were two canvas constructions that I took to be long drop toilets. A couple of canvas constructions were hung across the stream to provide a little privacy for those brave enough to wash.

The final descent into the camp was treacherous but fortunately a rope hand hold was in place to prevent us from entering the camp like skeleton bob riders in the winter Olympics. Andrea clambered down closely followed by our two new friends and I brought up the rear. We were greeted by a warm round of applause from the other students and sighs of relief from the adults who must have feared for our safety.

Most of the bunks in the shelter had been claimed already so Andrea and I could only get two together by negotiation. I let Andrea choose and set up my mosquito net and stored my dry clothing in my hammock. I also practised getting in and out of the hammock a few times in order to avoid embarrassment should I need to make a quick exit during the night. Andrea did very little simply standing and staring at her hammock. After a few taps on my shoulder I realised she wanted something and turned to help. She said nothing, just pointed at a black shape in the middle of the hammock.

There was no way I was dealing with this, it was a Sulawesi tarantula and I did what any self-respecting male would do

"You chose that hammock; I did give you first pick so I'm not swapping now."

"You made me come into this fucking jungle so you get rid of it."

A measured response I thought.

As we stood and stared at "Boris" Jenny, our Australian walking companion from the trek, appeared at our side.

"I love spiders Jim. I will get rid of it for you"

She carefully placed her cupped hands in the hammock and allowed "Boris" to crawl onto them. With equal care she walked out of the sleeping area and placed the giant spider onto the forest floor returning to us smiling.

"Bloody hell Jen. How the hell did you develop the courage to do that?"

"It's why I'm on this trip, to study spiders and bugs I just love them. I'm going to study them at uni next year. They are really quite gentle unless you scare them."

"Well we will take your word for that, but thanks so much"

Andrea and I looked at each other in total amazement, this tiny, timid looking little girl had more guts than both of us put together.

I explored the rest of the camp in the dry spell between storms and it was beyond doubt the most primitive place I had ever stayed. Like most people I had camped a bit when I was young and even then I found the idea of a toilet block with communal showers a pain in the arse but compared to this, that was five-star luxury. The stream that ran through camp was the only source of drinking water and had to be boiled. Thus the water had a smoky taste similar to Laphroaig whiskey without the kick.

The local guides did all of the cooking on open fires, and washed up in a designated area in the stream. All detergents were eco-friendly and consequently totally bloody useless. There were two closed washing areas in the stream and a natural pool that doubled as a communal bath and play area for the youngsters. The water was freezing which was fine in the afternoon heat but in the morning it was a shock to the system. The bogs were long drop holes in the ground but were un-lit. This meant at night head torches were the only option and, every trip to the loo became a bug attack trial.

The scientists, for whom we would be the "goffers", were an odd lot.

There was "Malta" No-one seemed to know his real name but he came from Malta we knew that much. He was catching and studying bats, and was probably the most enthusiastic person I have ever met. Without any trace of social skills, he was a genuine odd ball. The only time he ever spoke to anyone in camp was when he caught a bat and then he lit up. He would explain the hunting techniques, the use of sonar, its prey and everything else about the creature.

He would allow us to hold them and even release them. He used a tiny hole punch to mark the wing so that he would know if he recaptured the same animal. Each morning a different group of students would help him bait his traps and bring into camp anything they had been lucky enough to catch overnight. The rest of the day he lay in his hammock reading or snoozing. In the evening he repeated the process as not all bats are inactive during the day.

Malta was also one of the fastest and most voracious eaters I have known. When meals were served, he went to the front of the queue regardless of how long others had been standing waiting and took as much food as he was permitted. Whenever possible he took a bit more. By the time the second person in the queue had sat down Malta would have finished his meal. He would then re-join the queue and start over again. As most meals consisted of rice and precious little else at least it meant he didn't get the best bits.

Then there was Trevor the butterfly man. He was an American and we suspected he was a bit of a misfit. Andrea thought that had he not discovered butterflies and moths he may well have become a serial killer. He was so intense that most of the young ones were a little scared to work with him as he did not take errors particularly well and did expect everyone to know as much as he did. He was fighting a slight losing battle as catching butterflies in a net whilst prancing around in a jungle is not exactly a manly thing to do, and for that matter it's not a womanly thing to do either.

The students would always volunteer for every other activity and those slow of the mark got to help Trevor. I did try to befriend him as I felt a little sorry for him but that turned out to be a massive error as I was continually asked to examine another species. They all seemed the same to me, especially the moths and to be honest they were not even colourful. I did, however, learn that butterflies at rest have their wings closed whilst moths at rest have them open. Never again will I confuse moths and butterflies.

The entomologist, Saoirse, was, Irish, from Dublin with an unpronounceable name (she pronounced it Sersha) and an indecipherable accent. She had one very loyal disciple in Jenny. The pair were inseparable for the whole of our jungle stay. Even Jenny's teachers allowed her to work exclusively with the insect lady rather than moving her around the groups. Jen was in her element.

Saoirse was a stunningly attractive woman with dark hair and deep brown eyes. Her full lips hid two rows of perfect white teeth and her smile lit up the camp. I suspect she had no idea of her beauty and she certainly had no idea of style. She spent most days in ill-fitting jungle pants and a muddy t-shirt and was almost always to be found handling giant spiders or gruesome looking beetles.

Some of the more observant boys, and indeed the men, were quick to volunteer to help the entomologist and I guess she naively thought they too loved bugs. Mind you as soon as they saw the size of the bloody spiders Saoirse was usually left alone with Jen. I tried on one occasion to overcome my fear of spiders by holding a tarantula. Jen was patient and really tried to encourage me but I have to admit I never managed to let the grotesque beast crawl onto my hands.

There were two bird men and they were the oddest of the lot. Jack and Alex were the little and large of the jungle. Jack stood well over six and a half feet tall and had a mop of bright red hair, rosy cheeks and hands the size of garden shovels. Alex was about five foot two, blonde and chubby. He had clearly given up the ghost as far as his feet went and wore flip-flops even in the deep jungle. I'm sure he had trench foot, and was in pain all of the time but seemed not to care one jot about it. The two of them set mist nets in the jungle, ringed whatever they caught, (which was very little) and made bird jokes that kept them endlessly amused

. "Well guys we saw two pimps, a gimp and a wimp today."

They gave each other a knowing look and erupted into a fit of giggles. The boys explained to me over supper that they had invented their own abbreviations for the various pigeons. Pimp being pied imperial, gimp being the green and wimp the white. They found this to be hilarious and repeated every day to every new group. This meant I heard it at least once a day. I couldn't help laughing, not so much at the joke, but at the immense joy it brought to Jack and Alex.

The only other notable scientist in the camp was Anya the monkey lady. She was following a troop of macaques and this meant lots of walking and immense patience. It also meant that if you went with her for the day you got the most amazing insight into the lives of a family of monkeys. They clearly knew her, trusted her, and were happy in her company. The day Andrea and I spent with her was magical.

The adult monkeys ignored us and were happy to feed and play all round us. On two occasions mothers brought their babies down so close it was almost as if they were proudly showing us their offspring. They held the babies close to their chests but made certain that we could see them. Anya said it would be very dangerous to reach out and touch them and macaques do have massive teeth so we believed her without question. It was, however, a real privilege to even get this close.

The food in camp was awful, not because those on kitchen duty didn't try, but because rice is just not that interesting. Breakfast was fried rice, lunch boiled rice and supper boiled rice with green stuff. The green stuff looked like water weed and tasted of nothing. The only flavouring in the food was a thick sweet soy sauce or chilli sauce.

On some evenings there was a fried egg with the rice and these meals were the best ones. Despite this we all looked forward to meal times. Sitting around in the mess tent chatting to the students and scientists and hearing what bugs Jenny had found that day was brilliant. Inevitably after the events of the day had been thoroughly discussed thoughts turned to the first proper meal we would have when we exited the jungle. Lasagne seemed most popular, although I went for fresh bread with cheddar cheese and Angela opted for pulled pork. Night came early and by 6pm most people were tucked up in hammocks unless they were playing cards or writing essays for school or university.

On the penultimate evening in camp the scientists gathered us all together and explained that it was equally important to study night life and that to do this we were going on a river walk. It was voluntary but was likely to give us opportunities not available in the day. The plan was to walk downstream hoping to capture and measure amphibians, snakes and any other night creatures that we could find.

The Aussies were dead keen on the idea after all an adventure is an adventure. I was less sure but did not really want to miss out. Andrea, who by now was pretty much game for anything. Flatly refused to take part.

We were briefed on water safety and kitted out with large hand held nets, wet suit booties and insect repellent before we set off. The river was not deep or dangerous but the flow was strong. The main issues were created by overhanging branches and an uneven river bed. Occasionally, at the bends in the river, pools had developed. These were very deep, but equally they were obvious even in the poor light and warnings were given by the local guides.

At first we saw little, which was not surprising as a dozen or so students walking in a river at night is not a quiet thing. Laughter erupted every time someone fell over, or crashed into a branch. Screams broke the silence as we walked into giant cobwebs walked or as flying bugs dive bombed our head torches. This lasted for ten minutes or so before calm overtook the group and searching began in earnest. It is amazing how bright kids realise when the time has come to concentrate and en-masse change their behaviour.

Tiny brightly coloured green tree frogs were the most common amphibians we found and once captured sat peacefully on hands noses or any other part of the body they chose. Their sticky feet enabled them to leap from one student to another with great aplomb. The students quickly discovered that the frogs would leap directly onto whatever was in front them if you touched their back legs. The boys had endless fun making frogs jump onto the girls faces, heads and backs. The girls remained calm and dismissive.

We also came across lots of massive bull-frogs some the size of footballs. Each was weighed and rereleased. The release process was not welcomed by the local guides who clearly could not understand why good protein was being re-released into the jungle. I am certain I saw at least one of the amphibious giants being secreted away in a bag for later, but I chose not to expose the culprit.

The first snake we saw was high in a tree, curled around a fork in the branches. It was small and green and thankfully well out of reach. As we stood looking up a commotion kicked off a few feet down stream. Stuart, the reptile man had thrown himself headlong into the flow and was sitting astride a massive reticulated python. It was around eight feet in length and was clearly not too impressed at having its evening hunting trip interrupted.

Stuart skilfully secured his hands just below the snake's head to prevent the jaws locking onto any of us, while the guides secured the snakes body to prevent it from encircling any stray legs or arms. The beast was dropped into a large sack and weighed after it had been fully extended and measured. Within the group there was a mixture of great excitement, fear and bewilderment. I had never been that close to such a magnificent serpent and my thoughts kept going back to Harry Potter and the urge to try my version of parseltongue was almost too strong to resist.

Stuart caught three more smaller pythons over the next forty minutes along with more frogs and we caught a fleeting glimpse of a water creature that may or may not have been an otter. As the group splashed back to camp there was a general sense of having been part of something rather special and we all felt a bond. We had an Indiana Jones style of evening and one not to forget.

The camp was quiet when we returned, but not because everyone was asleep. We had a visitor, and no one dared move or speak in case it ran away. Under the awning of the mess tent was a civet snuffling along for any dropped food, some chance of that. Andrea stared in utter amazement as the small feline like creature examined the eating area.

The animal looked like a cross between a cat, a dog and a badger. It had a striped head and a spotted body but the long tail was curved rather like a lemur. Its face was pointed and it was silent. The civet is not especially rare in these parts but being totally nocturnal it's hard to see. We were indeed privileged and it crowned off a near perfect evening for us jungle folk. It stayed around for a good ten minutes and seemed not to be bothered either by the cameras or the photographers. One of the scientists smeared some jam on a rock and the civet loved licking it off. I am pretty certain every student in the camp would have been equally delighted to have the opportunity to lick the rock had they been allowed.

Anya who had not been on the river walk had spent the evening chatting to Andrea and the pair of them had made plans for the next morning. They were going to leave camp just before dawn and find tarsiers. These beautiful bush-baby like primates are one of the smallest of the primate species. I would have loved to have gone but Andrea was so excited by the prospect of a girly adventure and of doing something that showed she was coming to terms with her fears, that I felt it best to offer encouragement and no more.

When I stirred from my hammock she had already left camp but re-appeared in the middle of breakfast.

"We saw them of my god they were brilliant. We found their nest and the whole group was returning from a night's hunting. There were loads, a family group plus babies, oh they were Gorgeous. Anya was amazing she knew exactly where they would be. The babies were so tiny they could have gripped onto my thumb."

It was rather like listening to a machine gun as Andrea fired off words in a barrage that perfectly conveyed her enthusiasm and excitement. It confirmed to me that to let her have this adventure on her own was the right thing to do even although secretly I was so jealous.

Our last day in the rain forest was thankfully a dry day and we were able to at least rinse the worst of the mud from our day clothes. I decided that after nearly a week without a proper wash I would brave the river cubicle. The walk to the secluded wash areas was treacherous. The duck boarding was soaked and slippery as ice. I felt like I was in the trenches at Passchendaele as I picked my way to the flimsy canvas structure that spanned the stream.

Finally, inside the mini tent I looked down only to see a deep red stain on the front of my jungle pants. I wondered how I could have strawberry jam on my pants when we had only been eating rice, (its bizarre how one's brain works when robbed of the normal trappings of everyday life). As I slipped my pants down a massive leech fell into the water, swollen to the limit after gorging itself on my blood. It was the size of one of my fingers, the biggest leech I had ever seen.

The scar left by this bloody creature was on the inside of my thigh really close to my bollocks. Thank God it preferred leg meat. The bleeding simply would not stop and I began to panic that the blood in the water would attract other even more vicious creatures. For some reason I actually thought that sharks could swim hundreds of miles inland to get me. Imagination working over time again, the jungle does create wild illusions. I washed thoroughly and felt so much better but still the blood trickled down my leg, and it was a good twenty minutes before the anti-coagulant pumped into me by the leech stopped working and the bleeding stopped. Having dried myself carefully and almost fully dressed I attempted to put on my stained jungle pants and toppled off the narrow duck board back into the stream.

I must have looked like an upturned turtle as I struggled to regain my upright position and my dignity.

Our last meal in camp not only included eggs, but as it was the last night of the scientific season we were able to share some crackers and jam. Never had anything so simple tasted so good. We were also given the last of the oatmeal and powdered milk and Andrea created a very passable porridge which was wolfed down by everyone. It was the nearest thing to a pudding we had eaten all week.

The trek back to Labundo was just as tough as the trek in but somehow we were now jungle folk. Although we slipped, fell, sweated and grumbled we kept a good pace and made it to the pickup point a good hour sooner than we had made it on the inward journey.

Back in Labundo we raided the house front shop for any snacks available. I chose a Magnum ice cream and a tube of Pringles. Sheer decadent luxury!

Bed 18 The Slave ship!

Alan was there to meet us and explained that the jungle camp was closing as the rains were expected within the next few days. He offered us both the opportunity to join him and a few others on a small island where different studies were being undertaken. I looked at Andrea and she nodded

"Why not? I can't get any dirtier. Let's go for it."

We left Labundo and retraced our steps part of the way back to Bau-Bau before setting of across the peninsular towards the coastal town of Pasarwago. We arrived late in the evening and boarded a vessel that was immediately christened the "slave ship".

The slave ship was a medium-sized wooden craft with three decks. It looked barely sea worthy in the half-light so goodness knows what it would look like in the full light of day. As we boarded the crew told us to grab a mattress and find a space on the deck to sleep until the tide changed and the ship could put out to sea. In theory, this was straightforward, but in reality it was a nightmare. The top deck was spacious and the air clean but it was raining and sheltered spots were very hard to find. The hold was full with supplies for the destination island so that only left the middle deck.

This area was divided by shelves that were large enough to hold a mattress but with no privacy at all. We all huddled together and tried to get comfortable. Almost as soon as the jostling for position had concluded the captain turned on the ships engines. These were located on the bottom deck but the noise and the smell of diesel meant they could well been on the mid deck with all of us.

To make matters worse the captain allowed locals to board the vessel, which according to the Opwall staff was forbidden. They almost immediately began to smoke and eat foul smelly fishy snacks. This extra stench combined with the diesel smell was too much too bear. Andrea and I moved to the open deck and huddle up under a plastic sheet and tried to sleep, Oh for a jungle hammock!

At first light the vessel set sail and within the first hour the mid deck resemble a living hell. The sea was rough and the ship pitched and rolled to the extent that sitting on the deck was too dangerous. The smell of diesel fumes pervaded everyone's senses. Those with weak stomachs or with sea sickness were already throwing up through portholes or through the open loading bay at the side of the ship.

The boat ride to Hoga Island took over eight hours and some of the very ill threw up for the whole journey. The ship stank, but no-one cared. Those who were not ill sat and comforted the wretches who just wanted their lives to end. I was really concerned about Andrea; she had been sick so many times that nothing was left to come up but she kept retching nonetheless. I also had a genuine fear that the vessel would capsize and sink. Stories of capsized inter island ferries in South Asia are not uncommon in the press. In such a remote area the result would have been catastrophic for all of us on board.

Those who managed to sleep seemed almost numb with fear and nausea. Cockroaches crawled over prone bodies. I mentioned to one of the young student that a particularly large roach was sitting on their chest. The young lad looked down and in a resigned disgust just smiled and said "Oh Yeh! Cheers mate." He lacked the energy or the enthusiasm to flick the beast off his chest.

Never have I been so grateful to see land. The island of Hoga in the Wakatobi National Park came into view in early afternoon and we finally moored alongside the jetty at around 2pm. I expected a rush for the safety of terra-firma but the hours of sickness and fear had left everyone weak and almost helpless.

Those of us who had not been ill helped unload the packs and helped the others ashore. The island looked idyllic with the tropical sun beating down from a cloudless sky. Palm trees swayed in the breeze and gradually the horror of the crossing gave way to a mild hysteria. Andrea turned to me and with an honesty that comes from despair, said

"Thank God that's over I really thought I was going to die"

After a brief hug we walked to the briefing room.

The briefing room was set out like a classroom with desks and benches. At the front was a white screen ready to show a film or a Power Point presentation. Standing beside it was an oldish woman who looked like she had spent a few too many years on a desert island. Her leathery skin made her look older than she probably was. She was wearing a rather unflattering loose fitting and well-worn summer frock, the original colours faded to a dull grey/yellow, and flip-flops on her feet. Her name was Dr Mary Felix and she was the head scientist on Hoga. Her brief, for this short meeting, was to welcome us all and then tell us that just about everything on the island, and in the water that surrounded it, could kill us.

Sea snakes, mosquitoes, monitor lizards, sharks, jellyfish, spiders and of course the ocean itself. Her talk might have been mildly amusing had we not have just suffered the sea crossing from hell but she seemed oblivious to this and chatted away as if we had just arrived by private helicopter. The young students tried to listen but as an adult I felt obliged to speak up.

"Doctor Felix, sorry to interject but we have just been at sea for eight hours throwing our guts up. Would it be possible for us to have this chat later today when we could probably concentrate a little more?

Her response was sympathetic and we agreed to reconvene at 6pm. Everyone drifted off to their huts for a rest, a wash and some recovery time.

Andrea and I had been allocated a hut on the leeward side of the island some five minutes' walk from the main station buildings. It was basic, but after the last village hut the jungle, and the slave ship it was like checking into the Hilton. We actually had a bed with clean sheets and a mattress. The mandi was still devoid of running water but we had a sit down toilet. Andrea and I were very quickly learning that small things meant so much when stripped of the comforts of western middle class life.

Our first supper on the island included a small portion of fresh tuna caught by the local fishermen, and never has fish tasted so good. We also ate fresh fruit and had squash to drink. The water did not taste smoky. Best of all however, was a jar of prawn crackers they were delicious, so simple, but so satisfying. We really were in paradise.

Doc Felix resumed her briefing and explained in detail how we should best avoid the pitfalls of life on a very isolated island. There was a small medical centre and a doctor on the island but anything major could not be treated on site. The nearest hospital was many hours away by sea. Everyone took the briefing seriously.

It appeared that whilst on land the main issue was quite bizarrely, sea snakes. These beasties come ashore at night to sleep and become very aggressive when defending their space. We were advised to give them a wide birth. In the ocean they generally avoid large objects such as divers, or tended to show a non-threatening curiosity. I heard one of the students whisper to his mate "if it shows a curiosity in me non-threatening or not I'm bloody out of here."

Andrea and I soon discovered we had a few squatters in our hut, a couple of small lizards and some pretty big black ants. We also appeared to have a friendly gecko who announced itself by calling its name very loudly. These things no longer bothered us at all and we looked forward to our week in the hut.

The next morning and on all subsequent mornings our routine was the same. We met at the central admin block for breakfast. Nasi goreng was the breakfast staple but there were also bread rolls that could be split open and toasted and I still had some Marmite in my back pack, so all was right with the world.

After breakfast Andrea got kitted out and went diving with the students. Watching her try to get into a wet suit is always wonderfully amusing, the best bit being that as lots of young students were around, she couldn't swear at me when I laughed. I hate swimming in the sea and chose to spend much of my morning reading in the sun or wandering the island looking for birds. There were not many to be found on such a small island, but I did get great views of red bellied and hooded pittas (two very good spots) as well as a few smaller less colourful species. The peace and solitude was something it is hard to find in places closer to the beaten track and, it certainly was a privilege to be so far from anywhere.

Andrea is an excellent diver and loved the chance to experience reef diving in such an ecologically important area. The coastal coral reefs and the abundant life associated with it meant that every dive was different. She surfaced each lunch time with different tales of turtles, and nemos or hammer head sharks and coral snakes. Each dive was for a specific purpose to help the Opwall staff survey the reef and the students counted and logged all they saw. Andrea was excused the formal part of the dive and simply enjoyed herself.

The food on the island was good and it was thankfully plentiful. If the daily catch was good, we all ate fish. If not, it was substituted by tofu. Coconut milk was added to the rice, as were chillies and other flavoursome ingredients. The food was still unbelievably simple but it was delicious. The small admin area even sold cold beer so most evenings Andrea and I lounged in hammocks drinking cool beer and reading. Teaching seemed so far away. Occasionally when the wi-fi was working we could catch up with emails or even skype our daughters. They were amazed at how adventurous we had become. We were not entirely sure if they were jealous or concerned. India was very worried we would turn up to see her in flowing hippy clothes with tattoos and braided hair or a goatee beard. It was pleasing to know that even in absentia we could still embarrass our children. We had not lost the magic touch.

Close to Hoga was a globally unique settlement, constructed over the water on stilts. Here the Bajau people or sea gypsies lived. I caught a small fishing boat over to the village one afternoon while the divers were out enjoying the beauties of the deep. I was accompanied by Doc Felix who visited periodically to check on the pregnant women and the young children. Her visit was a highlight for the Bajau children as she often took across treats such as hair ties or small bangles and sometimes even a few sweeties. Today was no exception and as we docked we were welcomed like returning heroes.

The settlement was semi-permanent consisting of around 50 dwellings built above the coral reef and linked together by bamboo or wooden walkways. The whole structure looked incredibly unstable yet the Bajau people went about business as if it were the most stable structure on the planet. Children, who could not have been more than three, leapt over gaping holes in the walkways or threw themselves into the sea as if they had not a care in the world.

I had no common language with the Bajau but we got by with a mixture of hand gestures, smiles and pointing. Dr Felix had a basic grasp of the lingo and I tended to stick pretty close to her. As I waited outside the huts while she examined the mums I was shown turtles, octopus, star fish and many more seas treasures that were now living in any water tight container the youngster could find. I hoped beyond hope they were not destined for the cooking pot but were part of a greater plan to re-stock the reef. I knew deep down that my optimism was ill-founded and these creatures would sooner or later form a part of a family meal.

The reef under the village was all but dead and much of the surrounding reef was dying. In time these Bajau would have to move on and resume their gypsy life style. They could no longer rely upon ocean to provide for their every need. As Dr Felix and I looked out to sea, mighty Chinese and Malay trawlers were illegally fishing in protected waters and nothing was being done to stop the rape of the sea.

As we were about to leave excitement broke out and Dr Felix was summoned to a small hut on the far side of the village. A woman she had seen just an hour earlier had gone into labour. It was her fifth child and labour was likely to be very short. Sure enough less than an hour later a tiny Bajau girl began her life in this perilous place, perched on a reef in the Banda sea.

As the doc and I were transported back to Hoga we discussed the prospects for the Bajau and our conclusions were dismal. We both suspected that this new arrival would not grow up with the traditions of her forefathers and that the Bajau way of life, tough as it is, would not survives for much longer.

Bed 19 & 20. Island in the sun.

The ferry crossing from Hoga back to Pasarwago was very different to the outward journey. The small slave ship was replaced by a bigger slave ship. The weather was wonderful and the eight-hour journey was completed in less than six hours. Andrea and I spent much of the time on deck soaking up the sun. I, as always, taking great care not to burn by using my usual method of carefully timing the amount of sun light I allowed to hit my body. Andrea using her methods of liberally applying sun screen and missing bits. This time she chose to miss the bits in her parting and by the time we reached Pasarwago the red glow emanating from the top of her head indicated that she was in for a few uncomfortable days.

We said good bye to Alan in Pasarwago and thanked him for giving us such a unique opportunity. He was staying on Sulawesi for a few more weeks tying up loose ends and adding the final touched to his part of the scientific paper. He promised to let us know if and when this region was granted funding to protect the environment and its flora and fauna.

Our onward journey to Makassar and Jakarta was straightforward and getting a flight to Bali was easy enough. Jet Star were still cancelling flights but Air Asia for some reason was not. We flew down to Ngurahrai airport in Bali and looked forward to a few weeks of beach bum life interspersed with a bit of culture and a lot of pampering.

We booked into the Sunset, a quiet little hotel in Legian. It was cheap, clean and had excellent A/C. From the Sunset we could walk into Kuta for meals and shopping.

Kuta is where it all happens for the party set in Bali and to be honest it was not really what Andrea and I wanted, neither of us being particularly keen on drunken Australian youths, and tattooed yobs. It was a bit like being in the Benidorm of our youth. Clearly, the warnings about too much sun had escaped the great unwashed and all around us were blistered shoulders, Rudolf style red noses and legs so red they looked like the bars on an electric heater. Still at least Andrea, with her glowing bonce, did not feel to out of place.

Andrea and I have never had a very positive view of Brits abroad and in our slightly snobbish middle class way we had frowned upon drunken British men and women sprawled across bars and pavements with legs wide open and knickers showing, or threatening to fight anyone who dared look in their direction. Well at least here it wasn't British girls puking in the street or squatting in side-alleys, or British males abusing waiters and squaring up to locals. No, the Aussies have their own breed of underclass and if anything, they are worse than ours.

Andrea and I decided that it would be an excellent step forward if governments stopped issuing passports to those with an IQ below a certain level. I was beginning to turn into Victor Meldrew and I had only been retired a few months. We found the best thing to do in Kuta was to keep a very low profile and keep well away from the bars. We ate early and in local eateries and left the fun to the young.

The memorial to those youngsters so tragically killed in the Bali bombing back in 2002 is tasteful and well respected. We took the time to read the names of the dead and pay our respects.

The sunset from Kuta beach is magnificent and something every tourist should witness.

We arrived as the sun was going down and took our place at the top of the beach. A local bar gave us two chairs and beer crate for a table and we sat with cold beers and watched the world go by. The beach was busy but the atmosphere was great. The lunchtime drunks were long asleep and anyway sitting watching the sun go down was nowhere near cool enough for the Oz yobs.

Frigatebirds wheeled in the sky and as they flew across the setting sun. They looked almost prehistoric. All manner of beach sellers plied their wares along the sands. Andrea, never one to miss a chance to shop, spent a good fifteen minutes bartering with a watch seller before settling on a Cartier and a Rolex. At $20 for the pair I kind of figured that they may not have been genuine. They were well worth the money as they worked for at least long enough for the seller to be out of sight.

The sun slowly set and the skies changed from orange through red to purple and many colours in between. We finished our beers and set of back to the Sunset Hotel for a shower before supper. En-route we passed Jamie Oliver's Italian restaurant, who'd have thought it? From school dinners to pacific islands he certainly is a global brand. Mind you as his restaurant charged prices way in excess of the local food outlets we gave it a miss.

Just down the road from the Sunset hotel was a car park, which at night, became a foodie's paradise. About a dozen stalls opened up selling excellent local food. The tables were a tad low and the chairs seemed to strain under my weight and we were the only Europeans eating in the area but it was worth it. I opted for nasi ayam a chicken dish with savoury rice while Andrea had babi guling which is suckling pig stuffed with spices and vegetables. I did suggest we share half and half when I saw her dish arrive but was met with a firm and emphatic;

"Not a chance."

I put the terseness of the reply down to burnt forehead.

Kuta was not really our scene and we made arrangements to travel on to the Gili Islands, Gili Trawangan to be exact. Trawangan is the largest of the three Gili Islands the other two are Gili Air and Gili Meno. These tropical isles lay between Bali and Lombok and have long been the hang out for hippies and people who have simply dropped off the map. These days' students throng to the islands for relaxation cheap diving and plenty of sun.

We secured a cheap deal on our return crossing to Gili which included a pick from the Sunset, transit to Padang Bai, ferry port, the return crossing and finally a drop off in Ubud which was our next port of call. We had read so many scary stories on the internet about picks not arriving and the unsafe state of the crafts but after the slave ship we were sea hardened. Well the pick-up arrived on time and the boat was fine. I sat on deck while Andrea sat below not wishing to get any more sun exposure. The Ekajaya was a fast boat and including stops at the smaller islands we were in Trawangan in about 90 minutes.

Once on the island we could almost feel time beginning to stand still. There are no cars, just cycles and horse drawn carts. We climbed aboard a cart and were slowly taken to our home for the next week. I had chosen the Resota Twins which turned out to be a wonderful choice. The owner was a charming Italian lady called Simona.

Our room, up a flight of wooden stairs, was rather like a wood cabin. Everything we needed was there, a large comfortable bed, tea and coffee, a wardrobe and a TV. We had our statutory in-room gecko and ear plugs. These were to prove to be the most invaluable addition to any room on the whole trip.

The bathroom was en-suite and the shower powerful if a little chilly in the mornings. There was a small veranda where we took breakfast and sat in the early evening watching the sun go down. The Resota Twins was set back from the main strip but within easy walking distance and we settled in almost at once.

At 5am the next morning we quickly realised why ear plugs were supplied. The local mosque was about one hundred yards away and it was loud. I can pretty much sleep through anything but Andrea made excellent use of the plugs. The mosque did not appear to have an Imam calling the faithful to prayer, rather it was a recording that may well have been made in a previous century. If the chanting of prayers didn't wake you then the scratching on the recording did. However, would we stay at the Resota again? At the drop of a hat!

Breakfast was served by the young local staff and, it always came on time and with a massive smile. We had fresh fruit, pancakes, eggs, toast and chilled fruit juice. All of the staff were desperate to try out their English so we always had company at breakfast. Even Simona popped along for a chat and to give us tips for the day.

Each day followed a similar pattern. We rose and showered before taking a leisurely breakfast. Then we strolled along the beach-front checking out the shops and looking for the perfect section of beach to spend the day. The beach front shacks all served food and for the price of a beer and a snack you could use the sun-loungers for the day. We had to be careful to get the choice right as synthetic sun loungers got too hot, wooden ones were too hard. The bean bags were great, but it took us both about half an hour to get out of then. We must have looked like upturned turtles. The loungers with white plastic slats that are omnipresent at every hotel in the world were as comfortable as sitting on the bars of an electric fire. The perfect choice was a combination, an easily adjustable back, a firm base and a cushion cover proved just right and we found these on about the third day, bliss!

Some days we chose to snorkel. On others we simple lazed around and chilled in the ocean from time to time. We paddled with turtles and drank beer in the shade of the palm parasols. Time did indeed stand still.

During one cooling off period in the ocean we overheard a German couple chatting, in perfect English of course, to a local boatman. He was trying to persuade them to go out for the afternoon in his glass bottom boat to see the reef and swim with the turtles. Andrea being nosey as ever, joined in the conversation. The next thing I knew we had negotiated a price and the four of us were heading off in a small boat for the afternoon.

The reef fish were stunning and we did indeed get to swim with big turtles. I am not a great swimmer and being afloat in a massive ocean with only a small boat drifting nearby does not fill me with confidence. So when I looked up to see the boat about one hundred metres away I was scared. I tried swimming with my head up to watch the boat but got nowhere. Then I tried swimming face down which was much faster but after a couple of minutes of effort I discovered that I had been swimming off course or the boat had moved. The snorkel was a handicap and when I slipped it out of my mouth it kept poking me in the face or clawing at my nose. I tried the goggles and snorkel around my neck but this felt as if I was being strangled. By now a mild panic was setting in and I resorted to waving frantically at the boat, Mulia the boatman waved back cheerfully. When it finally became clear that I was not going to make it back to the boat Mulia steered towards me. Andrea and Karl and his wife Sylvia were on the boat which was lucky as it took all of their effort to drag me aboard. For the rest of the trip I satisfied myself by looking down through the glass bottom.

That evening we dined with Karl and Sylvia in the Thank You restaurant and had slightly too much to drink. It is amazing that when Brits and Germans get together the beer and wine usually flows. However, what a find the Thank You was. The food was excellent and was cheaper than anywhere else we had found on the island. It sits one row back from the main street and is a gem of a place.

Andrea become increasingly concerned about the plight of the island horses. Stories abounded of animal cruelty, lack of fresh water and indeed that horses were given salt water to drink. Certainly many of the beasts were pulling huge loads, some with building material and some with four or five very obese sun burned tourists. Mostly, however, the horses seemed in a reasonable state of health and based on the fact that they were very important to their owners I made the optimistic decision that they must be well cared for.

The horses were not the only animals coming in for scrutiny from my observant wife. She had noticed that the island was clear of dogs but occupied by dozens of cats and these cats were of the very odd variety. They were friendly enough though they never actually looked you in the eye, and it took me back to school when naughty boys seldom looked at you while receiving telling offs. These cats appeared to look at you but their eyes darted off in different directions. At first we thought we had come across a moggy that had lost a fight, but no they were all alike. They also had had tails that were either non-existent, very short or at right angles to the rest of their bodies.

Andrea was fascinated and I was mildly agitated assuming that some witch's curse had condemned these poor creatures to forever be the butt of people's jokes. They seemed happy enough with their lot and made a pretty good living from begging at tables and scrounging in the street. I guess looking like animals that had appeared of being created in the minds of mischievous school kids, had some advantages.

Gili Trawangan is one of the loveliest places we visited. There is a down side, and It needs to be mentioned. The beaches are sandy on first impression but they hide a secret. Much, if not all, of the sand is in fact coral and it can be sharp. This is not so much a problem until you try to get into the sea.

We tried everything, we carefully picked a route and then stood on a sharp bit and fell over. We shuffled out on our bums until the water was deep enough to roll over and swim. We tried floating and walking with hands as if in a wheelbarrow race but without a partner. Nothing worked. It was simply a painful experience. The up side was that while we were sunbathing or reading on our loungers we at least had something funny to watch most of the time. The best victims of the coral were the cool dudes, the beach gods and goddesses who tried so hard to pose in the sea. They stood aloof and bronzed in bright coloured swimmers, muscles rippling with beach bodies primed and ready. But whenever they got buffeted by a wave and moved a foot, the coral got them and they re-entered the realms of us mortals.

Bed 21 Classy Ubud

From Trawangan we caught the ferry back to Bali and transferred to Ubud. This small town in the central highlands is the centre of culture and crafts and a mecca for yoga buffs and those seeking spiritual enlightenment. The town is dotted with ancient temples, holy sites and magnificent palaces. Expensive hotels mix with tiny hostels and family home stays. Posh restaurants vie for trade with small family-run establishments that seat no more than six to eight people. Each evening traditional performances take place all over Ubud, local dance groups perform Balian dance while local musicians play traditional instruments in classic settings. The town is surrounded by lush forest and rice paddies which help to enhance the feeling that Ubud is a very spiritual place to visit.

Andrea and I opted for a homestay on the Monkey Forest Road. It was located behind the main shops in a small courtyard. Our room, one of three upstairs, was clean and central but had no air conditioning, it was bloody hot. It cost the princely sum of $10 a night with breakfast. The Sukuram family that ran the Sedona homestay lived downstairs.

In the centre of the courtyard was a small Hindu shrine painstakingly decorated with garlands of flowers and candles. It was dedicated to Ganesh and the statuette of the Elephant God took pride of place. Behind the shrine was a blossoming Jasmine bush which was constantly visited by glitteringly bright sunbirds. Chickens pecked around in the garden and the children of the various families around the courtyard played here in safety.

Mr Sukuram, later known as Hasan took our bags and led us to our room. He was very proud of his homestay and with a beaming smile showed us the "modern" bathroom and newly installed ceiling fans.

Ubud was a fascinating place to visit and there was so much to do. We were disappointed that the promised cooler climate turned out to be myth but apart from that Ubud was a delight. Everywhere we looked there were temples, shrines and buildings that had clearly been erected during a historic period when Ubud was the most important settlement on Bali. With so much to see and do we did not have time to waste so immediately after breakfast we started exploring.

We headed to the Campuhan Ridge Walk which began at the north end of the town. The starting point was not obvious but we eventually found the Gunung Lebah Temple and the pathway tucked behind this impressive edifice. The route is mostly paved and follows a ridge providing brilliant vistas of the surrounding countryside. Every guide-book we read talked about the cooling breezes that made the walk a pleasure. Well the guide-books are wrong and it was roasting. The sun beat down and we had finished our water supply almost before we had started the walk. We trudged along the ridge resting at every shady tree and watched the butterflies and colourful birds feasting on the nectar-laden shrubs and flowers.

We passed several small art galleries and painters studios and eventually we made it to the top of the ridge and the welcoming Karsa Spa. In the café overlooking the rice paddies we sipped chilled coconut water from the shell and followed this with fresh water-melon juice. Andrea ordered a fresh fruit platter of mango, papaya, melon, oranges, bananas and strawberries it was all a bit healthy for me but I did nibble at the papaya and mango.

The spa is situated in beautifully manicured gardens with small ponds full with ornamental carp and lilies. The thatched treatment huts tucked at the rear of the gardens are kept cool by fans and natural breezes. Soft music drifted through the rooms adding to the tranquillity.

I opted for a Balinese massage while Andrea had a manicure and pedicure. The cost was a little more than back in town but the setting and luxury of the surroundings made it money well spent. The only down side was we still had to face the walk back and in typical English style we undertook this at about two in the afternoon, during the heat of the day.

When we eventually got back to the Sedona it was a massive relief to find that the showers, renewed or not, only supplied cold water, and never had a cold shower felt so welcome.

Ubud is famous for being the focus of the ancient cultures of Bali and reminders of this are everywhere. It is also famous for the Sacred Monkey Forest which lies at the bottom of the town. The forest surrounds a complex of Hindu temples. The aim is to promote a greater understanding of all natures creatures, this forms part of the greater Hindu belief. The monkeys are tended by the monks and in turn they believe that the monkeys will protect them and their spirits. The Hindus call this Tri Hita Karana.

Well, the monkey forest is certainly not a misnomer. We had never seen so many monkeys in one place and I doubt we ever will. The little beasts in question are the long tailed Balinese monkeys better known to us as macaques and at the last count there were around 600 in a relatively small forest area.

Viewed from a reasonable distance of a few feet, the monkeys ranged from the babies that were cute in a very ugly way, to adults that were very ugly in, well in just an ugly way. The dominant males are fat and scary beasts, who carry the scars of battles lost and won and sport guts like English football supporters. The females are usually smaller and often have a youngster clasped to their undersides. To be honest it's a bit like walking around a council estate in any British city. The only difference is there are no obvious drugs on sale and the youngsters seem keen to learn.

All of the monkeys seem to have the common aim of grabbing as much food as possible from any unsuspecting tourist who is silly enough to look away for as much as a second.

Andrea and I were forewarned by our eldest daughter who had visited the forest the previous year. She had lost an earring and her packed lunch to a troupe in a matter of seconds. India had warned us to carry as little as possible and to avoid buying bananas from the street sellers as they simply attracted the braver macaques in hoards.

We walked along the paths and laughed as Chinese visitors wrestled to keep hold of their cameras, their daypacks and handbags and their small bunches of bananas. As we walked behind one chap a ninja monkey shot up his leg and stole a full water bottle from his day pack before running away down the path pursued by other excited monkeys keen to share in the spoils. They had not yet mastered the art of removing the bottle top but sharp teeth soon punctured the bottle and produced the desired effect.

Andrea thought this was hilarious and for a few moments lost concentration. Now I had told her not to take her handbag with her, but as often before had been overruled. It was a disaster waiting to happen and we did not have to wait long.

A young macaque clambered up her leg and to her horror tried to open her handbag. Andrea placed her hand over the top of the bag and refused the intruder easy access. The net result was one bitten knuckle, a loud scream, a startled monkey and a panicked troupe. As the rest of the monkeys shot up trees or dashed for cover Andrea continued to yelp. I stood and stared doing absolutely nothing to either help or placate. I knew not to laugh, but aside from that, was not immediately sure of the best course of action.

As she calmed down I ventured to say that if the monkey had been serious the bite mark on her hand would have been much deeper but strangely this did little to ease the tension. We duly visited the medical centre and a charming lady doctor explained that rabies was not an issue as all of the monkeys were rabies free and that the cut was minor and unlikely to get infected. She also said that if the monkey had been serious the bite would have been much deeper, I refrained from making a comment.

The Monkey Forest is a unique experience but it wasn't relaxing. When humans mix with wild animals the net result is usually disastrous for one party or the other. Here the monkeys rule and humans simply have to follow their rules. Eye contact with a big male will always result in a show of strength from the macaque. Monkeys like to climb and if they choose to climb on you then sitting still and not panicking is the only way to behave but it takes guts. Food is the most important currency in the forest and if you have it the monkeys want it. If, as a tourist you follow these rules then most of the time all will be well but they are all wild animals.

Our next venture out was to the yoga barn and I was not entirely convinced that it was a good idea from the outset. I have always found it difficult to fully appreciate the need to discover one's inner calm or to be able to get my feet behind my head. The thought of spending a day with a group of real world drop outs seeking to find themselves rather filled me with horror. I was much more of a rugby club, lad's night out type of bloke but Andrea was keen so off we went. I had to promise not to say anything likely to upset anyone or to fart loudly while trying to hold any difficult positions. I promised the former but said the latter would be down to nature.

On arrival we registered and opted for the Introduction to Yoga Class. This class was billed as a way of learning basic breathing techniques and positions in preparation for more advanced classes later on. After a somewhat lengthy introduction and explanation on the wonders of yoga we moved to the studio.

The room was open-sided with a thatched roof and stood on stilts some three feet above the garden area. The floor was wooden and beautifully polished. Our teacher was a middle-aged woman who appeared to be made of a mixture of elastic and leather. She had a deep European accent and from the long blond hair and white teeth I guessed she was from Scandinavia or Germany. It is often the case that a woman in a leotard can look very sexy, but this was most definitely not the case with Claudia. She was lithe and sinewy, but too many years in the sun had given her skin the appearance of a lizard and her shiny white teeth gleamed from her brown face in a slightly comical way.

There were 10 other novices in the class of, eight women and two men. We were all armed with a small mat and most of us had a look of amusement and apprehension on our faces.

After about fifteen minutes of breathing exercises I was knackered, so much for breathing being automatic. Clearly my diaphragm was not fully in tune with the world. After this, we settled down to stretching. I was a big fan of this especially in my PE classes at school. I was, however, a big fan of telling others to do it not of doing it myself. I had long lost the ability to touch my toes and, indeed prior to eating very little for three months I had lost the ability to even see my toes. Today, however, my toes did peep out from under my tummy but they may have well been a million miles away.

As we sat on our mats valiantly reaching down my fingers reached mid-shin, but I was by no means the worst in the class. Ingrid a large Germanic lady who occupied the mat in front of me sat bolt upright rather like a giant panda eating bamboo. I remembered the Weeble toys from my childhood that wobbled but would not fall down and, she certainly wobbled. As we rolled over onto our fronts to stretch our lower backs Ingrid let out a fart that would have woken the dead. Andrea immediately glared at me and threw me a look of total anger. Fortunately, at that moment Ingrid smiled and said

"Entschuldigen sie" and laughed.
Andrea still glaring at me returned to her stretching.

I spent the rest of the hour waiting and hoping for a second chorus from Ingrid but obviously she had cleared the decks with her first effort.

As we became a little suppler and the heat allowed us more movement we started to cross legs in unfamiliar ways and to combine stretches with balances. In the second part of the class we even assisted each other to maximise stretching. To an outsider it must have looked like a swinger's party engaging in a giant game of Twister. I partook but without a great deal of enthusiasm and made certain I was never in firing line of Ingrid. Andrea stayed on for a second class while I spent the afternoon relaxing in the Kafe with a cool drink and a book. I resisted the urge to eat, as none of the food looked remotely like food and all seemed decidedly uncooked.

Andrea spent the next couple of days at the yoga barn and claimed to really enjoy it. I used the time to explore the rice paddies and surrounding countryside looking for birds and generally getting to know the place. Ubud seems to cater for just about every interest, the scenery is spectacular, the food is cheap and tasty and there is culture, nature, shopping and of course, yoga.

Bed 22. VIP treatment in Nusa-Dua

We were both I little sad when we moved on to our final Bali stop, at Nusa Dua. We intended to spend a week of doing nothing before heading to Australia. As it turned out this last week in South East Asia was one of the oddest of our trip.

We arrived at the Mesten Tamarind Hotel and waved goodbye to our taxi driver only to find that the place seemed deserted it had a feel of the Mary Celeste. We rang the reception bell and even banged a massive gong in the reception area but no one came. Andrea then phoned the hotel and eventually the call was answered and a sleepy looking receptionist welcomed us to the Mesten.

The hotel looked magnificent, the floors were shining and the reception area was decorated with intricate Hindu statues, garlands of brightly coloured flowers and ornate furniture. The lift ran up the outside of the building giving great views of the surrounding countryside and of the coast some ten minutes or so away. Despite this Andrea and I felt that something did not feel right.

Our room was perfectly prepared and plenty large enough for our requirements. The bell boy who spoke little English did manage to convey that the wi-fi was not working. I think he realised that this was not good news as soon after he had left us there was a knock at the door. The hotel manager, Jonathon, stood apologetically outside our room.

"Sorry but we have no wi-fi at present sir, we're working on it as we speak."

"Any idea how long? we have flights and accommodation to book in Australia so we really need it"

Jonathon looked concerned and promised he would try to sort things out as soon as he could. In the mean time we were given a room upgrade for our troubles. Five minutes later we were in the penthouse suite, with a massive bedroom and a lounge area but no air conditioning. We did not have the heart to complain straight away so left it a while.

After an hour or so we phoned reception and asked how the aircon worked. Once again Jonathan appeared and assured us that a repair man would remedy the fault very soon. The next couple of hours saw a flurry of activity in and around our suite. Air conditioning repair men came and went, wi-fi repair men came and went and we were served tea as if we were royalty. Jonathan checked on us every hour or so and offered to drive us into town for supper as the hotel only served breakfast. Throughout this whole period, we did not see another guest.

By the time we got back from Nusa Dua after a lovely evening meal we had a cool room, functioning wi-fi and a note saying that breakfast would be served at 9am the next morning in the roof top terrace restaurant. It appeared that all was well.

Andrea and I duly took our places on the roof terrace ready for breakfast. We had pre -ordered eggs and fruit but received nasi goring and toast. We had both ordered tea but the coffee that arrived was just fine. There were no other guests at breakfast but we assumed that as we were in the penthouse suite we got VIP treatment while the hoi polloi ate below stairs.

After eating we strolled downstairs to the pool area to find two sun beds laid out with towels and a bowl of fruit set between the loungers, but still no other people.

We stayed at the Mesten for five days and each day followed a similar pattern. A mystery breakfast followed by a day in the sun by our private pool. The evenings were spent in town after being dropped off by Jonathan and collected after our meal.

One evening we were invited by Jonathan to join his family for a drink and some local snacks. We sat on his veranda at the rear of the Mesten and chatted to his parents and his wife and children. It was rather like we were family friends not hotel guests.

Each day Jonathans parents would spend countless hours preparing small offerings to the statues of the gods around the hotel or to place by the shrines that graced the pool area and reception. These small offering were all painstakingly handmade and consisted of banana leaf baskets with flowers, candles and sometimes food offerings. There must have been thirty or forty of these dotted around the hotel and it took the family hours to prepare.

I have never stayed in a hotel with no other guest before and it is a weird experience. We received wonderfully kind service and thoroughly enjoyed ourselves. We finished previously unfinished books, sent emails, planned the next leg of our trip and relaxed to the point of inertia.

Jonathan dropped us at the airport as if he was dropping off old chums and we sat and awaited the flight to Brisbane via Singapore. South East Asia had been magical and Andrea and I were better people for having experienced it.

We had seen extreme poverty, experienced wonderful service and been shown kindness by almost everyone we had met. We had seen spectacular examples of ancient temples, borne witness to the evidence of man's cruelty to his fellow man and spent time on some of the most beautiful beaches imaginable. We met people whose life styles had changed little from primitive times living alongside the modern cities of the 21st century.

Now after all of this we were heading to Australia and had so much to look forward to, including meeting up with our daughters who we had been missing so much.

Bed 23. Brisbane and beyond

Every flight that we took seemed to increase Andrea's insecurity. She was not in the least bit worried about flying, but held a certain belief that eventually our luggage would be lost by one airline or other and that we would be faced with the prospect of having nothing to wear for weeks on end. No matter how much I tried to assure her that Australia did in fact have shops selling everything we could possibly need she was convinced that Qantas could not be trusted.

Well the big silver bird touched down at Brisbane airport and as usual our bags tumbled off the conveyor belt safe and sound. Getting through customs in Australia can be a pain in the arse as many items seem to be prohibited. I opted for declaring everything from a part chewed piece of gum to my anti-diarrhoea tablets, I reckoned I might still get searched but at least they couldn't accuse me of hiding anything. Sure enough, I was sent to the search channel but to my amazement when I explained that the medicines were prescription drugs and I had a doctor's note and that we were carrying no wood, fruit, food or plant materials they let me through. Andrea who decided that declaring things was silly and that her couple of boxes of paracetamols did not constitute drugs joined the other queue. I was on my second cup of coffee and had read most of the newspaper by the time she got through into the arrival lounge.

The sun was beating down as we left the terminal building to wait for India who was due to meet us on arrival. We had not seen her for over a year and were very excited. When she arrived she looked every part the Aussie girl. She was so brown and her hair was sun bleached blonde. She was looking fit and clearly had taken to the Australian life style. Best of all she had not developed an Aussie accent and l kept her sentences endings level rather than the annoying Australian way of making everything sound like a question. She did not, however, seem happy and Andrea spotted this at once.

After the initial tears of joy and hugs and kisses we sat down to have a drink before driving into the city. As their coffee and my beer arrived, India broke down.

"Mum this bloody country is doing my head in. I love it here but they just make everything so difficult. I just don't know if I can stand it much longer"

India explained that the visa system was driving her mad and she was at her wit's end. She had been forced to stop teaching at her school because she had reached her six-month employment limit this, despite the fact the school was short of teachers and no-one wanted to work there because it was so tough. She now faced with the prospect of working on a farm for three months in order to get her next visa and there was no guarantee even then that it would be granted.

"Don't worry about the farm work dear I'm sure you will find some and it will be Ok." Andrea said.
India's face dropped even further and tears welled up again.

"I've already found some Mum and I start in a few days. I've been so looking forward to you coming and now I won't be here to be with you. Plus, I won't get to see Sophie and Harry is still going to have to stay in Brisbane to study. I will be all on my own when everyone else is together it's just horrible."

Andrea tried to comfort India but I stopped her short and suggested we drive to her flat and come up with a plan once we had all settled down and had time to think. I had no bloody idea what my plan would be but planning was what I did. At least I had a bit of time to think as Sophie was not due to arrive for two weeks and India's farm work was a week away. Much as I liked India's boyfriend Harry he might well have to be lowest priority when trying to solve this one.

Brisbane is a beautiful city, sitting on the river of the same name. I guess it helps if everything has the same name. It reminded me of the Monty Python sketch where everyone was called Bruce. India pointed out some of the landmarks as we drove back to her suburban apartment, but it was clear her heart was not in it. Andrea and I had plenty of time to explore so we didn't ask too many questions.

India's apartment was a little pokey but was central to pretty much everything and reasonably priced. Automatically Andrea set about tidying up and once again I had to stop her. India needed us passing judgement like she needed a hole in the head. We decided to spend the afternoon at Brisbane South Bank trying to come up with a plan.

The South Bank is a manmade city centre beach and lagoon. It is surrounded by cafes and bars and has shady to chill out in and well-kept lawns for those who wished to tan. Australian are quite rightly obsessed with sun safety so pretty much anyone sitting in the sun light could be deemed a tourist in the city. Thus the three of us sat with the tourists and did our best to maintain out vitamin D levels.

Certain parts of the plan could not be adjusted and India had to travel into the heart of Queensland to undertake her farm work. She had to leave the following Tuesday as her airline tickets had already been purchased and the farmer expected her. She had no option but to be away from Brisbane for three months as it was far too remote to come back for a visit. This was an issue as Andrea and I planned to be in Australia for six weeks or so and faced the prospect of not seeing very much of India at all.

As the afternoon wore on and the sun started to slip behind the sky scrapers of the CBD Brisbane took on a healthy glow. Light reflected of the glass buildings and the river side tower blocks reflected their images towards the South Bank. It was a beautiful city scape and with obligatory beer in hand things did not seem so bad. It was, however, a temporary lifting of spirits as we had still very little in terms of a plan.

My initial thoughts of bribing the farmer to say India had completed her work was shot down. An appeal to the immigration department for a stay of execution was as India so succinctly put it;

"Bloody pointless dad. Do you think I haven't already tried everything with immigration? They are a bunch of faceless, heartless nobs."

As we strolled back to her flat for supper it just hit me. There seemed no chance of India avoiding her duties on the farm to spend time with us in Brisbane, but there was nothing to stop the family going with her to the farm. Andrea and I were battle hardened after the jungle adventure and surely a farm in Queensland could always use a few more pairs of hands to help out?

Over supper I revealed my master plan and the shock on the faces of both India and Andrea was something to behold. They both looked at me in an incredulous manner and tried to speak with no success. So I carried on.

"If you travel up to the ranch India and explain to the farmer that we would like to do voluntary work for a couple of weeks, all we need is accommodation and food. Travel to and from would be down to us and we would not expect to be paid at all. I reckon he would happily say yes and then we all get to muck in together. It will be a bit hard on Sophie but since we paid her airfare anyway she won't be losing anything. What do you think?"

Silence echoed around the room.

India spoke first

"Are you sure? You two are not exactly the manual work types are you? Even if the framer says yes it won't be much of a holiday."

"Your father and I are tougher than you think young lady. We survived the jungle we can survive this"

Andrea said. Followed by a loud "hmph!" Marge Simpson was back, which I understood as decision made.

We spent the rest of the evening going over the endless possibilities and eventually decided that we should warn Sophie so that she wouldn't arrive in Oz with four bikinis and summer party clothes. She would need clothes suitable for a couple of weeks roughing it. We also decided that waiting until India reached the cattle station was not a good idea and resolved to phone the next day.

In the meantime, using Google maps we located the station and to say it was off the beaten track would have been one of the greatest understatements of all times.

India called the farm mid-morning and, unsurprisingly, Bruce was out at work. His wife Tracy answered the call and we listened as she and India chatted through what to bring and how to get there. It was not a totally manual labouring role that awaited India. She was to spend each morning tutoring Tracy's daughter and then help out on the farm in the afternoon.

After about ten minutes. India asked Tracy if it would be possible for me to have a word with her.

"Hello Tracy, Jim speaking India's dad."

I burbled through the whole scenario and then eventually asked the million-dollar question.

"Would it be possible for me and Andrea along with our youngest daughter to travel up to the farm and work for two weeks. We don't want paying just a roof and food."

"You bloody POMs are bloody crazy. Do you really want to spend two weeks in the blazing sun working for bugger all when you could be relaxing on the Sunshine Coast?"

"I won't tell Bruce. He'll laugh so much he might fall of his bloody horse."

"So is that a yes then Tracy?"

"Corse it is mate. You are more than welcome. We can put you up and feed ya, we can even pick you up at Emerald Airstrip. I never need much of an excuse to get into town and do some shopping"

I knew Emerald was a good three hours from the ranch so was delighted to have this part of the journey sorted.

"Right then Tracy. We will sort out some flights and get back to you. We will be with you a week after India arrives."

Time passed quickly and within a couple of days all of the plans were in place. Sophie had been told the news, India had left for the Lochnagar the very Scottish sounding cattle station and Andrea and I were settled in India's apartment with her partner Harry. Harry was studying at Griffith University most days and we spent the time getting to know Brisbane and the beaches of the Sunshine Coast. We spent a lovely day at the Lone Pine Koala Sanctuary and walked around the Karawatha Forest looking for birds but we saw bugger all. We drove out to Mount Tambourine and had a lovely lunch at the Heritage Estate winery.

On the Friday evening we visited the iconic Eat Street market over by the Brisbane Cruise Liner dock. What an evening this was. Live music drifted across the site as we walked around examining the dozens of food stalls. Food from just about every nation was represented, from Mexico to the Far East via Argentina, and Europe. The choice was endless. I opted for a spicy Mexican selection while Andrea chose Greek. We both had a massive ice cream sundae and a couple of beers before strolling back home. Eat street seems to be a local thing, similar to Borough market back in the UK but the warm weather and chilled beer raises it to a whole new level. It was an evening to remember.

Sophie arrived the next day and although there was a definite undercurrent of disbelief that we were going up country it was fantastic to see her after such a long time.

"So let me get this straight I take two weeks' holiday from work and fly 12,000 miles to see you all. Only to be put to work on a farm."

"That's about right pet, good isn't it!"

"I can think of other ways of describing it." Sophie said "but since you don't think I swear I will keep them to myself."

"Well you will get a tan working outside."

"Not if I'm in bloody wellies and dungarees I won't." Her face broke out in a massive smile and she gave me the biggest hug.

"It's fine. It will be an experience and there wasn't any other solution! Was there?"

Bed 24 Home, Home on the range.

Our journey to Lochnagar was interesting to say the least. The plane looked more like a child's model and to be honest it did look as if it had been stuck together by a child. I was convinced I had made more sturdy planes during my Airfix years. There were only six passengers on the flight plus a steward and the flight deck crew. There were no tannoy announcements the pilot just stuck his head through the curtain and told us we were setting off. En-route they served us a carton of orange and a sandwich, anything in a cup would have ended up all over the inside of the plane as we seemed to be buffeted by everything from bird's farting to high flying butterflies. It was not one of the most comfortable flights I have ever been on.

Surprisingly we did arrive on time at the tiny Emerald airport. We walked into the single story terminal building and were greeted by a smiling India but no sign of Tracy or Bruce. India and Sophie burst into tears as soon as they saw each other. India's year in Australia was the longest they had been apart and they missed each other so much. After endless hugs and a quick catch up we wandered out into the blazing sun. The central highlands of Queensland were certainly hot.

India took us to a massive SUV that she was driving and our fortnight on the cattle station was about to begin. The drive to Lochnagar was about three and a half hours, made longer by stops to see kangaroos, birds and even the odd snake slithering across the road. We eventually arrived late afternoon and with everyone else out working India was able to take her time showing us around.

We were staying in a "donga" which was a sort of prefabricated portable building a minute or so from the main homestead. It was pretty well equipped with two bedrooms and a bathroom and a small but functioning kitchen. There was air conditioning but it was so noisy that the ceiling fans were less intrusive and pretty effective. India made it clear that life at Lochnagar was full on and we would not be in the rooms a great deal. The rooms were clean, in total contrast to everything outside, which seemed to be covered in a thick layer of red dust. It had not rained significantly at Lochnagar for over two years and it appeared to me that all of central Queensland was blowing in the wind.

India showed us around the house yard and introduced us to Pepper and Ace the two Jack Russel dogs. The two dogs were very capable of tackling snakes and had learned well from their mother who was an expert, until she was sadly taken by a wedge tailed eagle. I expected to see lots of cats but India informed me that they wouldn't last very long with snakes and dingo's on the prowl.

When Bruce and Tracy arrived back from a day on the station they looked like typical cartoon cowboys but spoke with Aussie rather than American accents. Tracy had a leather hat, but no dangling corks, and she wore a dust-covered checked shirt and riding pants. Her boots were leather and could have been any shade as they were so covered in red dirt. She greeted us as if we were long lost family and at once we felt at home.

"Come in and have a beer. You must be bloody bushed after such a journey. Bruce will deal with the horses and then join us."

Bruce smiled. He was a tall wiry man with a deep tan developed over years of working outside. His forearms were massive. Clearly manual labour was not something he shied away from. He walked with a slight limp, later explained as the result of a kick from a fiery colt that he was trying to break. When he eventually joined us for a beer, he had a relaxed manner that put us at ease but also made it very apparent that he was totally the master of the Lochnagar station and everything in it. Both he and Tracy had the broadest of accents and almost every second word was a swearword. They didn't do this for effect or to offend, it was just the way it was and like everything else on the farm it was something we had to get used to.

Over a few drinks we got to know the Robertson's a little better and were given some idea about what to expect over the coming days. Their eldest son was away at boarding school and their youngest child, Molly was at home and was waiting to start at Rockhampton School with her brother. In the mean time she was home schooled and that was India's responsibility in the mornings. Many of the lessons were online, in virtual classrooms. India's main role was supervision and encouragement although she did tell us very proudly that she taught geography and some science lessons to Molly.

The Lochnagar day was not ruled by the clock but by the day light so we were to expect very early starts and early nights. The three of us were not given defined roles but it was clear that much of our work would be based close to the property as we could not ride whereas, Sophie might get to roam a little as she was perfectly capable on a horse. This meant that we didn't work too much with India as she had developed her riding and often set off to help muster cattle. We were surprised how quickly she had settled into the outback lifestyle.

The evening meal was delicious and very hearty. We ate home grown steak fried in butter with spuds and vegetables followed by an apple pie with cream. The portions were massive and during a quiet moment when Bruce and Tracy were in the kitchen India told us that meals were never smaller than this and often much bigger.

We were all back in the donga by 8.30pm and fast asleep within the hour. Sophie had been quiet during the meal but began to chat when we were alone. I expected her to be less than enthusiastic about her working holiday but to my surprise her mood was excellent, especially as there was a real chance she would be spending a few hours a day in the saddle. As we slipped into sleep India shouted to us.

"Don't bother setting an alarm guys we will all be up by 4.30am and you can come running with me and Tracy if you fancy it."

Sure enough we were awake to see the sun rise. Not because we wanted to be but because the noise from the donga kitchen would have woken the dead. The girls were clomping around getting ready to go running. The laughter emitting from their room made it clear they were making up for lost time. India was regaling stories from Oz while Sophie related life on the wards of a busy hospital. Suddenly without too much warning a smiling faced peered around the door.

"Coming running"

"Bugger off," I said "maybe tomorrow."

"You will regret it. It's the best time of the day and you see so much wildlife."

That was enough for me and I leapt out of bed leaving Andrea half asleep. I had no intention of running anywhere but a walk and a bit of birding seemed a great call.

As the sun slowly rose and watery daylight spread across the outback we set out, three women trotting off into the distance with two little Jack Russell's excitedly yapping at their heels. I followed instructions and stuck to the path thus reducing the chance of bumping into a brown snake or walking into a spider's web.

There were kangaroos everywhere, either bouncing along like some strange children's toy or just standing staring at me like an inquisitive nosey neighbour. Standing still they were so odd looking but on the move their power and speed was something to behold. The walk was productive, I saw black cockatoos, kookaburras and numerous other smaller birds. Sulphur-crested cockatoos wheeled overhead and the Major York's, with stunning pink heads cackled away in the tree tops. As I turned to walk back for breakfast a majestic wedge tailed eagle rose into the sky riding on the early morning thermals. It circled around and then with one mighty flap of its enormous wings cruised off into the distance.

As I neared the donga and the runners came panting up behind me I felt ready to tackle the day. Andrea was still asleep much to India's disgust.

"Mum wake up. You can't sleep when everyone else on the farm is up and ready to start."

"Bruce and Tracy will be working soon and they haven't been lazing on a beach in Bali for the last month."

Nothing changes, India had always been the bossy one and usually it was Andrea who bore the brunt of it. Mind you she did have good point.

Breakfast was simple, porridge and toast. India did say we could have eggs from the "chooks" but we were still full from the night before. The donga kitchen was pretty well equipped and India had kept it very clean and tidy.

By 6am we were all up and running. Bruce took Sophie to the barn to get the horses. She was buzzing until he let slip that today was a big ride and she might not be up to it first day. Sophie had to settle for cleaning and filling troughs. India set to work with Molly, who like most kids was not wild about the idea of spending too much time studying. Andrea and I were tasked with yard jobs while Tracy oversaw our handy work.

There were half a dozen calves who had been orphaned at birth and these had to be bottle fed. The very young ones had to suck on your finger first to practice before using a bottle. The pigs needed feeding. The sow pig was massive and was called Maggie. Her piglets were in a different pen just in case she rolled over in the night and crushed them. The pigs received a mixture of chick peas, left overs and slop it looked revolting but went down well especially with Maggie. The farm yard chickens roamed around pecking at grubs and seeds and we threw out handfuls of corn to supplement their foraged diet.

By mid-morning we were starving and knackered but Tracy was like a human dynamo. It was abundantly clear that life on a property was no walk in the park and the people who were tough enough to make a go of it were special, with a work ethic the likes of which I had never encountered before. We did stop for "smoko", this traditional break at 10.00 was never missed regardless of the task at hand. It consisted of brew and a large chunk of homemade cake. Then it was back to work.

In the afternoon Bruce returned from checking the cattle and immediately set about the next task. Rain had not fallen for a couple of years and the priority was to try and drought-proof the property. Lochnagar was lucky in many ways as an underground aquafer was substantial and with the system of bore holes, pipes and troughs the property was still in good shape. Many of the properties in the area had been abandoned or sold as farmers found it impossible to make ends meet in the extreme conditions.

I spent the next four hours helping dig channels while the women laid pipes and moved troughs into position. It was back-breaking work in temperatures that were close to 100 degrees but the time passed quickly. The sun was starting to slip away by the time we called it a day.

The beer that followed may well have been the tastiest drink I have ever had in my life. As we sat on the veranda watching the sky turn red and then purple and orange few words were spoken. The cicadas called and the sound of happy slurping and deep contented sighs were the only things that broke the contemplatory silence.

Over the next few days we continued to go about the chores that made up a day on the station. I kept calling it a farm and India got more cross each time I did.

"Dad it's not a bloody farm it's a station or a property, farms are what you get in England and this place is bigger than Kent so how can you call it a farm."
She had a point but it didn't stop me.

Sophie spent more time riding out with Bruce and she loved it. She had always wanted a pony or a horse, like most girls, and we had steadfastly refused to get her one. Now she was up early and doing whatever had to be done to a horse to make it road worthy. She was often gone before we had eaten breakfast and seldom re appeared before mid-afternoon. Andrea and I were delighted that she was having a great time as we had felt guilty about robbing her of two weeks on the beach.

As our first weekend at Lochnagar approached Tracy announced that we would be going to a "camp draft" some three or four hours away. We had no idea what this was. India explained it was something like a rodeo but without the bull riding.

We drove to Clermont, picked up some supplies and moved to the camp draft site. We had travelled in a couple of horse trucks and spent a good hour or so feeding the horses and getting them watered and settled before we even thought about getting ourselves comfortable. Andrea and I looked around for the potential accommodation blocks but said none. India then explained;

"Mum, dad, you need to clean out the blue horse truck. That's where we are sleeping tonight and Sophie and I can't help cos we have to help Tracy and Molly get ready for tomorrow and we need to be done and dusted before it gets dark."

We would have panicked had we not already experienced roughing it in Labundo. It took us an hour to sweep and clean but by the time Tracy had handed us our swags the horse box was ready. As the evening drew in we set up z-beds in the back of the box and opened the side to allow a breeze through.

We all sat around the camp fire and chatted while our meat cooked in a massive cast iron pot suspended over a fire. Every sense was stimulated, the sky changed colour, the smell of cooking meat drifted towards us, cicadas started to call and the horses and cattle seemed to chat to each other. Kangaroos appeared in the half-light like old men tentatively trying to assess whether to approach. As darkness fell the light from the fire reflected in their creating a ghostly presence. It was easy to see why the indigenous people give them a spiritual importance.

Sleep came remarkably easily. I think we all felt a sort of connection to the land. Before we drifted off Sophie poked her head in and said;
"This is so much better than sitting on beach. I could have done that in Spain"

Andrea and I felt a warm glow and would almost certainly have cuddled had it not been impossible whilst cocooned in a swag.

I would love to say that I understood what went on the next day but even with careful explanations from Molly and Tracy it all seemed a bit like organised chaos. The general idea behind a camp draft is that a rider has to isolate a cow from the group and then guide it around a course between pegs. This is timed and marked for both speed and accuracy. Well, despite the best efforts of some very skilled horsemen and women the whole thing did seem to depend almost entirely on the mood of the beast when it became separated from its mates.

Molly did brilliantly when it came to her turn and the cow seemed very compliant as it dutifully trotted between the pegs and through the finishing gate. Her smile was so wide that I guessed she was in line for a prize. Some of the other younger riders faced entirely different beasts. We saw grumpy cow, jumpy cow, stubborn cow and perhaps worst of all aggressive cow, all of which meant that at the end of the afternoon Molly was awarded the junior champions trophy.

Throughout the day there was an energy in the in the site. Sausage sizzles fed the men, while small pop up bars served beer to the thirsty. Jaxonbilt cowboy hats were on sale but despite both Andrea and I really wanting to buy one of these authentic outback fashion items, they were just too expensive. We both expected to see indigenous art and crafts but India was quick to point out that these types of get together were very much the domain of the white farmers.

It was a very happy Molly and a very contented group of POMs that spent a second night in the horse boxes in the Australian bush. It was not a lifestyle that I was strong enough to survive for any length of time. The mental and physical toughness needed to farm in the outback was beyond me and indeed beyond most people. People like Tracy and Bruce are a dying breed. I cannot see Molly or her brother staying on the station after they finish school. The weather is cruel, either no rain at all for months on end or flash floods. A constant heat in the summer months, unpredictable prices for the livestock and isolation that is hard to cope with. I have total admiration for these people and as I drifted to sleep I felt deeply honoured that they had let us into their lives even if for a very short period of time.

Before we left Lochnagar to travel back to Brisbane, Bruce took us on a flight over his land. He had a small single engine plane that he flew when he needed to reach the far flung corners of the ranch. As we circled the house and then flew out over the land the true size of the place became apparent. It was simply massive. To me it looked like an arid wasteland but to Bruce who knew every waterhole, every hill and every shelter it was his backyard. It was a wonderful way to finish the fortnight and we were really sad to leave.

India drove us to Emerald airfield the next morning and we flew back to the city. Sophie stayed at the airport to catch her flight back to the UK and we picked up a hire car ready to move on.

It was very clear to Andrea and I that India was now an independent and confident young woman who could handle pretty much anything that was thrown at her. Her time at Lochnagar was going to stand her in good stead when she eventually returned to the city in search of another teaching post.

Bed 25/26. Our first hot Christmas

Going north from Brisbane we spent time in the charming town of Montville which resembles New England but with more sunshine. Interesting delicatessens can be found alongside art galleries and cute little cafes. The buildings hark from a bygone age and the people move at a pace that suggests they may well have been there since the buildings were erected. The pavements are dotted with ornate tiles designed by the primary school kids to illustrate pictures the history of the village. Montville sits high in hills behind the coastal fringe and the views over the valley towards the sea are beautiful.

It is not on the normal tourist route but it probably should be. It's not the sort of place to spend a week but for a few days break it is lovely. We had a pool attached to our accommodation, so time never dragged and we were able to rest our aching limbs after the strenuous work of the previous fortnight. Many of the local farms sold homemade jams and fresh fruit and dairy products. We had great fun trying different cheeses and yoghurts. The local bakery made the most wonderful bread each morning. It went down so well with raspberry jam from farm shop.

Close by was the more modern attraction of Australia Zoo. Now sadly without its figurehead, the charismatic Steve Irwin. The Zoo is concentrating on conservation and the enclosures and exhibitions make it very clear that this place was a labour of love for Steve.

The crocodile show was the highlight of the day and the prehistoric beasts did not disappoint. The crocodile wranglers that introduced the massive reptiles make it very clear to the audience that crocs are not to be trusted. I guess a creature does not survive for millions of years without being good at what it does.

The culmination of the show was the appearance of the monster croc, attracted by a rhythmic banging of the wranglers foot on the side of the pool. Agro, the croc, was close to 15 feet long and weighed in at 1000kgs. It was impossible not to be impressed. Despite his size Agro was still able to propel his huge body up out of the water to grab a frozen chicken held enticingly by the crew. I made a vow to avoid all watery areas that could be inhabited by Agro's extended family.

From Montville we moved to Noosa for Christmas and spent the holiday period lounging by our private pool and walking along the Heads or up to the cliffs. We scanned the seas every day in vain search for whales, but did at least see pods of Dolphins cruising along the shoreline.

On our so un-British Christmas morning walk in the parkland we saw our first koala in the wild, it was sleeping in a tree. It was the perfect start to an Aussie Christmas.

We had begun our walk at sun rise and by 7am we were in the sea along with half of the population of Noosa. We had coffee on the boardwalk and returned to our condominium for our traditional Christmas breakfast of ham and eggs. Of course we had a BBQ lunch and we did throw shrimps on the barbie, except they weren't shrimps they were Moreton bay bugs and they tasted magnificent. Not being a royalist I did not miss the Queen's speech one iota but otherwise Christmas traditions were upheld as I fell asleep after the meal and dozed until early-evening. Andrea woke me when we received a skype call from Sophie and wonder beyond wonder we managed a three-way link and chatted to India as well.

In the fading evening light, we were sitting on the veranda overlooking the inlet on which our unit was constructed. The waterway was busy and many of the boats were decorated with fairy lights and inflatable Father

Christmases. It was all very colourful and added to the delight of Christmas especially for the numerous children who were around.

Opposite us, across the water was a massive house that appeared to be occupied by a Greek couple and their extended family. There was certainly a lot of them. One of the men boarded a jet ski and pushed away from the jetty in front of the house. I had watched crafts go up and down the water all afternoon and it was clear even to me as a non-resident and non-water person that there was a speed limit. It was not clear to our Greek neighbour, however, and he revved the jet ski and sped down the inlet.

At the sound of the revving engine several people appeared on their verandas and started to shout to the young man that he was well out of order. His reply was to turn the jet ski around and give everyone the finger before speeding even faster in the opposite direction. Well this went down like a lead balloon and more shouting ensued before one guy started to video the clown on the jet ski.

"Mate I've got you on tape and we will have you thrown out you bloody dingo"

With this the jet skier returned to his jetty and rather sheepishly re-entered the house. Then all hell broke loose and it was brilliant to watch. The family elders sat the guy, who must have been in his late 20's, down in front of the house. They proceeded to take turns to berate him. These elderly Greek men were scary but their female counterparts were a different class altogether. This went on for the greater part of the evening. I have to admit I used my birding binoculars to get a better view of proceedings but I needed no assistance to hear the telling off.

Andrea and I guessed they must be renters, like us and may have feared being evicted for bad behaviour. I have no idea if the video was every presented to the police but I suspect no-one could not have issued a telling off as severe as that given by his own family. This was far better entertainment than Christmas TV.

Bed 27. Laid back in Byron Bay.

From Noosa we headed south aiming for Adelaide, via all points in between. Our hire car was certainly no luxury vehicle but it worked, at least it worked for the time being. We really did feel like students on our gap year as we headed to the beaches of the Gold Coast and Byron Bay.

The beaches to the south of Brisbane are stunning, miles of golden sand, with waves crashing ashore to provide hours of entertainment for the hordes of surfers drawn here like moths to a flame.

The beaches at Byron Bay are no exception and during the post-Christmas holiday period they were heaving with locals and tourists alike. The locals were naturally beach ready, surf board under arm, sun screen splashed all over and a confidence that comes from a life by or in the sea. The tourists were a different breed altogether. They seemed to fall into a few clearly defined categories;

Firstly, the ageing hippies appeared to have dropped out of some society or other in the late 70's and not found their way back in. They arrived at the beach in battered Volkswagen campers usually accompanied by a scraggy pooch or two. The men wore cut-off denims and ill-fitting wife beater vests. Long greying hair flopped from their heads often tied in pony tails and more often than not sported goatee beard kept tidy by an elastic band or a small bead. The women wore flowing dresses cut low under the arms which allowed unsupported bosoms to make occasional appearances whenever any type of movement was undertaken. Their hair was worn long and often dyed purple or green. Mostly these peaceful folk congregated under trees and played soft guitar music to while away the hours. They seemed to claim an affinity with Bob Marley simply because they knew the words to "no women no cry". I am willing to bet that the only person on the beach who had actually seen the great man in concert was Andrea who had been at several Marley gigs during her time working at the Rainbow in the late 70's.

Those not sitting under trees set up small roadside stalls selling handmade trinkets or pieces of art. I never saw anyone buy anything but I guess they must have sold something at least enough to buy some food and a drink.

Next there were the posh gap year students. Going by their accent, it would appear that the children of the rich and famous were having a wonderful time on the beaches of Queensland and New South Wales. It seemed that just about every school leaver from King's Canterbury, Wellington and the like was bronzing themselves as part of the great adventure. This group did not appear in the early mornings like the hippies, they were almost certainly sleeping off hangovers or awaiting daddy's next cash transfer in order to have eggs benedict for breakfast.

When they eventually arrived on the beach the loud somewhat embarrassing chatter began.

"Gosh Anthony did you see Charlie's tits last night. She was showing them to everyone."

"No way Jasper far too stoned man. You know I made out with Becca before I crashed."

"Are you meeting her for lunch? The little Mexican place is lovely."

"Probs not, thought I would chill here and then try a few moves on the surf board later."

"Great plan Jasper Might have a go myself when the effects of the dozen lagers and a bottle of vodka have worn off."

Andrea and I cringed and hoped beyond hope that the Aussies didn't think all British youngsters were as shallow as these guys. Still I guess most countries have their fair share of wankers.

By far the largest group frequenting the beaches were real backpackers and they arrived daily on buses that spilled these wide eyed students onto the road side about every two hours. Most of them looked slightly unwashed, very hungry, and over tired but the glint in their eyes showed that they were having a wonderful time. English was the common language but they came from all four corners of the globe.

After they piled out of the buses and gathered their battered backpacks from the hold they sat on the grassy area behind the bus stop. Here plans were made for the coming days and weeks. Around the grassy areas were a couple of travel bucket shops which offered free wi-fi along with an enormous number of short and long trips including cheap flights to other parts of the antipodes, buses to Airlie beach and the Whitsunday islands and excursions to Frazer Island, Cairns and the Barrier Reef. For those heading south there were various ways of getting to Sydney and Melbourne or inland to Uluru and the red centre. Sitting on a bench close to this hive listening to them make enthusiastic plans and carefully calculate costs to the last dollar was fascinating.

Andrea and I were certainly not alone as representatives of the Grey Nomads but at Byron Bay it was easy to feel alone. We did not fit into any of the groups and found ourselves being critical of almost all of them.

We felt sorry for the hippies who were still searching for something that they would probably never find. We wondered what it would be like to be a 70-year-old with no income and no fixed abode. What the hell would they do when they became bored with Bob Marley?

We disliked the posh prats who seemed oblivious to all around them and seemed to assume that everyone in

Australia wanted to know who they were shagging and what cocktail of drugs and booze helped them to do it better.

We enjoyed chatting to the gappies and comparing stories of where we had been and where we were heading. Often they seemed genuinely pleased that we had undertaken the adventure and hoped that their mums and dads would do the same. We always kept a look out for any students that we had taught in out mid Kent Grammar school, but either they saw us coming and went the other way or they had not yet reached Oz and were working their way across Asia.

Beds 28 & 29 Celebrating the new year at 10pm?

From Byron Bay we headed towards South Australia via interesting little places like the Glenwood Tourist Park in South Grafton, and Port Macquarie where we saw in the new year. Most travellers would probably have aimed for Sydney for the new year fireworks but we opted for the Port Macquarie youth hostel. This may have been a slight error in retrospect but the company was great.

After arriving in the late afternoon, Andrea and I had a nap to make certain we would be ready for the big night. We were woken mid evening by the noise of great hilarity from the common room in the hostel. We ventured in and were greeted by a dozen or so drunk Aussies and a few drunk Scandinavians. They offered us drinks and immediately made to feel welcome, despite the obvious age gap.

We resisted the temptation to join in the game of strip jenga that was in full swing and settled for a spectator role and a gin and tonic. Modesty was clearly not high on either Aussie or Scandinavian agendas and before long the room was full of naked or semi naked youngsters most of whom were in pretty good shape it has to be said. Andrea turned to me a said. "Jim I'm just not sure where to look" "I know exactly where to look." I replied before receiving a playful slap on the cheek.

After a few G&T's and many laughs we set off for town for the firework extravaganza at the beach front. Now for some reason the port Macquarie New Year's fireworks don't happen at mid-night. They are all over by about 10pm and we both found this bizarre. Added to this the extravaganza lasted about five minutes and reminded me of a back yard firework display from my childhood. The only thing that was missing was my dad sticking a garden fork in his foot and a rocket flying sideways into the wall of the house narrowly missing an open window before exploding and setting fire to the rose bushes.

Port Macquarie may have lots going for it with lovely beaches and a pleasant life style, but celebrating New Year's Eve is not something it does well and Andrea and I wished we had pushed on to join the revellers at Circular Quay. Still we wound our way back to the hostel and toasted the New Year with our last drop of gin before I fell asleep and missed the magic hour.

From the NSW coast, we skirted around Sydney and headed off across the hinterland towards the Hay Plain. We stopped in in the quaintly named town of Gumly-Gumly part of Wagga-Wagga and unlike New York it certainly was not named twice because it was so good.

The Hay Plain is desolate and seems never ending, as we set out across it, our sat nav read. "in 364 miles keep left."

The great disappointment was that in 364 miles the "keep left" was simply a bend in the road and I felt somehow cheated. The plain is flat and broken only by a few tiny settlements consisting of a few grain silos, community hall and a few houses. The homesteads and farms all seemed deserted or in the process of becoming deserted God alone knows how people could make a living in this place.

We occasionally met a vehicle coming the other way and even more occasionally either overtook or were overtaken by cars going our way. We were in constant fear of running out of petrol, especially as both Andrea and I had watched the 70's horror film The Hills Have Eyes, and could imagine similar types of weirdos living in the bush country.

The highlight of the drive was spotting emu's and therefore another tick off my list but Kangaroos still proved very elusive. Maybe they only live on cattle stations! There were plenty of dead ones, indeed they seemed to replace mile stones at the side of the road. I was becoming even more convinced that these creatures so symbolic of Australia were in fact mythical and that the corpses along the road were dummies placed by locals to keep the myth alive.

On the drive towards Canberra and before the trees disappeared and the vastness of the Plain took over, we drove along the Remembrance Driveway. This stretch of road, commemorated in 1954, by the Queen is a tribute to Aussie servicemen who fought in WWii or subsequent conflict.

The rest areas on the road are each dedicated to those awarded the Victoria Cross either in the World War or Vietnam. Andrea and I loved this idea and read all of the notices in the rest stops we visited. Such a simple idea but one that should certainly be copied back home and one that keeps the memory of these incredibly brave young men in the forefront of people's minds.

Eventually after what seemed like an eternity on the Hay Plain we started to descend into Adelaide, the city of churches. The final fifteen or so kilometres are downhill and from the warnings on the road signs you could easily believe that you were driving down the side of the Alps rather than on a well maintained highway. Still we had reached our destination and it did appear to be a very impressive city.

Bed 30/31 & 32 Why is it called kangaroo Island?

Like many UK residents we had family in Australia and ours were based in Adelaide, or rather Andrea's were based in Adelaide. We spent a few days catching up with them and seeing the local sites in a sedate and fitting fashion for people of our age. We ate on Rundle Street, visited the koala and wildlife park and relaxed by the family pool.

We spent a few hours in Harndorf, which is a magnificent German settlement set in the Adelaide hills. The town is beautifully preserved and on a sunny day could not have been better. Andrea and I visited the Harndorf Hill winery and had a stunning cold lunch of smoked cheeses, meats and German sausage accompanied by a bottle of Compatriots Cabernet Sauvignon. In the afternoon we sat in the shade and ate ice cream and watched the people go by. Sheer luxury.

However, we were not on holiday we were travelling and too long living the easy life was likely to change our mind set. The never-ending quest to see Australian nature took us to Kangaroo Island, surly in a place so named we would be lucky and there would be hundreds of the bouncy buggers for us to stare at and take photos.

We drove the couple of hours to Cape Jervis and boarded the Sealink ferry for the forty-five-minute crossing. The sea was calm so there was no need for Andrea to get a seat near the loos or to take her sea sickness tablets. We were joined on the crossing by two massive sheep lorries, full with bleating and pooing sheep heading for, well we hoped open fields but feared something far worse. The smell was awful and the mixture of poo, wee and general sheep smells was enough to make everyone on the ferry sick. Andrea and I moved to the front outside deck and braved the spray and sea air rather than loose our breakfast.

KI as the locals know it, is a haven for wild life and outdoor lovers and we booked into our small cabin close to Seal Bay with high expectations of not only getting our fill of roos but generally enjoying good food, good wine and plenty of nature. Over the next few days we visited Seal Bay and got great views of southern sea lions and southern fur seals. We lazed on Vivonne beach and visited the national park to see the Remarkable Rocks and Admiral Arch. We were lucky enough to get within touching distance of five wild koalas, and they were just as cute as we had imagined they would be.

Despite using binoculars and taking evening and morning walks we managed to visit Kangaroo Island and not see a single kangaroo. Now I know they are real because we saw them on the ranch but bloody hell they are hard to spot in the wild. Whoever named Kangaroo Island so must have been permanently pissed or hallucinating.

We checked out of Seal Bay Cottages which had been an excellent place to stay. The rooms were comfortable and the kitchen well equipped. Out cottage was quiet but the small terrace caught the sun in the afternoons. Parrots and cockatoos roosted in the trees surround it.

We drove back towards the ferry terminal via American River. Where we had another great lunch. Both Andrea and I had tasted oysters in France and had reached the conclusion that they were not really for us. I know we among the minority and that they are a delicacy as well as essential part of any great food lover's diet but I think they taste of the sea and are truly disgusting.

However, at American River, they are smoked and tasted rather good. Fortunately, we were able to sample them free before ordering them for lunch with a crisp Islander Sauvignon Blanc. Our last hour or so before the crossing was spent hoping to catch a glimpse of fairy penguins but sadly they were all at sea and we had no luck.

We left Kangaroo Island on the ferry, thankfully without sheep lorries on board. We drove off the ferry at Cape Jervis heading back to Adelaide and started the long climb away from the port. Dusk was almost upon us when Andrea screamed at me

"Stop Jim Stop."

I assumed I had hit a pedestrian or run over someone's cat and screeched to a halt. Fortunately, the emergency stop did not inconvenience anyone as the road behind was clear.

"There back in that field didn't you see them?"
"Didn't I see what?"
"Kangaroos, loads of them."

Sure enough as we reversed back along the road a field full of kangaroos came into view. There must have been well over a dozen. Some stared at us while others continued to graze on the grass. The sun was setting behind the field and these strange animals appeared almost in silhouette.

"At bloody last. I assume they are waiting here to get tomorrows ferry back to Kangaroo Island. "I exclaimed, as Andrea leapt from the car, camera in hand.

Our onward plans from Adelaide were already made although but we had not booked accommodation. The idea was to take a slow drive around Great Ocean Road to Melbourne and then back to Sydney before flying out to New Zealand. Sadly, our plans were thwarted by the Australian weather.

There had been a massive shortage of rain in Victoria this summer and this had led to massive bush fires. These fires were so intense that the Great Ocean Road was closed in parts and we could not get to Melbourne via that route. We had little alternative either drive inland to Melbourne and miss the coastal route or go directly to Sydney across the dreaded Hay Plain.

We decided on the latter even though we knew it would be so dull and repetitive. We left Andrea's kin folk after a fantastic evening of barbecued steak and plenty of McLaren Vale wine and set off up the long hill out of Adelaide. As we drove out of the city our car made a strange whirring noise for five minutes or so and then the air conditioning started to blow out hot air instead of cold.

We both fiddled with the dials and turned the air conditioning off and on but to no avail it was knackered. Still we only had three days driving ahead of us in temperatures in the high 40's so it couldn't be too bad. By early afternoon as we approached a small town of Balranald we were both reduced to balls of sweat. The seats were soaked through and we were out of water. We had no option but to stop for the day. When we checked into the very comfortable Balranald Club Motel we must have looked like half-drowned refugees. The girl on reception resisted commenting on our appearance but the lad who showed us to our rooms said helpfully

"You know cars in Oz have air conditioning don't you mate?"

I replied

"So do cars in the UK but at home the bloody system works."

"Cripes mate what a bummer. You should have put some bottles of water in the freezer overnight to keep you cool in the car."

It would have been so easy to lose it at this point and scream.

"I didn't know the fucking a/c was going to pack up on us."

But I resisted the temptation as it was a bloody good idea.

Andrea and I duly filled all of our water bottles and froze them overnight ready for day two. We must have looked odd to cars passing the other way as we sat with bottles of frozen water stuck behind our necks as we drove across the near deserted plain. They did help and we made it to Sydney late the next day, still looking like workers coming off shift from a steel smelting plant but at least closer to being alive than the night before.

Bed 33. Beautiful Avalon

We were not staying in the city of Sydney, as we had the use of a friends annex in the northern suburb of Avalon. Now Avalon is just down the road from where they film Home and Away and it is just how most POMs imagine Australia and the idyllic life style.

Golden beaches are battered by white topped rolling surf. Bronzed youngsters ride these waves with consummate ease on brightly coloured surf boards. The streets leading to the beaches are lined with cafes and bars and everyone looks a million dollars. In fact, to live in Avalon probably takes a good bit more than a million dollars.

Our hosts were charming people and even though we did not know them especially well we got on straight away. Andrea and I had taught their youngest son indeed he had resided in our boarding house when we had been house parents. Peter was very bright but I recall he was no angel and was always full of mischief. He was one of those lads who you desperately wanted to tell off but found it impossible to stay mad at and I invariably broke into a smile whilst in mid rant, thereby breaking the spell. Peter knew this well and would take any punishment handed out in good grace probably spotting that he had dodged a bullet.

His mum and dad were perfect hosts, welcoming us for drinks and food when it felt right but giving us space to explore and be by ourselves when we needed it. We chatted about school and how things were going but it was never a chore and both Andrea and I felt totally at ease. It was a great stop.

From Avalon we explored the city and did all of the tourist things that every visitor to Sydney dreams about. We walked around Circular Quay, to the Opera House. We had seen this iconic building so many times in movies and documentaries and to stand next to it was special. The sunlight reflected of the roof and the shadow of the building was reflected in the clear waters of the harbour. We had a coffee and a snack in one of the numerous cafes that run alongside the Opera House.

It was great fun watching the other customers trying to protect their chips and sandwiches from the ever hungry gulls that seemed to know where to get an easy meal.

From here we walked through the botanical gardens around to the stands that had been erected for the New Year celebrations and were still to be dismantled. These gave a wonderful platform for getting the perfect Opera House and harbour bridge photo. The short walk was well worth it.

Workers and day trippers sat eating picnics in the gardens, we wondered if there was a more special place, anywhere in the world, to eat a sandwich and drink a soda. In my opinion there may not be.

There was a plethora of buskers performing in front of the ferry terminals. On one a young woman seemed to be able to fold herself up and clamber into a tiny Perspex box. Closer to the water a group of indigenous people played the didgeridoo and exhibited art works and crafts.

We contemplated the Harbour Bridge climb but neither of us are great with heights and it looked hard work. We contented ourselves with a ride on the Manly ferry.

David Bowie passed away while we were in Sydney and one of the local radio stations dedicated a whole show to his music. We were lucky enough to be in the car at this point. listening to one of the world's most iconic singers whilst driving in one of the world's most iconic cities and it is something I will remember for ever. As we drove across the Harbour Bridge we were indeed "sitting in a tin can far above the world" and "Planet earth was blue."

Bed 34 & 35. The land of the long white cloud.

Our flight from Sydney to Christchurch was a late one and we arrived in the South Island of New Zealand just about in time for bed. Our hotel was very convenient We were met at the airport and within 45 minutes of landing we were sound asleep at the Sudima Hotel in preparation for our travels in Aotearoa, the Land of the Long White Cloud.

The following morning, I popped into Juicy Car Rentals and picked up our quaintly named "El Cheapo" and returned to the hotel to collect Andrea. Juicy seemed a pretty good bet for car hire in the South Island and the El Cheapo car worked perfectly well so as they say Down Under "no worries".

Our first destination was the adventure centre of New Zealand, Queenstown, and the drive across Central Otago was spectacular. We passed crystal-clear rivers, radiant blue lakes and snow-capped mountains. We knew we would be returning on the same route so kept a good pace leaving photos and sightseeing for the return trip. As we neared Queenstown we stopped at Mrs Jones's Farm Shop to try some local fruit, wine and ice cream. This road side stop is a magnet for all tourists in the area and one that I had visited before on a rugby trip. Andrea had never been to New Zealand so it was new to her. The fruit was delightful, with so many varieties to sample. The usual peaches, cherries, apples and the like alongside golden kiwi fruit, which were new to us, as well as ripe mangoes. Andrea was just about to dig in when a coach load of Chinese turned up. Within a couple of minutes, the samples were devoured in a feeding frenzy unlike anything I had seen before.

I had seen David Attenborough's programs about animals at a kill but a pride of lions or a group of sharks had nothing on a bus load of Chinese. Andrea frightened to try and pick up a piece of kiwi in case her hand was bitten off. Standing back and watching was great entertainment as manners and social niceties seem to have failed to reach this particular group of travellers. Not only did they push past the likes of us and other visitors already in place but they shoved each other as well. They grabbed anything they could and if they didn't like it they just threw it on the floor. I was amazed at how much food little Chinese women could force into their mouths at one time. Half of them left the shop looking like hamsters with food pouches well and truly stuffed.

When calm eventually descended on the farm shop we both opted for an ice cream and what a great choice that proved to be. Fresh mangoes crushed into vanilla ice cream and then piped onto a cone. We chose one each but they were massive and we could almost certainly have shared. We made certain to keep them well shielded in case any more Chinese were still lurking in the shop.

From Mrs Jones's we drove over the pass along state highway 6 and arrived in Queenstown in late afternoon. We had booked a home stay through Airb&b and found the address without difficulty. Our hostess was a tattoo artist and after welcoming us to her home and showing us around we never saw her again for the whole time we were there. This meant we were able to use the kitchen at any time and made catering very easy.

The home stay was a perfect base to explore and there was so much to do. The adventure activities are mind-boggling and actually cater for all ages and all fear levels, but they are not cheap. You can parachute jump, luge, jet boat, bungee, zip line, canyon swing or just about anything else you can image that is guaranteed to raise the heart rate and get the adrenalin pumping.

Andrea and I, being a little more sedately than the eager young bloods swarming around the town. We opted for a jet boat ride out at the Shotover river. It cost $135 each but my God it was worth it. The bright red jet boat hurtled up the Shotover canyon clipping the sheer cliff walls and pirouetting in the icy water. Spray drenched everyone in the boat but somehow the pilot managed to keep a good enough view of his route to avoid killing us all.

At first Andrea clung onto me with such force that I thought a trip to casualty would be necessary. By the midpoint of the ride she was screaming loudly with her arms held gleefully above her head as we span again and again.

It takes a good few minutes to come down to earth at the end of this experience and we seemed to stand looking at one another just going "wow". I still have no real idea how you train to be a jet boat pilot but all I can say is thank goodness the training is good and next time I'm in Queenstown I will be back for another go.

The jet boat is symbolic of the town but there are other must dos and we set about doing as many of them as possible bearing in mind that the aged bodies that we now possessed did not lend themselves to certain activities.

We drove to the old mining town of Arrowtown for lunch and then to the AJ Hackett bungee jump at the Kawarau bridge. I had no intention of even thinking about making a jump but Andrea was buoyed by her mornings exploits and was at least considering throwing herself off the bridge attached to a large elastic band. We stood on the viewing platform for fifteen minutes or so and with each passing minute I became more and more certain that only a complete bloody idiot would ever make the jump. The young jumped and the screamed or screamed and then jumped. Some were dunked into the river while others were jerked back skywards just before being dipped into the freezing water.

Andrea had gone very quiet and occasionally popped off to the ticket desk without involving me. After one of these visits, she reappeared with black marker pen on the back of her wrist.

"What is that?" I asked

"It's my weight."

"And the reason is?"

"I'm jumping."

"You are kidding me? You must be bloody crazy"

"Maybe but I won't be here again and Sophie and India have both done it so why not me?"

"Why not you. Isn't it bloody obvious? They were in their early 20's and you are… well you are not in your early twenties."

"Listen. you said at the outset that this would be the adventure of a lifetime so don't get funny now just because I am trying new things."

"I'm not trying to be funny but I just thought…."
Andrea was off up the steps towards the bridge.

"Make sure you get a photo when I jump, then we won't have to buy the video."

Then with a wave and a smile she confidently marched half way across the Kawarau bridge to the jump station. I stood in total amazement while she waited for her turn and to be honest I did expect a last minute wimp out. How wrong I was, Andrea stood on the small wooden jump deck that resembled a plank from the old naval ships. She turned, smiled and shouted something incomprehensible and leapt into the void.

The jump itself was a success, but I guess once you have left the platform there is bugger all you can do; you certainly can't turn back. Climbing into the rescue raft at the bottom was however a totally different matter and it has to be said it was not something that Andrea made look easy. Dangling upside down on an elastic band, over a freezing cold river trying to grab a pole and pull herself into the rubber launch whilst still buzzing from the jump was beyond her. All I could hear from the viewing platform was near hysterical laughter, and an expletive full rant

"get me fucking down."
More laughter
"I can't grab the fucking pole. I can't even see it"
More laughter
"Oh bloody hell I'm gonna fall in"
More laughter

Eventually the crew hauled Andrea unceremoniously into the tiny craft and brought her safely ashore. What a day and what a transformation. When she finally climbed the hundred or so steps back to the viewing platform the realisation of what she had done began to hit home.

"Can we have a cup of tea in the café before we set off?" was all she said for a good few minutes.

The following day was less adventure packed and more stomach packing. We rode the gondola to the skyline mountain top restaurant for a scenic lunch overlooking Lake Wakatipu and Queenstown. The view from the restaurant is mind blowing. At eye level you look across the valley at the beautiful mountains that ring the majestic lake. The winter snow had gone under the strong summer sun but the rugged peaks make it easy to imagine what the vista must be like in mid-winter. Looking down the lake shimmered in the midday sun and the water was clear, clean and still. The surface was broken only by the waves cut by the paddle steamer Earnslaw as it chugged majestically across the lake. Queenstown itself looked like an alpine village going about its daily business.

Lunch was excellent and as buffets go, this one was right up there. Sushi, soup, salads, green-lipped mussels, prawn's, cold meats and salmon were ample choice for starters. This was followed by roast meats and casseroles, even meat pie. The choice of sweets was equally varied l with coffee to follow. We certainly ate more than enough to keep us going. The restaurant was full with guests from around the world and once again it was the Chinese who came to our attention. I was beginning to think that we were being followed by some anti-social bus trip. It was as if Chinese were intent on gate crashing everything we wanted to do.

Despite having been given very clear seating times which were printed on their tickets, they simply tried to barge their way into the seating area without taking any notice of the staff, other guests and even one and other. Once at a table they loaded up with food and then after using the glasses and cutlery they moved to other tables simply to get a better or different view. This made it a nightmare for other guests. When a family of four appeared at our table while we were selecting our main courses Andrea almost lost the plot. I did think she would physically remove the unwanted interlopers. Instead, she asked them politely to move, pointing out her handbag and coat on the back of the seats. When they ignored her, she sat on the lap of adult male in the group and amidst much gesticulating and loud Chinese burbles, she reclaimed our table. I am sure the staff wanted to applaud and certainly she got a few smiles and congratulations from those around us. The rest of the meal much to everyone's relief was far less eventful.

As we stood to leave one of the young Kiwi waiters came over to us and apologised for the situation. We smiled and indicated that it was fine and that we felt really sorry for her and the rest of the staff who had to put up with.

"Maybe your wife could stay and help us during service. I have never seen anyone do that before. It was brilliant"

I replied

"It's a brave man that gets between Andrea and her lunch I can tell you."

In the early evening as we sat by the lake watching the ducks and catching up on some reading. Much later we ventured into the Patagonia Ice Cream store. I chose my usual chocolate and vanilla and Andrea had dulce de leche. If you have never tasted this, you are missing out big time.

No visit to Queenstown would be complete without a drive over the mountains to Glenorchy, and so "El Cheapo" set off the following morning to visit this quaint, charming little settlement at the head of Lake Wakatipu. The hills tested the poor old car to her maximum, but she pulled through. One does not visit Glenorchy for the excitement but the there is plenty of that to be found in Queenstown. It is a place where time almost stands still. Children plunge into the lake, almost all wearing wet suits which gave us a good indication of the temperature of the water. Hikers, called trampers, in these parts set off on long walks and return after a few days in wilderness. They all looked tired and weather beaten but had smiles that made it clear their exertions were worthwhile.

It was gone 4pm when we made it back to Queenstown and just about time to sample the famous Ferg burger. Ferg's is certainly not for the faint-hearted but it is a must do when in town. The queues outside give some credence to the notion that these burgers are amongst the world's best. I can vouch for the fact that they are delicious and massive. For about £14 we had a southern swine burger and a Ferg with cheese plus fries. We queued behind a dear old lady who must have been in her 80's and was travelling around New Zealand. She was wonderstruck by the burgers and although not totally au fait with the protocol of a fast food joint seemed to love the whole process. The staff in Ferg's did everything to help her and all around left with a rather warm feeling.

The drive back to Christchurch from Queenstown is one to be savoured. We stopped at the Church of the Good Shepherd on Lake Tekapo and although I am not in any way religious this little place of worship nestled between the mountains of the Southern Alps and on the shore of a beautiful lake was very tranquil and peaceful. I could understand why believers would be drawn to this place to give thanks.

Bed 36 & 37. A city at the mercy of nature.

We broke the journey in two by spending a night at a lake side motel in Twizel. After a quick visit to the local store we sat on our terrace with a large drink and some olives before eating a perfectly fine microwave supper. We were becoming very good at making the best of what we had and travelling was by now what we did, rather than something we endured. I was loving it and Andrea was more relaxed and at ease than I had seen her for years. The trials of teaching, marking, Ofsted and the like were as far removed from this place as anything could have been.

A couple of the big Christchurch schools had rowing groups staying on site. Some were in the campground and others in larger accommodation units. I had in the past taken many sports teams on overseas tours and knew only too well what senior students could get up to given half a chance. I expected to see boys sneaking in with cans of beer and boys and girls creeping off together for a sly fag or a bit of romance. Well I was wrong. These upstanding representatives of Christ College and St Andrews were so bloody knackered after a day of full on training that they hardly had the energy to walk to the shower blocks. Even as night was beginning to fall the stragglers were still returning from what appeared to be a monster cross-country training run.

We reached Christchurch by late afternoon and checked in with some friends that I knew from my rugby coaching days. You can save a massive amount of money if you have friends around the world and any travellers worth their salt should look people up en-route. Sometimes it just so nice to be in a family home, eating home cooked food and relaxing and our friends in Christchurch made us feel so welcome.

I had first met and befriended John and Karen some twenty years earlier when they had been living near Cape Town. They had left their beloved South Africa in the hope that they would be able to give their children greater opportunities in New Zealand. Now they were well settled and the children grown up. They still visited home most years but they were now very much Kiwis even though their South African accents had not left them.

Christchurch is a city unlike most others, elegant and with an old world charm that few places in the southern hemisphere can match. It is a city that has somehow kept its dignity and class despite being almost raised to the ground by two massive earthquakes. For us both the aftermath of the 2011 quake was hard e to come to terms with. Somehow devastation in a first world country just seems so wrong. We have all become accustomed to seeing wrecked cities in Nepal or Pakistan and although we care, we feel somehow detached as the buildings do not look like our buildings and the people do not look like our people. In New Zealand it just looks like home and feels like home and the effect is to magnify the feelings of horror because it is easy to picture something similar in London or Birmingham.

I was even more shocked by the devastation then Andrea as I had visited Christchurch before the quake. I had walked around the cathedral before it became a symbol of ruin and heartbreak. I had eaten in river side cafes and walked along tree-lined streets. Christchurch today is not lying down and accepting its fate it is fighting back and rising like a phoenix. In a similar fashion to Londoners after the Blitz the people have rallied and refused to allow their city to die.

A new Cathedral constructed from cardboard has sprung up and it attracts worshippers and tourist alike. A new test cricket venue sits proudly in Hagley Park and welcomes the world's best. A pop-up shopping mall made from shipping containers is a popular drawcard and the designer outlets and food stands make a roaring trade most days.

Christ College seemingly untouched sits on the edge of the devastation like a bastion to the private school system, copied from England. Majestic buildings, smartly dressed young students and Dickensesque masters add to the air of tranquillity and old worldliness, alongside the River Avon. Serene cricket matches are played in Hadley Park and with cucumber sandwiches and a nice cup of tea one could imagine standing on Grantchester meadows.

Highlights on a trip full of highlights are hard to quantify and often it is the simple things that leave greatest impressions. As we sat in the lounge of our friend's house discussing all manner of things and enjoying excellent wine. We were disturbed by a strange snuffling noise coming from the garden through the open French windows. The light was failing and we could not see anything obvious but the noises continued. Armed with a torch John and I ventured in the garden and discovered two hedgehogs busily hunting for grubs and generally getting acquainted. Quite how hedgehogs get acquainted with so many spines remains a mystery to me, but they did.

In my youth growing up in Kent I had seen hedgehogs regularly, very often squashed on the road. I had not seen one back home for at least twenty and Andrea as a London girl had never seen one. I felt oddly privileged to be able to spy on their world as they went about their business in John and Karen's garden.

Our "El cheapo" vehicle had to be returned in Christchurch but it had served us well and covered plenty of miles. I returned it to Juicy Cars and walked half a mile to Avis car rentals to collect one of the bargains of our trip. I had discovered, purely by chance, relocation vehicles and had been lucky enough to book one. Avis gave me one of these cars to drive from Christchurch to Auckland free of charge. I had seven days to conclude the trip the ferry crossing to the north island was included as was full tank of fuel. This my friends is known as a result! If only we had discovered relocation vehicles while we were in Oz we could have saved a fortune.

Bed 38 & 39. Birding heaven and a big birthday.

We left Christchurch heading north. Our first stop was in the coastal town of Kaikura and by a stroke of good fortune this coincided with a momentous birthday for me. Once Andrea I checked into the local youth hostel and as usual our evening routine of a large G&T and some nibbles raised a few smiles among the younger guests eating pasta and drinking cans of cheap lager. We wandered into town and feasted on delicious fish and chips, they may well have been even better than Harry Ramsdens.

Andrea had booked me a boat trip for the following morning and as the weather was pretty grim and there was a distinct possibility the seas could be rough we did not overindulge. Andrea also decided that it would be better to postpone a birthday supper until the following night in Picton.

I was up early and down at the boat company with fingers and toes crossed that the trip would actually take place. Now Kaikura is one of the best spots in the world for watching whales. The ocean shelf plunges into the deep very close to the shore line and the upwelling currents bring the krill and plankton, that whales love, to the surface. The whale watching boats are popular with tourists but today I was not going to be one of them. I had a trip on the Albatross boat to look forward to and the thought of it not going out was hard to bear. The signs at the boat house quite simply read "decision delayed until a weather report is in."

Andrea and I bought a coffee and waited, Andrea was no joining me on the boat as her tendency to get sea sick when taking a bath did not lend itself well to the rougher waters of the Southern Oceans. I was beginning to lose hope when a smiling young girl came over and advised me that the seas were just about Ok.

"Do you think I should take seas sick tablets>" I asked

"Depends if you are prone to sea sickness." she replied

Kiwis are so straightforward.

There was a sudden commotion as the dozen or so potential albatross spotters gathered wet weather gear and telescopes and who know what else. I had my binoculars and wore shorts and jandles, think it would be much easier to dry wet legs than wet clothes. The other birders gave me some very funny looks as we climbed into the mini bus to head to the boat yard.

As our small boat left the harbour and ploughed through the waves and the spray lashed over the whole craft. Our female pilot kept a tight hold on the wheel and seemed to really enjoy her battle with the waves. She made certain not to get hit side on but the rise and fall was still too much for the German couple next to me and they very soon puked their breakfast over the side much, to the delight of the gull's.

As we got further away from the breaking waves the pitching became less violent and up above the sun started to make a watery appearance. Even this did not help the Germans who by now had rid themselves of breakfast and were making every effort to get rid of yesterday's supper. It has to be said they were making a pretty good job of it. Another couple quickly followed suit. I was unsure if these were sympathy pukers or maybe the trip was full of Teutonic bulimics. Those of us with stronger constitutions tried to keep up wind of the pukers to avoid the spray and the smell.

After about 45 minutes our boat slowed and came to stop. We were just about out of sight from land and the ocean seemed to dwarf us, but it was relatively calm. The pilot came to the back and attached a chum line to the rear and threw it into the sea. The frozen fish gunk did its job and within a matter of seconds we were the centre of attention for any albatross in the area.

It was unbelievable suddenly we had, wandering, southern and northern royal albatrosses as well as several small varieties almost within touching distance. They were magnificent. These majestic creatures are capable of circumnavigating the globe on the southern winds and here they were sitting next to the boat like ducks on a village pond.

As well as albatross there were petrels, shearwaters and prions almost all of which were life ticks. As we moved to different areas so the mighty birds took to the wing and followed us. We were the Pied Piper of birds and I loved it. At the third stop the chum was once again thrown over the back of the boat and the birds assumed their place in pecking order. Without warning the chum was blasted out of the water closely followed by a two-metre-long blue shark. A minute later it repeated the trick. We all enquired as to why it did not take the birds and our pilot explained that the risk of getting its nose badly pecked was not one worth taking.

Then as if nothing more could happen a small raft of little blue penguins surfaced close to us adding another life tick to the list. This natural spectacle was just the icing on the cake on what was a magical morning. Before we returned to the harbour the pilot offered us hot chocolate and biscuits and buns. The Germans politely turned these down, thankfully that left more for the hardy types.

My actual birthday was spent in Picton which in all honesty is not one of New Zealand's great places but it is where the ferry to the north island sails from so we had little choice. The Picton Yacht club was a very pleasant place to stay but it pissed down with rain all day so walking around town was damp affair. We ate a birthday meal at the Barn where the lamb was delicious.

Bed 40. So proud in Wellington

The following morning, we boarded the 9.05am ferry to cross the Cook Strait to Wellington. The scenery in the Marlborough Sounds is spectacular and although flying is much quicker, sights like these are worth taking the extra time. As the ferry glided through the Sounds we were accompanied by all manner of sea birds but hard as I looked I could not spot any dolphins. Houses perched precariously on hillsides that plunged into the water, life seemed dependent on the water. Fishing boats and transport boats and leisure boats and sailing boats cut white furrows through the blue waters of the sounds. It was tranquillity personified.

We arrived in Wellington on a dull but dry afternoon and found our way to the city centre youth hostel. As it happened we were in Wellington for what was to prove a busy weekend. The World Rugby 7's circuit was in town and the fans seemed ready to enjoy themselves. The 7's did not come as a surprise to us as we had planned to be in town to see them. I was like a proud father as one member of the England team was a former boarding student of ours, we had at the time, as houseparent's, been like a surrogate mother and father.

Ruaridh met us at the team hotel but not before I had sat with Andrea star spotting as players from around the globe milled about waiting for team meetings, training runs and final practice sessions. I spotted Sonny Bill Williams the Kiwi superstar and pin-up boy along with countless other big names none of whom Andrea had heard of. Just before Ruaridh arrived the lift doors opened and out stepped a group of men who were bigger than any humans I had ever seen before. The Samoan and Fijian players entered the room with an air of South Pacific nonchalance. They looked cool in flip flops and Bermuda shorts but their battered faces and phenomenal muscularity made it plain they had descended from the same warrior race that greeted Captain Cook centuries earlier.

My only advice to Ruaridh was to try and avoid being hit by any of them

"Yeh! Thanks for that Jim. Samoa are in our group!"

Andrea and I took up our places in the famous Cake Tin stadium for the first day of the tournament. The authorities had deemed that the Wellington leg of the world series should be fancy dress and some of the costumes on display were brilliant. We took our seats surrounded by super heroes, Flintstones, burlesque dancers, William Wallace lookalikes and Maori warriors. There was one small group that not only looked unique but strangely disturbing. Six men had dressed as giant babies complete with realistic but hugely oversized heads. Each baby had its own distinct facial expression, one smiling another in tears and so on. They were the stuff of horror movies but incredibly fascinating. Andrea spent as much time photographing the babies as she did watching the 7's.

England duly won two games and lost to Samoa but topped the group. Ruaridh played well and scored a couple of tries and I went back to the youth hostel as proud as I had ever been.

We were not in for a peaceful evening. As the revellers returned from the 7's it was clear that they had drunk one or two shandies and as Andrea and I sat over a very simple but pleasant pasta supper we were entertained with renditions of rugby songs I had last heard at university in the 70's. I feel we were remarkably tolerant but sadly the same cannot be said of some of the other codgers staying in the hostel. I really felt like having a word with some of them Let's face it if you check into a youth hostel there has to be at least some chance that a few of the residents will be youths. Plus, if it's the weekend of a major sporting event it's an equally fare bet that beer will be involved. If you put youths and beer together the net result is likely to be noisy. Well noisy they were but at I no time did I witness anything remotely threatening and it all seemed pretty good humoured to us. Perhaps spending so much time in youth hostels was making us young again. My hangover the next morning indicated perhaps not.

Bed 41/ 42 & 43 Maori culture and geysers.

The rest of our time in the North Island was to be spent catching up with old pals and playing at being tourists rather than the experienced travellers that we had become. We headed to Rotorua to stay with the first set of our friends.

I had not primed Andrea about the single most noticeable feature of the town so as we neared the city she began to look accusingly at me and turn her nose up. Andrea generally accuses me when any strange smell appears anywhere in our near vicinity, and now and again I have to admit that she does have a case. On this occasion, I was able to keep a straight face and deny any guilt. The smells grew stronger until eventually I had to tell her that Rotorua genuinely smelled like this. The slightly rotten egg pong that hangs over the town is a product of the enormous amount of geothermal activity that makes this such a magnet for tourists. It does take some getting used to and if the air is heavy as it was on the day we arrived it seems as if there is no escaping the stink.

We visited the Te Puia Maori Village which an ideal way to enjoy Maori traditions, learn about the past and experience the non-worldly geothermal activity. It is hard to explain how strange this landscape is and certainly Andrea had never seen anything like it before. We all learn at school that tectonic plates move and the surface of the earth is unstable in some areas of the planet. Nothing however can prepare you for this. The mud seems to bubble and boil like a casserole on a cooker. Streams flow and the water steams as it boils. I half expected Captain Kirk and his crew to appear from the mist as the scenery is far more akin to outer space than it is to planet earth.

We approached the big one, the geyser known as Pohutu, as it was about to explode and we watched in amazement as jets of boiling water and steam were blasted 30 meters into the air. The rocks around the geyser took on a sulphurous yellow colour as the waters crashed back down onto them.

It was very hard to drag ourselves away from the mud pools and geysers and as we walked around the park we were drawn back by their magnetic quality. The blipping and blopping of the mud, and hissing of escaping steam, and the moisture dripping from the ferns and palm trees enhanced the feeling that we were somewhere other worldly and mysterious. We sat for a good hour or so just watching, exchanging few words, but I am certain we were thinking the same things. This was just another amazing experience on a journey that had been full of amazing experiences

From the mud pools and geysers, we moved to the Maori heritage area of the park and watched traditional skills kept alive by the indigenous peoples of Rotorua. We saw weavers, wood carvers, canoe makers and stone polishers. It was both fascinating and educational. We each bought a greenstone tiki for good luck and we bought two more for the girls.

Our afternoon ended with a hokey pokey ice cream, the traditional treat in New Zealand. They are good but not as great as the Kiwi's think they are. To me it's a vanilla ice cream with a Crunchie bar in it. To your average Kiwi it is described as something just short of heaven. Still each to his own.

Andrea and I spent the early evening wandering around lake Rotorua watching the jet boats and taking in the scenery. We ended up at a small church in Ohinemutu just outside of Rotorua. Saint Faith's Church, as it was called, was completed in 1914 and is part of the living Maori village. The building sits overlooking lake Rotorua and boasts two rather unique and moving attractions.

The stained glass windows inside the church depict religious scenes, which of course is common in all churches, not that I go inside too many. This one however was different as Jesus was depicted wearing a Maori cloak and set at such a height that he appeared to be walking across the surface of the lake. Outside the church is a small graveyard for soldiers who fought and died in the Maori regiment. It is a simple but very moving resting place for these men who often died so very far from home. Those who made it back from the various overseas conflicts can also be buried alongside their fallen comrades when their time finally arrives.

As the sun set we drove to the Mitai Cultural Visitors Centre for an evening of dance, music and perhaps most importantly food. We were welcomed onto the sacred ground, in the traditional manner, by a warrior and the enchanting singing of a Maori woman. After rubbing noses with all and sundry, a greeting known as a hongi, very un-British and slightly unnerving we moved into the Great Hall. Here members of the tribe performed dances, sang songs and explained the elaborate tattoos that adorned all parts of the men's and women's bodies.

The men's skills with spears and clubs, even in this sanitised setting, was amazing. They looked so fearsome. Their facial tattoos and ability to extend their tongues half way down their chests added to the feeling that one false move in the audience could spark a massacre. It must have been a scary sight for Captain Cook and his men when they encountered these warriors for real back in the mid 1700's.

After the show the guides walked us, in the dark, to a crystal clear stream where with the use of torches we could clearly see trout and other fish. As the lights were turned off glow worms glittered in the trees and bushes it reminded me of Christmas. An eerie chanting could be heard getting increasingly louder and from the mists appeared a fully loaded war canoe being paddled down the river. The canoe or Waka was manned by a dozen massive men in woven grass war dress with tattooed faces and the obligatory long tongues. Andrea and I did wonder if somewhere in the distant past these warriors were related to lizards.

The feast that followed was the result of a pretty good attempt to recreate the traditional methods of cooking. The food was prepared underground in a hangi or pit oven. Meats and kumara wrapped in leaves were placed on the hot stones over a fire, the pit closed and the food left to cook. The result was moist and succulent meats and perfectly cooked veggies. The puddings were less authentic but nonetheless delicious. We had pavlova and sticky date pudding, but in all honesty no one in the massive eating hall was in the least bit concerned that this part of the evening had departed from Maori tradition.

As we drove back to our friend's house Andrea and I both felt that we had really taken in the Rotorua experience and gone at least a short way down the path of understanding how the traditions of the Maori people have pervaded into modern Kiwi life.

The next day we dropped the relocation car off in Auckland and picked up a hire car before setting off cross country towards Tauranga. No visit to the North Island is complete without experiencing the film set of The Lord of the Rings trilogy. Andrea had seen the films and loved the stories. I had not seen the films and the books were too long to make them worth reading. Thus when we arrived at Mata-Mata the starting point for the tours Andrea boarded the tour-bus to Hobbiton while I wandered around the town and had a quite beer and a pie.

When she got back she was buzzing and the rest of the car journey to Tauranga was filled with excited chatter about things that I had little knowledge of and even less interest in. It is strange how when I chat about sport Andrea interjects "not interested" and the conversation stops. When she talks about Hobbits or shopping I am expected to listen, ask questions and show a real interest.

The port city of Tauranga is nothing special but the surrounding area is as it's lush and fertile. Another set of rugby friends provided us with a very comfortable bed and once again we were extremely grateful for the now familiar Kiwi hospitality. If there is a more hospitable race on the planet I have not yet met them. Not only did Ron and Jenny put us up but they organised for their friends to provide us with accommodation on the Coromandel Peninsula which was to be our next stop.

With Ron and Jenny, we explored the rich farm land around the city. We saw kiwi fruit and avocado plantations, Andrea and I found it odd to see these exotics growing so widely, as we had really only seen them in Tesco and Sainsbury's previously. We climbed the Mount Manganui volcanic plug and had a spectacular view across the bay and we popped into Ron's school for the first assembly of term.

Of course we had experienced well over fifty first day assemblies between us during our teaching careers but nothing like this. Tauranga Boys College or TBC is a big all boys school in the city, catering for lads from across the social and economic spectrum. It has a proud tradition in sports and academia many great games players are among its former pupils. They include Sam Cane a current all black and Kane Williamson who stars in the Kiwi Cricket team and would probably make any world best team selection. Add Olympic gold medal winning sculler Mahe Drysdale and the quality is clear.

The school also embraces its Maori traditions and culture and has its own Marai on site. The school Marai was beautifully decorated with carvings and totems associated with tribal meeting houses. There are specific teachers to cater for the needs of the Islander and Maori children. The first assembly of the school year clearly embraced and celebrated this diversity.

We entered the main school assembly hall, through the back door and stood with Ron and the other staff. The whole school was present, and sitting cross-legged on the floor, save for a large gap at the front of the hall just below the raised dais where the senior staff were to sit.

The hum of noise that only a thousand plus boys can create was very evident and certainly took me back to my teaching days. As the senior teachers entered the hall the noise stopped and the vast majority of boys sat up straight. I would hesitate to say the students looked smart. They certainly didn't look English Grammar school smart. Uniforms varied from white polo shirts with shorts and jandles to smart suits and school blazers with highly polished, new term shoes. Some of the teaching staff wore suits while others looked rather like cast rejects from to 70's sit-com "Please Sir" or the film "To Sir with Love."

I am not certain whether the silence represented respect or a little fear but it was certainly a silence. It was very different from my final years in a mid-Kent Grammar school where the students disliked the new head teacher with such a passion that whenever he entered any room the noise levels escalated with a good deal of that noise was made by the staff.

The principal stood and asked the school to stand and greet the new year 7's in the traditional TBC fashion. As the tiny new boys entered the room looking lost and overawed a thousand boys broke into the school Haka. The noise shook the building and almost lifted the roof off. Rhythmic foot stamping and body slapping accompanied the

Maori chants of welcome. As the Haka ended the students sat and the formal part of the mornings proceedings began.

The principal spoke in a commanding and enthusiastic way welcoming one and all back for a new school year. The new Head boy, a Samoan, was greeted with nose-rubbing and garlands of flowers. This young man addressed the school with a mature confidence one associated with students chosen to lead.

Andrea and I bid farewell to Ron and slipped away before the nitty gritty started and before we could be asked to cover lessons. We headed north to the Coromandel Peninsular.

We were travelling north to the most beautiful part of the North Island at least that is what we had been led to believe. Others would claim that honour belongs to the Bay of Islands or Milford but we had high expectations of what awaited us. We had found pretty much the whole of New Zealand to be worthy of a page on a calendar so if this was to be even better we were in for a treat.

It was pissing down with rain as we left Tauranga and it was still pissing down as we passed through Kati-Kati and stopped for ice cream. It was still pissing down as we drove through Thames, the gateway to the Coromandel, and it was pissing down even harder when we reached our beach front accommodation in Hahei.

When we awoke the next morning, it was still pissing down in almost biblical fashion. We contemplated beginning work on an Ark and both signed up for swimming lessons at the local pool. We got especially worried when animals started to line up in pairs on the front lawn but then I realised that my brain was waterlogged and I was hallucinating.

We had a simple choice stay indoors and watch the rain fall or get on with things as we had planned. Trust me it was not an easy decision. The rain fell so hard that it almost hurt, plus the clouds were low and seeing anything was pretty much hit or miss. Having given the day an hour or so to clear up we decided to brave the elements and set out.

We arrived at the car park for Cathedral Cove and much to our surprise there were plenty of parking bays vacant. The houses on the approach road that advertised "on drive" parking at extortionate rates were not making money on this particular day.

Andrea and I were so much fitter than we had been when we left England and a short walk of a couple of kilometres or so no longer bothered us in the slightest. The path was clearly signposted and it even gave approximate distances via route one and routes two and three. The car park was high on the cliffs and we guessed the cove and beach would be somewhat nearer sea level. Luckily, like most PE teachers, I had taught geography as well as Phys Ed, and we opted for route one which was the shortest.

Ten minutes later we realised we had made somewhat of an error. The rain had caused the pathway to become a small torrent and the loose underfoot conditions made the walk more of a scramble. There was bugger all to hang on to and there was a real danger that one or both of us would slip, fall and plunge into the sea below. Just as we were beginning to panic a little the path turned inland and although it was still difficult fear of an early doom in the stormy sea, was removed. I would have loved to have seen a video of the pair of us intrepid explorers trying to reach the beach. I suspect it would have been akin to watching Bambi's first attempts to walk on ice from the classic Disney movie. We made it down and chose not to speak about the return journey.

Te Whanganui-A-Hei as the cove is known by the Maoris, is a bit special and reminded me of my geography field trips to Lulworth Cove. The waves crashed ashore and the wind blew but from the shelter of the sea arch created by the pounding waves we were able to appreciate the rugged beauty of the coastline. It is hard to describe the power of the sea, but as the massive white rollers pounded the cliffs it was easy to see how the cove had been carved over the centuries. I am sure the outlook would have been better in sunshine but this lasting memory created by mother nature at her most fearsome would take some beating.

We chose route three on the way back to the car park and although it was much longer at least we didn't fear for our lives. It took us a good hour to struggle up the slopes to the car. We had not seen another soul on the walk both ways and during our spell on the beach. We had this place all to ourselves, and although we were soaked, cold, and bedraggled we were pleased we had made the effort.

Having checked the tides before we set out, we knew that the afternoon was the best time to visit Hot Water Beach on Mercury Bay. The geothermal activity beneath the sands leads to an upwelling of warm water and when the tides are right it is possible to dig hollows in the sand and wallow in the warmth. We arrived at a bright weather interlude and the rains had eased slightly so that the torrents were now just a drizzle.

Andrea and I were by now self-proclaimed experts in predicting how groups of tourists from other countries would behave and we used this to our advantage at Hot Water Beach.

From what we had observed during our travels, Chinese almost always arrived at a tourist spot in coaches and had a very limited time to do whatever it was that needed to be done. They would wear bizarre brightly coloured clothing, white socks and sandals, massive peaked hats or visors and have sufficient white sun block on their faces to prevent even the strongest sun beam from reaching their skin. They have a herd mentality and many have a total disregard for all around them. Part of this is rudeness, but I am certain that the tour reps only serve to exacerbate the situation with frantic shouting and flag waving. Their main aim seems to be to take a photo whist giving a Winston Churchill two finger salute and then to get back on the coach as quickly as possible.

The Russians are never in large groups but travel in style. They arrive in hired people carriers or large cars and look blingtastic. They are wasteful, and have little respect for local customs, traditions or people.

Russian women invariably wear the most inappropriate clothing for the situation, high heels on the beach, hot pants and boob tubes in temples or smart restaurants. They have peroxide dyed hair that looks so brittle that a mere touch would break it off. Rolex watches and thick gold bangles are everywhere. They just ooze unsophistication and brash showy wealth.

Many Russian men look like thugs with shaven heads and muscular arms protruding from overly tight shirts. They wear neck chains that wouldn't go amiss on Chicago pimps and have gold crowned teeth. They tend to park across parking bays taking no heed of others. They almost all smoke even inside buildings and get most upset when asked to stop. Thankfully we came across very few Russians in New Zealand.

The children are dressed like little dollies and are carbon copies of their parents. They are usually sucking on lollies or eating unhealthy foods. Whatever the latest hand held accessory on the market is they have it and appear to take no care of it.

Mind you when you see the way their illustrious ruler behaves it is not surprising that they are the way they are.

There is however a sinister side to the Russians as they not only dress like they own the world but they behave like they do and God help you if you get in the way.

We did meet some younger Russians students in Bali and they were much more aware of things around them so perhaps there is some hope for the future.

The Germans are altogether different and in our experience a pleasure to be around. Super organised, polite and aside from their innate drive to reserve sun beds at some ridiculous hour of the morning, very aware of those around them. They are always happy to share a table, chat over a beer and much to our embarrassment they all seem to speak impeccable English.

Germans are so like the Brits and it is hardly surprising that Andrea and I made more temporary holiday friendships with our European neighbours than anyone else. Even the young German travellers have a class and maturity that makes them stand out from the crowd. They seem to be able to drink without puking, look beach ready without appearing cheap, and understand about a tourist site before the guide even opens their mouth.

The Aussies, of whom there are many in South East Asia and New Zealand, seem to fall into more than one stereotype. The mature Aussies are great fun to be with, and by mature I am not talking about age, rather a behavioural manner. They are chatty and knowledgeable about customs and traditions and generally make a good day into an even better day. They have a sense of humour that is infectious and I defy anyone not to enjoy the company of these people. The younger ones like a beer but do not abuse local waiters, they know how to have fun but not at other's expense and they, for the most part, have a great national pride, but do not let their country down.

The bad Aussies are a different kettle of fish. Known as "bogans" by other Aussies these people are well worth avoiding. They are class-less, manner less and generally obnoxious. Fortunately, they don't travel too far, but when you encounter them you'll never forget it. They are abusive, racist and totally inappropriate in almost every setting. Andrea and I had the misfortune to encounter them on the Gold Coast and in Bali, but not in New Zealand.

Anyway back to hot water beach, the Germans had arrived before us and with no sun beds to claim they had set about digging bathing pools with an energy and skill unlike we had seen before. We would not have been surprised if each group had a civil engineer with them to plan and monitor the job. Before you knew it, the beach was dotted with beautifully crafted hot pools that would not have been out of place in a luxury spa. The rest was simple. We just waited until they got bored and then jumped in after them. We had a perfect hot pool with no digging, no hiring or carrying spades, and no hard work. It just goes to show that the EU can work for everyone.

The rains soon returned as heavy as ever, and although it was not cold, thanks to the hot water, we did feel a bit like idiots sitting on a beach in a hot pool whilst the heavens opened above us so we headed back to the beach house in Hahei.

So our excursion to the Coromandel had begun in pouring rain, continued in pouring rain and concluded in pouring rain. I would love to be able to paint a glorious picture of the place but to be quite honest we really didn't see much of it' especially as visibility was never much above 50 feet. None-the-less we still had one highlight to look forward to before reaching Auckland. We were heading for Miranda to watch shore birds and with any luck see a few rarities and get a few more life ticks. My excitement was palpable, as I suspect was Andrea's, but she did hide it well.

We set off early the next morning after checking the tide times. Tidal patterns are vital when shore bird watching as if the sea is too far out you can't see the birds and if it's too far in they have buggered off. We arrived early and had time for a coffee and cake in a local roadside café before heading off to the bird watching hides.

The Pokorokoro Shorebird Centre is one of the top places to watch shore birds especially if you want to see wrybills. These strange little waders with a twisted beak are not easy to spot unless elsewhere. Here, however, they are abundant with half the world's population gathering on the shoreline.

I had a wonderful time and saw so much. Andrea had an ordinary day and saw the same as me but with less enthusiasm. I am not about to record my full day's list but suffice to say with Godwits, sandpipers, stints, plovers, spoonbills and of course wrybills it was a morning to remember.

The birders at the site were just like birders at home. They wore camouflaged jackets and trousers and carried massive telescopes along with binoculars and guide books. Those who really knew their stuff kept to the secluded spots and offered advice that was both educational and somewhat secretive. The pretend birders whizzed around in groups trying to identify species that they had never seen before. They continually mis-identified common species as rarities a practice known as "stringing". I personally always count a species as the most common one around unless I can positively identify it. The Chinese just seemed to shout a lot and scare off anything that got too close.

Bed 44. The City of Sails.

Auckland is a beautiful city that deserves a few days of anyone's travel time. The city fringed by the Pacific is rightfully known as the City of Sails. Andrea was bitterly disappointed as she thought it was the city of sales. Along the water front are marinas that hold hundreds of sailing ships. Ships range from the small sail boats used by families at the weekend, to luxury yachts used by the rich and famous. The waterfront area is alive with cafes and restaurants and people throng here to see and be seen. It is possible to sit with a coffee and a cake and watch the former America's Cup yachts move silently in and out of their moorings as they give rides to eager tourists.

The magnificent Harbour Bridge, nearly as impressive as the ones in Sydney or San Francisco, stands as a majestic reminder of man's engineering skills. The bridge holds an eight-lane highway which acts as an artery in and out of the heart of the city. There is even a bungee jump from the centre of the bridge into the waters below.

As we only had a few days left in New Zealand we were determined to enjoy them to the full. This meant leisurely lunches, chilled white wine and sumptuous seafood suppers. We stayed with old friends in Epsom one of the suburbs of the city and it would have been hard to have a better in those final few days.

Sam and Marie's house was tucked away in a quiet road and was typical of the lovely houses in the area. The rooms were spacious and airy and the garden sported the obligatory barbecue and a hot tub. Sitting in the tub in late evening watching the stars and sipping white wine took our minds off the long flight that lay ahead of us in a couple of days.

We drove over the bridge to the seaside suburb of Davenport where the sandy beach makes bathing easy, but my goodness the water was cold. We had lunch overlooking the harbour and wiled away the afternoon sipping beer and chatting about the old days when Sam and I had been in the sports department together in Kent and we had been neighbours and close friends.

The final highlight was a day trip to Waiheke Island, an old volcanic plug set in the Hauraki Gulf about ninety minutes from downtown by ferry. Waiheke is all about food wine and stunning scenery and we did all we could to enjoy these. We hired a driver for the day and set off to explore the island, via various wineries and scenic beauty spots. We probably spent as much money in a day as we had in a week in South East Asia but it was worth it.

Our first stop was for lunch at the Mudbrick Winery. perched high on a hillside the cellar door restaurant overlooked the island and was an ideal spot to just sit and enjoy the view. It was however even better for sitting and eating great food and drinking crisp dry white wine. We had two food platters between us, one showcasing kiwi cold meats and cheeses and the other fruits of the sea. It came with a basket of fresh bread with we ordered a bottle of pinot gris. The lunch set us back close to $200 dollars. Andrea shocked me by announcing that the view alone was probably worth the money, but as we munched on fresh bread and stuffed ourselves with green lipped mussels we were very glad we had opted for an enhanced view.

Mid-afternoon saw us reach Cable Bay Winery. We walked the short distance between the two sites and enjoyed some Waiheke rose while sunning ourselves on beanbags on the winery's manicured lawns. We really felt as if we were somewhat older extras in the Auckland equivalent of Made in Chelsea.

We spent the late afternoon and early evening driving around the island and snapping pictures of the sun slowly sinking into the Pacific. The ferry journey back to the harbour probably took another ninety minutes but since we both snoozed most of the way it passed in a flash.

One added bonus of the Auckland leg of our trip was a fleeting visit from India who flew down from Brisbane for a couple of nights to see us before we set off for South America. It was a brilliant surprise and rounded off the leg of our adventure absolutely perfectly.

Bed 45. In the shadow of the Andes.

The flight from Auckland to Santiago is long, nearly twelve hours and as luck would have it the screen on my seat wouldn't work so I spent most of the flight restlessly trying to get comfortable or doing exercises in the space at the back by the aircrew kitchen. Despite the fact we had nearly flown around the globe I was no nearer to finding a way to sleep on planes. I have tried everything from drinking a lot of alcohol which makes the next day a mess, to drinking only water which means I continually have to visit the loo. Nothing works for me. I don't dislike flying, in fact I love airline food, I just cannot ever get in the correct position to sleep. What I really need is a chin hammock that would hang from the overhead locker. I am sure that If an entrepreneur could invent such a thing they would be a best seller. Just lolling my head forward with a fluffy chin strap for support would send me off to sleep in an instant. I wonder what the people on Dragons Den would think of my idea?

I was really looking forward to getting to South America and re-visiting places and people I had met through rugby and teaching years before. Andrea and I had lived in Montevideo for a couple of years in the mid-80's while I coached rugby at The British School. We had made some excellent friends and I was secretly hoping that our planned date to return to the UK would be put back and that we could spend a couple of months or even longer travelling through Chile, Argentina and Uruguay countries we knew well. Hopefully after this we could move on into Peru and Bolivia and see a very different part of this many faceted continent.

I was detecting a change in Andrea and this change did not bode well for what I had I mind. She was beginning to talk a lot about getting home and starting to plan things relating to our arrival back in the UK. I knew in my heart of hearts that for her the journey was coming to an end and her enthusiasm which had developed massively over the time away was beginning to ebb. I could understand this, but it did not make it any easier to come to terms with.

Sure enough, somewhere over the southern oceans, she began to open up and questions fell from her mouth like the waters over the Iguacu Falls, which we were soon to visit. There was no particular order to these questions and no answers were required from me. It was simply an outpouring of emotions that had clearly been building up and could no longer be held in check.

"What are we going to do when we get home?" she asked

"Where will we stay until our house is ready to move back into?"

"What if our tenant has done lots of damage to the house and we can't move in straight away?"

"When shall we give him notice to move out?"
The questions were backed up by rhetorical statements;

"We will need new carpets you know. The painters will have to do most of the rooms in the house. It is going to be so difficult getting the right containers out of store."

I could not see that any of these issues were particularly hard to overcome but I had learned that solutions or answers were not needed, and all I had to do was listen and nod at the appropriate time. The solutions would come later when Andrea had formulated her thoughts and started to plan in earnest. I just listened and agreed that these issues needed to be thought about and suggested we make a to-do list and spend time over the coming days trying to resolve them. This seemed to work in the short term but I knew for sure that Andreas thoughts were now fully on getting home and anything beyond the very straightforward would not be possible in South America. I was disappointed, but having spent so much time together, I knew that trying to stretch our trip beyond the pre-planned date would cause huge anxiety and probably lead to neither of us enjoying it.

We landed in Santiago and travelled into the city centre to an apartment that we had booked. It was clean and spacious and very handy for the city's underground railway system. Santiago, although being a city of over 5 million, does not somehow seem as hectic as some other Latin American capital. Getting around is easy and the views, on days when the haze is not apparent, are spectacular. The Andes sit some 30 kilometres inland from the city and provide an unforgettable backdrop. A comfortable bus journey in the other direction sees you reach Vina del Mar and Valparaiso on the Pacific Ocean. Both of these places have a great deal to offer the inquisitive traveller.

Andrea and I had visited Santiago 30 years ago and like all people we were interested to see what had changed as the city had grown in the 21st century. The first thing we noticed was that more of the city was standing. We had visited in 1987, a couple of years after the 1985 earthquake, and at that time the damage to the city was immense. Now there were few reminders of the devastation caused by the quake. We both hoped that Christchurch would be able to re generate as successfully.

I am not sure why but neither of us had remembered Chile as being an especially hot country, perhaps the name gave us a false impression. Chile in summer is hot and the summer is long. This was an added bonus and we took every opportunity to top up our tans before returning home.

Back in 1987 we had spent a lovely day on the top of Cerro San Cristobel, at an open air swimming pool. We decided to retrace our steps and firstly see if the pool still existed and if so spend a day lounging by it. The cable car was not running due to an upgrade being undertaken, which is always good news if you are scared of heights or just don't fancy riding a tele-cabin in an earthquake prone city. Fortunately, the funicular railway was still in operation so we did not have to undertake the long walk uphill in the Santiago sun. The funicular commenced from the Pio Nono entrance to the park which Andrea and I reached using the very efficient local buses. From here the train climbed majestically up the 300-metre hill and conveniently stopped at the public pools en-route.

The views over the city were quite simply breath-taking providing the smog stayed away. Thankfully this phenomenon is more prevalent during the winter months and we had a wonderfully clear view over the metropolis below. A magnificent statue of the Virgin Mary watches over the citizens of Santiago from the hill top. The statue is as tall as a cricket pitch is long and there is a small chapel in the base of the construction.

Despite visiting religious buildings during our trip, including cave temples, temples dedicated to Hindu gods or reclining Buddha's, from small chapels and the giant ancient temple cities at Angkor, I was still no more of a believer than I had been when we left England. One thing was true, however, and that was that many of these religious sites and monuments had been erected in places of outstanding beauty and the Virgin on San Cristobel was no exception. There was a feeling of serenity and peace at the Virgin and despite the hectic nature of the tourists clamouring to take the great photos.

The late morning and early afternoon lounge by the pool was a real memory jerker. We even tried to re-create a photographic moment from 30 years prior. Andrea lay prone by the side of the pool with her arms pushing her body towards the sun while the hill top breeze gently blew her hair.

One leg straight and the other bent completed the pose and despite the passing years the effect was still good.

We ate a simple picnic lunch of empanadas de carne, roughly translated as a small meat pie, and a soft drink before taking in a quick visit to the zoo. On our previous visit to Chile we had been to a few zoos and found them very similar. It did not seem to matter greatly what was written on the enclosure whether it be lion or bear. Almost every enclosure seemed to house a llama. We assumed that either the original occupant had passed on to animal heaven and been replaced by the cheapest possible option or that the zoo curator had been rather too optimistic in his approach to animal recruitment and had never actually had a lion or a bear in the first place.

I am pleased to say things have changed in Santiago Zoo and now a high proportion of the animal cages do seem to house the correct beast. That is about as good as it gets, however, and I have to say the conditions and the enclosures are not what we have come to expect in Europe. There was far too much concrete and not enough stimulation for the animals. Andrea and I left fairly quickly, and will not be returning.

Over the next few days we re-explored the city and took every possible opportunity to eat great food. We had always planned that the South American leg of our journey would be a culinary delight and despite Andrea's growing desire to get home we saw no need to change this part of our plans

The highlight came with a visit to the much heralded Mestizo Restaurant which sits close to the San Cristobel hill. The restaurant is rightly proud of its food but with a panoramic view across the city in one direction and a vista towards the towering peaks of the Andes in the other makes for a visual as well as a culinary experience.

Andrea and I started with a dish of ceviche and a barbequed octopus platter, which we shared, accompanied by a local white wine. The ceviche was unbelievably delicious and considering that I had never eaten much fish before let alone fish that was in essence raw, I was blown away. We had no intention of ordering ceviche, at least I had no intention of ordering it. Our waiter, however, sensing my reluctance to experiment, came good and did what good waiters should do.

"Sir the sea-food is the star of our restaurant and I am certain you will love it."

"Nice try Carlos", I replied looking at his name badge., "But what if I don't? I will have wasted money and still be hungry"

"Then let me bring you a small taster to try before you order."

This short conversation did two things. Firstly, it totally shocked Andrea who did not think my Spanish was up to anything more than ordering a beer and secondly, it opened my eyes and taste buds to the world of truly fresh and delicious fish.

After sampling the tiny dish of ceviche that Carlos brought to the table I ordered in confidence and his recommendation proved to be the right one. We stuck with Carlos throughout the meal and he recommended salmon for the main course which was equally excellent. We rounded of the meal with panna cotta and a selection of local fruits. The meal was remarkably well priced for a city restaurant and after thanking Carlos for his expert guidance we strolled back to the apartment feeling sophisticated and full. I was very pleased with myself for overcoming one of the few remaining hurdles in my gastronomic journey I was not yet ready for bugs in Asia and Africa or strange un-food like things in China.

The next day in bright sunshine we set off up the Andes by bus to visit one of the more accessible ski fields. There was of course no snow due to the season but it was a trip we felt we had to make.

The bus battled through the early morning city traffic and painstakingly made its way towards the foothills some twenty or so kilometres out of the urban sprawl. I thought of my mates, Stu and Dave, back at home. Both avid mountaineers and how they often struggled for days just to reach the mountains in remote places of the world. Here we were driving into the second highest mountain range on earth without any fuss, or hardship. I couldn't help thinking that we had got this one about right.

I remembered drinking a beer of five with the two of them hearing how they had hiked for more than two weeks into the mountains of Kyrgyzstan accompanied only by a lone wolf, in order to climb previously unclimbed peaks. Here in Santiago they could have caught a bus pretty close to Aconcagua and climbed the highest peak outside of the Himalayas. It did, however, confirm my opinion that mountaineers are a breed apart from normal humans.

We reached the Val Nevado ski station which was the end of the line for the bus and my first impression was how desolate the mountains looked. Of course when there is no snow ski areas look so different but this place looked like a desert. No trees grew and the ski runs were just dust fields. The ski lifts looked weirdly out of place in this moon scape. Despite the height and in my opinion the greater closeness to the sun it was bloody freezing and dressed in shorts, a t-shirt and jandles I really felt it. The wind was cutting through us like a knife but when we did find a little shelter the sun was strong enough to warm us. As the morning passed the temperature did rise and we were able to explore a little.

We could see El Plomo far in the distance. Standing over 5400 meters high, this peak is always snow-capped and stands out in bright contrast to the dull grey of the surrounding mountains. In the distant past this peak was part of an Inca trail where a 500-year-old mummified body of a young girl was found. This mummy, now housed in the city's natural history museum is a morbid reminder of the days when children were entombed in the high Andes as offerings to the sun god, only to be re discovered in a different lifetime by climbers or archaeologists. Andrea and I had seen the mummy back in the 80's and to now gaze upon the mountain that had been her tomb for half a millennium was very poignant.

As we looked down the Andean chain a shadow drifted across the slope directly opposite where we were standing. The image of a giant bird was silhouetted against the dust and rocks of the mountainside. We both noticed it at the same time and turned to each other.

"What the bloody hell is that? Its massive."

We looked around and saw nothing due to the sun, but as the shadow moved further away the cause of the apparition appeared in the clear blue sky. A male condor was using the thermals to gain height in its quest for food. The massive black bird with a huge white collar soared and wheeled in the sky. As it banked to change course the white almost silvery wing feathers shone in the sun's glow. As we looked more carefully, we could see that his bird was not alone. Two other condors had caught the same thermal and were gradually ascending into the heavens. It was a truly majestic sight and one that even Andrea, still a reluctant birder, also found mesmerizing.

Condors close up, are ugly members of the vulture family. Lacking head plumage they have a head that resembles Abe Simpson. On the ground they are cumbersome and noisy. Once airborne they become a totally different beast with a mastery of the air that few other birds can match. They can soar for hours with hardly a wing beat as they scour the high Andes for a meal of carrion. The condor epitomises the cordillera and we were truly fortunate to be able to watch these birds at such close range.

After a couple of hours on the mountain tops we caught the bus back down to the city. We saw mountain hares and two of foxes, as well as several other mountainside birds. These were too small and too fast to identify and went down in my book as mystery "brown jobs."

The traffic was still bad in the city and with so many cars and the close proximity of the Andes it was easy to see why air got trapped over Santiago causing dreadful fog. I tried to explain that in winter the air would be moister and heavier therefore increasing the likelihood of fog. I got the distinct impression Andrea was thinking about carpet cleaners or kitchen fitters so cut my geography lesson short and continued the return journey in a contemplative silence.

Santiago is the perfect city to find your South American feet. English is widely spoken, although my Spanish continued to stand up well under pressure. The food is excellent and the wine is both delicious and inexpensive. Lunches became a leisurely half-day pursuit and rather than consume one big course, we usually opted for small dishes and local beverages. The transport infrastructure is reliable and easy to access. Once you get over the fear of earthquakes the underground system is efficient and straightforward. The people of Santiago are classy, the women dress to impress and the men just look sharp in smart suits and highly polished shoes. It might not be Milan or Paris, but a scruffy git like me did stand out a bit.

Our apartment over looked the Escuela Militar. The buildings were impressive and the lawns would not have gone amiss at Wimbledon. As we sat on our balcony the young students could be seen working hard on the assault courses and marching across the parade square. The Escuela does not have the same dark past as the Escuela Naval in Buenos Aires but none-the-less South American soldiers do have a way of looking very menacing even when they are not trying. Chile, of course, has its mysterious past under a military rule and many of the senior officers in the military school were probably around in the Pinochet era. Political dissidents had been locked away in the main football stadium and as many as 27,000 civilians suffered human rights violations and Pinochet accepted that 3500 were murdered. It was hard to believe this had happened in the quite so recent past.

When Andrea and I had first arrived in Santiago back in January 1988 we had come by train from Temuco. The train was delayed and we did not arrive in the central station until after midnight. We had been forced to rest in the station because of a military curfew and fear of arrest. How different it all seemed now.

Our final day trip from Santiago, was organised for us. We were planning to leave the city and visit old friends in the central town of Curico. Before we had even contacted Maria and Juan Pablo in Curico they had reached us. Maria told us her sister lived in Santiago and would love to take us out for the day. Partly this was to practice her English and partly because she would use any excuse to drive out to her seaside house for the day. We were certainly not going to refuse a chance like this.

So the next day we were met by Vivien and driven at breakneck speed to the seaside town of Algarrobo. Vivien must have been nudging sixty-five but she drove like Lewis

Hamilton. This did not cause us concern whilst on the motorways but once we hit the one lane roads nearer to the coast I felt like we were on a white-knuckle ride. I can honestly say I have never been so relieved to join a traffic queue, as I was when we reached the outskirts of Algarrobo. As I released my grip on the edge of the car seat and the colour began to return to my fingers I did wonder if I had done permanent damage to the cars upholstery. Andrea who had not spoken for well over half an hour said rather quietly, and probably out loud to herself, "well that was in interesting journey."

A slight smile crept across my face, one borne out of relief and amusement.

Algarrobo is like many seaside towns across the world in that, in summer when it is busy, it is a buzzing place full of tourists and Chileans alike out to enjoy the beaches and the seas. There is however one massive difference in Algarrobo. It is not that the sea is absolutely freezing all year, which it is. It is not that the seafood served in the local eateries is fresh and delicious, which it is. It is not the pelicans floating and flying everywhere like a squadron of miniature aircraft. It is that Algarrobo boasts the second largest manmade swimming pool in the world and it is huge. The pool which is the frontage to the Alfonso del Mar Resort is big enough to have sail boats, kayaks and smaller private beaches. It is lined by the ocean on one side and high rise apartments on the other. The pool is over a kilometre long and covers eight hectares. It was the largest in the world for many years before something more massive was constructed somewhere in the Middle East.

I managed to persuade Andrea to join me in a kayak, although I did require a little help from Vivien to convince her it was a good idea. I have to say it was not one of the great successes of our gap year experience. First, it did not seem the Andrea had any real sense of balance, despite being a perfectly capable skier. She appeared to develop an unfathomable fear of falling in, despite being a good swimmer. Indeed, she is a far stronger swimmer than me.

Second she seemed incapable of getting to hang of paddling and steering. Consequently, either I did all of the work or we simply moved around in circles. My aim of reaching the far end of the pool and examining the restaurants and apartments there was soon overtaken by the desire to get back to the jetty before Andreas screams and expletives led to us being arrested or sectioned by the Chilean mental health board. On our return to terra firma, Vivien had wine waiting for us on the table and a face that suggested she had been in tears with laughter.

Bed 46 & 47. Great friends and great sorrow.

We left Santiago with slightly heavy hearts and headed south, by bus, towards the central city of Curico. We had met and become friends with Maria and Juan-Pablo whilst living in Montevideo. They had come to visit our school in Uruguay, she being a headmistress, and stayed with us for a few days. We had kept in touch and indeed Maria had been to England to stay with us. I had been to Curico once before but Andrea had not so we were both really looking forward to renewing our friendship and spending a week or so in the wine growing region of Chile.

We were met at the bus station in Curico by Fernando, Maria's eldest son, and driven the couple of miles to the house. I had vague memories of what it looked like but clearly my memories had faded much more than I had thought. In front of the l house was a small paddock with a couple of magnificent looking chestnut horses and a rather less magnificent looking donkey. It was the donkey who greeted us with her comical braying and lip curling in a vain attempt to win a carrot.

The homestead was a bungalow although not a bungalow as we know it. Just about every bungalow I have been in is been occupied by an elderly couple and decorated accordingly. The aged like these homes due to the easy access but I have to say I have never liked single story houses.

Maria's front room was loving decorated with memorabilia of gauchos and the farming heritage of the area, old black and white paintings of grizzled cowboys on horseback, and men branding cattle or sitting around camp fire, adorned the walls. The chairs and settee were leather and looked invitingly well-worn and comfortable. There was an open fire at one end of the room with logs already stored for winter. At the other end there was a small bar with a sign, in

English, simply saying "man cave". On the bar were bottles of whiskey, gin and pisco. Above the bar were small mementos collected during family holidays or given as presents by visiting friends.

A screen at the side of the room pulled back to reveal a large dining area with a polished wooden table that would have comfortably sat at least twelve diners. In this room the photos were mostly of family. The black and white images were of grandparents and great uncles, almost always working in the fields or on horseback. The colour photos showed the six children Fernando, Paula, Maria-Pia, Magdalena, Soledad and, Sebastian their youngest. They were a handsome lot and our two friends were so proud of all of them. Paula and Maria-Pia were no longer at home. Paula lived with her husband and new baby in town while the Maria-Pia was away in Santiago studying.

There was no direct route from the dining area to the rest of the house but it was already clear that the house had a tardis like quality. The rooms seemed never ending, even at first glance there seemed to be five or six bedrooms and at least one other sitting room. The kitchen was massive and through the back door there was a small living area for the maid, who although an employee seemed very much part of the family.

Lucia the maid, was a ruddy-faced, cheery woman in her mid to late fifties who was, as it turned out, an excellent cook, and fiercely house proud. Her kitchen was her pride and joy and woe betide the child who left things lying around after a drink or a snack. The kids seemed to treat her with great respect and her status appeared to us to be somewhere between governess and second mum.

In the garden there was a sizeable pool and various seating areas as well as a quaint old fashioned hot tub. This tub was not a new-fangled affair with bubble blowers and heat jets. It was a massive barrel with a waterproof log-fuelled heater. Most of the time it was kept empty but when needed the log fire was lit and water piped in. Andrea and I felt that with daytime temperatures in the low 30's the last thing we would fancy in an evening was a hot tub How wrong we were.

The crowning jewel of the homestead was the outdoor living and dining area. It was the size of a small house in the UK and had everything you could wish for in terms of summer living. There was a small comfortable sitting area with a square coffee table and bench seats. Behind this was a bar and a cooking area, consisting of a parillada, and an electric stove top. We would call the parillada a barbecue but to Chileans and Argentines the parillada is a thing of beauty. To be able to cook well on the parillada is essential skill for young men.

The main eating area was centred around another huge wooden table which, if anything was bigger than the one indoors. It could have comfortably sat sixteen. The covered area was well equipped with glasses, cutlery, and table decorations. There was a beer and white wine fridge and a seemingly unlimited supply of red wine to boot.

The house had air conditioning but given design of the rooms, we never used it. The house was always pleasantly cool and extremely welcoming and comfortable. We dumped our stuff and sat on the bed before turning to each other with massive smiles and simultaneously saying, "Bloody hell I didn't expect this, it's wonderful."

We had no idea how wonderful and tragic this week would turn out but it will always remain one of the most memorable in our lives.

It was around 9pm on the first evening when Maria knocked on our door and asked us to join them in the garden. The family along with a few cousins, and a girlfriend or two were gathered in the outdoor living area. We apologised for being asleep most of the early evening but as it turned out everyone had been asleep. It was comforting to know that siestas were still part of Chilean life.

Andrea and I certainly felt very refreshed so when a glass of bubbly was suggested we wholeheartedly accepted. Over the course of the next hour or so we chatted in both Spanish and English, ate cold cuts, cheese and various other nibbles and drank several bottles of fizz. At about 11pm Juan Pablo without ceremony stood up and asked how we wanted our steaks. The parillada was, he said, at about the correct heat and so he would start cooking.

The children scurried around collecting salads from indoors and setting the big table. They did not need instructing. They each knew their jobs and carried out the tasks without fuss. It was a bit like being in a Hans Christian Anderson tale about an idyllic family. I should point out it was still school holidays so the next day was a rest day. We eventually retired to bed at around 2am and found it impossible to sleep. I was stuffed full, I think India would have said I had a food baby, and could not get comfortable, and my restlessness kept Andrea awake. It was however a contented restlessness if there is such a thing. The evening had been one to remember.

Our first few days in Curico were simply a delight. Leisurely breakfasts, simple lunches, siesta and then scrumptious dinners eaten late at night with wonderful company. We tried Juan-Pablo's pisco sour, a Chilean specialty, made from grape brandy, and they were strong. Juan claimed he made the best pisco's in Chile. We had nothing to compare them with but it would have been hard to beat these. Sometimes we sat in the hot tub watching the stars and passing the time. It was as if we had been transported into a different era where time was almost irrelevant and thoughts of home, even for Andrea, were pushed well into the back of our minds.

During the day Maria would often pop into her school to check things were ready for the new school year which was now only a week away. Juan would leave early despite being up until all hours. He oversaw the harvest of apples, pears and corn on the farm and spent most of the day in the saddle. His next project was to be introducing Kiwi fruits to Chile and he was planning a trip to New Zealand to buy trees and look at cultivation methods. As we had spent several weeks in the Kiwi growing area of the North Island we were able to give him a good heads up and even suggest a couple of our friends he could stay with in and around Tauranga.

This meant that during the daytimes we were left to chill by the pool or be entertained by the youngsters. Sebastian and his elder brother suggested a trip out to a local waterfall for a swim. Andrea declined but I thought it sounded fun plus there was always the chance of picking up the odd life tick or two. We set off in the SUV with me in the front with Fernando, while Soledad and Sebastian and a couple of mates piled in the back. We had made a small picnic and chilled a couple of bottles of cola for the trip. It was hot and the sky was clear so I guessed that when we arrived the waters would be sufficiently warm to make bathing a pleasure.

Well on arrival I realised at once that what the pups thought of as an easy walk was going to be akin to climbing a major mountain for me. The waterfall may well have been well known to the youth of Curico, but it was hardly a tourist destination. We started by scrambling down a steep dusty slope that was barely wide enough to squeeze through. I managed this section pretty quickly by slipping over and sliding down about twenty meters on my arse, much to the amusement of all. They jumped and half ran the rest of the way while I cautiously picked my way down using every tree branch and protruding root as a crutch.

"Jim we can jump into the water from here. It is good fun."

With that Sebastian was gone, quickly followed by the gang, except for Fernando who had spotted my terror.

"Do you mind if I jump Jim? There is the only way back so the others will come this way."

"Go for it, but count me out. It's far too high."

I looked over the edge and it must have been twenty feet to the plunge pool below. Sebastian and the others were already scrambling up the rocks ready for a second jump.

"Jim are you not going? Its great fun."

"Its bloody madness if you ask me. "

I doubt he heard as he was already in mid-air laughing with joy.

After twenty minutes or so of trying to encourage me to jump in, the pups got bored and gave up, we carried on through the trees towards the waterfall.

It took at least another fifteen minutes before we reached the falls. By the time we did I was a sweat ball, covered in dust and panting like an excited labrador. The pups were fine and still in high spirits. The cascade was beautiful and the pool created by the falling water was crystal clear. Sadly, the surrounds of the pool were not so pristine. South Americans are good at many things but looking after nature is not one of them. Litter was strewn around and there were remnants of camp-fires and drinking sessions that really took away the beauty of the spot. The pups were almost as shocked as me.

"It is terrible why don't people clear up?"

I was inwardly delighted with their attitude and even more impressed when they spent ten minutes gathering rubbish and putting it in a pile away from the pool.

Now my actions at the jumping spot had not done much for my credibility but this is where I came into my own. The water in the pool had come directly from the mountains and was bloody freezing cold. My physique, less well-honed, than any of the pups, meant I had a far greater tolerance to the cold water. As they tip-toed into the water and almost at once retreated to the sunny spots on the rocks I was able to fully submerge and indeed remain in the water without too much discomfort. If I was to draw a parallel with mother nature the pups lounged on the sun-drenched rocks like reptiles trying to warm themselves up. I lay in the icy water like a large sea lion awaiting the arrival of fish. The pups were impressed at my endurance and some credibility at least was restored.

That evening over a delicious paella and an even more delicious bottle of Carmenere wine Maria and Juan explained plans for the coming weekend. Would we like to join them on a trip into the mountains to visit old friends? They said we were invited and that everyone in the family spoke good English so we would not be at a huge disadvantage. We had no idea what to expect but said we were delighted to tag along providing we would not be in the way.

Thus began one of the best weekends of our lives. We set off for the mountains and naturally I assumed that would mean the Andes since they did seem to be rather obvious from just about anywhere in Chile. This wasn't the case as upon reaching the town of Rancagua we turned right towards the coast and up into the hills that run almost at right angles from the Andes towards the Pacific. The car journey to Rapel took around two and a half hours at break neck speed. Andrea commented that clearly every driver in Chile fancied themselves as a Formula One star.

The single lane highways were had been constructed in an era when not everyone in Chile could afford a car and I suspect in those days driving was a rather pleasant experience. Now, in the post-military era the general level of wealth has increased and most families own cars and consequently the roads are crowded. Many of the cars are old and many of the drivers are older still. This led to the slow cars clogging the highways while the drivers in the faster cars played chicken to overtake. They did this regardless of oncoming traffic or a place to pull back into. We had thought Vivien was a fast driver but she had nothing on Juan Pablo.

We were off to meet Crystal and her husband Patricio, known friends, as Pato, who were great pals of the Maria and Juan-P. During the journey Maria explained that Crystal and Pato lived in Santiago but had the lake side retreat for summers and weekends. They described it as a quiet and slightly remote place to get away from it all. I formed an impression in my mind's eye of a cabin style structure lacking mod cons but being step back into nature.

As we got close to lake we got totally lost and but for mobile phones we would probably still be roaming around in the hills in central Chile. We saw the odd llama and some of their smaller cousins which were either alpaca or guanaco but to be honest I am not certain if they were wild or farmed. Still it was great to spot them. There were birds of prey everywhere but no more condors. The ground was dry and barren but had a rugged beauty that mountainous areas throughout the world possess. I imagine it is what attracts the hikers and the climbers, although it is all a little too much like hard work for me.

There had clearly been a bush fire in the area as much of the vegetation was charred black and the few remaining trees, had been burned to stumps or at least blackened beyond any likelihood of being able to cling to life. The extent of the fire was hard to estimate but it certainly stretched as far as the eye could see on both sides of the road. The fire, stretching as it must have done, up the hill sides must have been both impressive and terrifying. We both assumed it must have stopped naturally as it would have been impossible to contain in the semi wilderness. Fortunately, there were very few farms or settlements in the area and we witnessed no damage to buildings or the like.

Eventually, and a couple of hours late, which by the way is perfectly acceptable in Latin America, we arrived at the "cabin" and two things struck me as we got out of the car. Firstly, the fire seemed to have stopped about one yard from Pato's property as if by divine intervention. He later explained that this had indeed been the case. They had left the house to the mercy of the fire and retreated to the lake only for the fire to peter out for no apparent reason. No water had been used to douse the flames and no fire wall cut in the vegetation. It had simply gone out. Andrea being left footed, (Catholic) herself, just smiled at me and said "oh you non-believers."

Secondly the "cabin" was anything but a cabin in the woods, it was impressive to say the least.

There were two sections to the house, the first was the main living quarters, which clung to the edge of the steep hillside overlooking the lake. The house was built into the rock and was on three floors. It was not big, but it was well designed. It had three bedrooms and a kitchen diner and a remarkable well-stocked beer fridge and wine rack. Outside the living room was a balcony with a great view across the valley and the lake. There was also a flight of steep stairs leading down to a second ledge on which sat a massive barrel shaped hot-tub really similar to the one at Maria's.

The stairs carried on down to a secluded lawn with an outside table and parillada. As we opened the windows the smell of roasting meat drifted up from the parillada reminding us that it was time to eat. The meat was being prepared by the resident parillista Jesus. This rugged little man not only prepared wonderful meat but looked after house and the grounds while the family were in Santiago.

We all descended to the lawn and while finishing touches were added to the late lunch. Crystal showed Andrea and I the second part of the house. Some thirty or forty meters below the main house and right on the side of the lake there was a boat-house. The ground floor of the boat house was a workshop and general store room housing, water skis, jet skis, and everything you could possible need to keep the mechanical crafts going.

The second floor was a small dining area and a bedroom and the top floor created in the attic space was a second bedroom. This was to be home for Andrea and me for the weekend. The facia of the boat house was designed to look like a ship complete with port-hole windows and a pointed front like a prow of a ship. There was a jetty in front of the house where two speed boats were tied. It was rather like a film set in California or Florida and we loved it a first sight.

Lunch was a long drawn out affair consisting of beef steaks and chicken along with salad and crusty bread. The beer was chilled and the red wine, although not vintage, was perfectly drinkable. What's more the company was excellent. Crystal was a charming and beautiful hostess. She must have been in her sixties and had clearly been a stunning woman in her younger years. She had lost none of her charm and elegance and ruled the roost over lunch. Pato, (which means little duck), clearly an oxymoron, spoke perfect English and had a good grasp of English humour.

Two of Crystal and Pato's four sons were at lunch but ate little as they were pre occupied with getting out on the lake. The two absent sons were already on the lake on their catamaran waiting to compete in the Chilean national catamaran sailing championships. The afternoon race was due at any time and clearly the brothers wanted to get out and support their siblings. Pato was laid back and seemed certain that the lack of wind would delay the race so there was no rush until late afternoon when the wind usually picked up. His local knowledge proved correct and the winds did not pick up until lunch had finished.

We did eventually set off towards the speed boats and loaded up ready for a late afternoon session of sail boat race watching. Andrea and I could not really speak as we sped across the lake as the noise of the powerful motors drowned out conversation. I knew from looking at her that she was loving it. The speed boat flew across the lake, the afternoon sun beat down and the wind blew in our faces. I even had to turn my cap around in the fashion of the young and in these circumstances I did not look like a dick. It was almost impossible to drink our champagne as the boat bounced around, but we tried hard.

The fleet assembled and waited, re-assembled and re-waited and eventually got going. Pato's sons came third and gained enough points to add to the weekend total and place for a silver medal. The mood in our speed boat became even more buoyant. We continued at a slower pace and moored at the Lake Rapel Sailing club for evening cocktails. Money never seemed to change hands and I got the distinct impression that Pato and Crystal were pretty important people in these parts. Over a beer, and while Andrea and the ladies sipped G&T's Pato explained that he was the main race sponsor for the Chilean Catamaran series and that these races had been the culmination of a season's racing. Sadly, his two sons would not be racing in Rio as this particular class of boat was not an Olympic class. He was, however, hoping that it might be included at Tokyo in 2020.

We returned to the house for a quiet, but delicious evening meal, cooked on the fire but served indoors as mosquitoes had come out in force as evening drew in. The sunset across Lake Repel and as it did the light changed from a deep orange glow to low purples and reds. The lake looked beautiful in the fading light surrounded by mountains. As the last rays of the sun caught the dozens of crafts still afloat they appeared to dance to mystic music. Once the sun had finally gone the lake appeared as a black stone covering the landscape. Pato explained that the lake was man made. Located behind a reservoir dam on the Rapel river, it was the largest man-made lake in Chile.

The next day was spent playing about on the water, drinking and eating wonderful food. In the early morning we took the speed boat out along the full length of the lake eventually reaching the dam. We all swam but the water was to say the least a little chilly. It was as if we did not have a care in the world.

In the afternoon I tried fly-fishing and it would be fair to say that the fish of Lake Rapel had little to worry about, at least from me. I have, of course, seen so many fishing programmes on TV and the act of casting never seemed very complicated. Well, trust me it is. The idea is to flick the line across water and then reel it back in. The fly on the hook becomes irresistible to the waiting trout in the water.

No matter how hard I tried I could not get the line to fly evenly across the water so consequently it landed in a lump and any fish in the area were immediately warned that fishermen were about. The only thing that I did not do wrong was fall in after the line but I came bloody close to that on a couple of occasions. Some hundred yards or so along the bank Juan-P and Pato were having little trouble in pulling good sized fish from the water, so at least we had lunch.

As the afternoon wore on and evening approached people could be seen snoozing in all manner of places. Hammocks in the grassy area by the parillada were fully occupied and sun loungers on the balconies were a popular second choice. Andrea went for a stroll along the lake shore and sat to watch the sun go down. We knew all too well that not only our time at the Lake was coming to an end but the Chilean leg of our adventure had only days left. I thought seriously about bringing up the subject of extending our travels but it seemed pointless. Andrea was content and relaxed both because of the current situation and the fact we were within a couple of weeks or so of our flight home. I did not have the heart to ruin the moment by adding stress. I only hope that she was not sitting by the lake hoping that I would bring the subject up.

The weekend ended with hugs and handshakes as we said goodbye to our new friends, all that was left was the white-knuckle ride back to Curico. Maria took the wheel and we knew what to expect having been in a car with her big sister the week before. We arrived back at the house to find that all of the kids had friends staying. We fully expected to find carnage in the house, as you would if you had left your teenagers unsupervised for a weekend back home. Maria and Juan-P did not seem in the least concerned as we unpacked the car. They were right. It seems like youngsters in Chile can have a great time without wrecking the place or hosting boozy parties. Indeed, quite the opposite, on our return we were told to take a rest while they prepared the evening supper and got the hot tub ready for later.

It was very sad to leave Curico and the family behind but we had to move on. We caught the overnight bus to Puerto Varas from where we planned to cross the Andes into Argentina at Bariloche.

As we checked into our hotel in Puerto Varas and reconnected to wi-fi, Andrea's phone let out its by now familiar beep. I assumed as always that the noise represented one of the girls checking in or rather checking up on us to make sure we were safe. They had been brilliant and very dedicated in checking on the progress of their mummy and daddy throughout the months we had been on the road.

Andrea did whatever one has to do to receive a message on a phone, not ever having owned a phone, it remained a mystery to me, and her face visibly dropped. She slumped down onto the bed and burst into tears. My mind was working overtime, what had happened and to which of the girls!

"For god sake Andrea. What is it?"

"It's from Maria Jim. Sebastian is dead."

"Oh my God. I thought it was one of our girls."

My relief was immediately crushed by the realisation of the situation.

"How can he be…What has happened? "

"Yesterday evening after we left for the bus, he went out on his bike with a friend and was hit by a car. Maria had to give permission for the hospital to turn off the life support. Jim how will she ever get over that? I want to go home"

We sat in silence for what seemed like ages and neither of us knew how to feel, what to do or what to say to each other. We were totally numb. Sebastian was fourteen and full of life. An excellent rugby player, a handsome charming young man with his whole life in front of him. Those fucking Chilean drivers!

The day spent in Puerto Varas remains a bit of a blur. We walked down to the lake and stared at the mountains beyond. We had a coffee and cake in one of the numerous German style coffee shops that proliferate in Varas. I booked a crossing to Bariloche via the lakes route for the next morning. But mostly we were in silence and just thought about the fragility of life.

We discussed going back north to attend Sebastian's funeral but decided against this course of action. We had no reason to reach this decision but I guess we felt that we could do nothing to improve the situation and having house guests was not what Maria needed at this time. Andrea and I wrote a letter to the family expressing our deepest sympathy to Juan-P and Maria and the children knowing full well that it would serve no purpose at this time. Later when they had time to reflect we hoped that our words of praise for Santiago would provide some small grain of comfort. We were leaving Chile, a country that we both loved, with deep sadness in our hearts.

As we boarded the bus in Puerto Varas Andrea turned to me and said "I do hope we can come back here one day Jim."

My smile was the only reply, but she knew what I was thinking.

Bed 48. Beautiful Bariloche.

Our bus left Puerto Varas on time and headed towards the Andes. The first stop was Petrohue on the shores of Lake Llanquilhue. Along the route the towering peaks of Vulcan Osorno and Calbuco came into view. Despite being mid-summer both peaks were snow-capped and the volcanoes were shaped so perfectly that they actually looked like every child's depiction of a volcano in geography tectonic plate class. At times clouds drifted past the tops of the volcanoes giving the impression that the peaks were smoking in preparation for eruption.

We saw the impressive cascades in the Vincente Perez national Park. The vivid blue waters crash through gaps in the jagged rocks where the foam forms like windblown snow. These falls are not high but the force of the water creates a roar that is deafening and very impressive. Andrea took some wonderful photos of the cascades and I suspect that when we get home at least one will find its way onto a bedroom wall.

I had read an article in an old copy of the South American Handbook and giving some very sensible advice for the area around the falls. Apparently in summer the area becomes alive with very big horse flies. The article said that these same horse flies were attracted to the colour blue. It became very apparent almost as soon as we reached Petrohue that this was fact.

I had chosen not to wear anything blue just in case. Andrea knew best and had worn her normal travel clothes which were indeed blue. Well, these bloody horse flies really did bite, but they did not bite me. The only saving grace was that they seemed slow and generally sat on Andreas arms or legs for a few seconds before attacking. She manged to hit a few and flap a few away, but not all of them. She was very glad when the onward boat arrived and we could move on.

The next leg was by boat across the Lago Todos Los Santos. The reflection of the snow-capped Vulcan Osorno on the surface of the lake gave the impression there were two volcanos one reaching to heaven and the other down to who knows where. It is almost impossible to describe such beautiful views but there is no doubt this was on a par with the temples at Angkor and Sydney Harbour. How lucky we were that the sun shone.

We exited Chile at the mountain boarder post enroute to Puerto Frias and the process was remarkably fast for Latin America. A second boat trip across Lago Frias took us to Puerto Alegre where we once again boarded a bus this time to Puerto Blest. The final water leg of the journey was to cross Lago Nahuel Huapi before a bus trip into San Carlos be Bariloche. We arrived in Bariloche at around 7.30pm, after what had been a long but spectacular day. I had booked us into a hostel about 7km outside the town and by the time we reached La Luna we were totally knackered. The journey and the news of Sebastian had taken it out of us and we slept long into the next morning for the first time on the whole trip.

Bariloche reminds me of the Austrian alps, the buildings are European in design and the quaint coffee houses and cafes are very Germanic. The scenery is breathtaking, the food is so good and then there is the chocolate and oh my God there is a lot of chocolate. Both Andrea and I knew that time was beginning to run short and we still had so much to see and do. Perhaps for the first time on the trip we did not have quite as much time to stand and stare.

We decided to explore the town first and within minutes of getting off the local bus we were in an ice-cream and chocolate house. We chose Rapanui although we could have selected any number of places along Bartolome Mitre Avenue. Andrea opted for a quaintly named Incendiado. It was to all intents a small baked Alaska, with two scoops of ice cream covered in meringue and then blow torched at the table. It was enormous and only cost 55 Pesos which was about £2.50. I opted for my usual two scoops, one of vanilla and one of chocolate. We would have dearly loved to buy some chocolate but it was still 80 degrees outside and chocolate and strong sun do not go well together. We did splash out on a box of alfahores which are Argentine specialities. They are soft chocolate cookies filled with dulce de leche.

We strolled along the lake front and ended up in the main square. Like in many busy town centres there was all sorts of things going on. The human statues, jugglers, buskers and the like mixed with hordes of tourists. The square its self is impressive, surrounded by Disney-like buildings, is was easy to forget you were actually in Latin America. The paving slabs were covered with graffiti but not the usual crap. There were what appeared to be white headscarves painted on the floor. These simple designs commemorated the Madres de los Desparecidos from the dirty war of the 70's and 80's. The Madres have walked in a dignified silence outside of the government building in Buenos Aires for over forty years in the vain hope of discovering the fate of their loved ones. It was good to see that other parts of Argentina were mourning as well.

The next morning was Sebastian's funeral back in Curico and over breakfast Andrea and I talked about the young man whom we had known for such a short time but who had made such a positive impression on both of us. Andrea dug deep into her Catholic roots and said a short prayer. I had no religious beliefs to cling to and simply remembered him in my own way.

We decided a quiet walk was the most fitting way to spend the morning and we set off for Cerro Cathedral, which in winter was the heart of the Argentine ski fields. I secretly hoped we would catch one last glimpse of the mighty condors but I was out of luck. The short walk turned out to be about six miles and when we got there the ski lifts were closed and there was no way we were in any state to try and walk up the mountain. There were plenty of honourable types sporting ski poles and walking sticks intent on the climb but we were never going to join them.

We visited the small shrine known as the Virgin of the Snows. The shrine is up a flight of stairs and lies embedded in the rock face. She is believed to protect the climbers and mountain workers of the area. The Virgin is surrounded by hundreds of plaques placed by those who believe she has in some way helped them, or their families. As always I found it hard to understand why people found such solace or placed such faith in these things. On this day of all days however it seemed even more confusing. I asked Andrea how something perceived as so good and so protective could allow something so awful to happen.

Andrea chose not answer and I did not push the issue. We both had tears in our eyes as we walked back down the stairs towards the road to our hostel.

The La Luna Hostel was a really welcoming place and the people in the surrounding shops and cafes seemed delighted that English tourists had taken the trouble to find accommodation outside of the tourist honey pot that is Bariloche. There was certainly no anti-British feeling here but we both wondered if it would be the same in Buenos Aires.

We only had a couple more days in Bariloche and spent them by the lake side catching the last few summer rays. We took a boat trip out to Victoria Island where it is claimed that Disney found his inspiration for the forest scenes in Bambi. Whether this is true or not is open to debate but the trees in the forest were majestic and the calm of the forest was a lovely break from the hustle and bustle of the town.

I caught an old steam train from Bariloche to Esquel. The journey that's heaven to steam train enthusiasts. La Trochita chugged along the line for about four hours billowing out great plumes of smoke and hissing like an angry cobra. There seemed to be so many stories about his part of Argentina and at least two of them centred around Esquel. The infamous American Bandits Butch and Sundance lived peacefully around these parts so it is said. Whether true or not it was easy to see why they might have chosen such a place as a hide away.

The mountains and the lakes covered such an impressive area that just about anyone could lose themselves if they truly wanted too. The second hideaway is far more sinister and I guess anyone who lived through the WWii would desperately hope that the tales were untrue. There seems to be some evidence to suggest that Adolph Hitler did not die in the bunker in Berlin, but instead, fled Europe for Argentina and lived out his life in Esquel. I cannot say that my day trip made me any more convinced that this was the case but people in these parts certainly believe it. There are allegedly some still alive who remember him well but I guess we may never know.

By the time it came for us to leave we were well rested and ready to move on. We had both liked Bariloche but felt that it had seen better days. The battle for the tourist dollar had almost taken over to the extent that the true beauty of the place was in danger of being lost. We both suspected that in winter under a coating of snow the charm would return but for the time being at least that would have to remain in our imagination.

We caught a morning flight to the city airport in Buenos Aires known as Jorge Newbery. Landing at this particular airport is a memorable event. Planes approach over the city centre and building seem close enough to touch. I even saw the River Plate Stadium which hosted the world cup final in 1978.

We hung around in the airport for an hour or so before flying to Puerto Iguacu. We were so excited by the prospect of visiting the Cataratas de Iguacu probably the most spectacular waterfalls on the planet.

Bed 49 Cataratas de Iguacu.

We had pre booked another hostel having had such a good experience in La Luna. This one was called Bambu Mini and it turned out to be another pretty good choice. We did not anticipate spending a huge amount of time in the hostel as we really were on a whistle stop tour and we wanted to see the falls from both the Argentine and Brazilian sides. Our private double room was however clean and comfy if a little basic. We ate in on the first evening as we were tired after a full day's travel and the noodle dish which came highly recommended by another guest did not disappoint. It was also a change from the steak diet that we had been on in Bariloche.

We decided to see the Argentinian side of the falls first and caught the bus from the nearby station. We could have booked a full day tour but by now we were far too experienced to waste money and had total confidence in our ability to sort the day out without help.

Once we reached the national park and the falls, it became abundantly clear why, way back in 1542, the Spanish explorer Alvez Nunez had found them. The noise from the falls was deafening. He must have heard the thunder from miles away.

Both Andrea and I had watched the film The Mission so we had at least a picture of what to expect, but the noise simply blew us away. We decided to catch the little train out towards the main fall. The Devils Throat or La Garganta del Diablo. As the tiny train wound through the jungle the roar and the expectation grew exponentially. By the time we clamoured down from our seats we could hardly hear each other speak.

We walked along the boardwalk towards the roar and as the jungle parted so the falls came into view. At la

Garganta the Parana river and the Iguacu River plunge down a narrow chasm into the depths bellow. It is as if a giant mythological creature is swallowing the rivers.

The spray rises into the air and soaks everything. The observation platform is directly on top of the cascade and seems so flimsy in the face of such power. The whole experience was difficult to take in. All around were fascinating things to see and experience. The jungle, the wild life, boat trips but whatever else we did, it was the power of this waterfall that dominated our thoughts

There are two paths on the Argentine side of the falls and both gave great but differing views of the natural wonder. There are around 350 separate falls at Iguacu, and together they are majestic. As a loud American tourist said

"This place makes Niagara look like a kid taking a piss over a wall"

Quaint and colourful description but he may well have hit the nail directly on the head.

The crowning glory of the falls comes in the myriad of rainbows that form in the spray. To see these arching between the trees of the jungle and diving down into the mighty rivers is simply beautiful.

The natural beauty of Iguacu does not stop with the falls themselves. There are so many creatures to see if you just keep your eyes open. We did not see the illusive jaguar although they are in the national park but we saw plenty of great stuff including caiman crocodiles sunbathing in shallow rock pools.

In all we saw five and although they were not as big as the ones we had seen back in Australia Zoo they were still impressive beasts.

The birding was excellent. I saw colourful red and yellow caciques, plush crested jays and the masters of the air the great dusky swifts which flew through the falls to nest in safety behind the torrents of water. The highlight came later in the day while we were walking along the forest path. I saw the bill first followed by the birds. a pair of toco toucans nesting in a hole in a tree. The female could not be seen just her brightly coloured bill protruding from the trunk of the tree but the male sat on a branch in full view. He was a deep black, blue with a white bib and this insane bright yellow beak.

Memories of the Guinness advert from years ago came back to me but seeing it for real was a million times better. The bird sat still as if posing and I was even able to see it's purple eye ring. When it did fly away it was so much bigger than I had imagined and rather clumsy but with a bill that size flying could not have been especially straightforward.

As we approached the café by the station we were met by a large green iguana that looked almost as prehistoric as the caiman, and then by any number of coatimundi. These inquisitive and forever hungry mammals look like racoons and are so used to tourists that they have lost all of their natural wariness. After Andreas experience with the biting moneys back in Ubud she was not at all keen to allow them to come too close. The coatis, however, were not aware of the biting incident and seemed naturally drawn to her. I tried hard to keep Andrea calm but my efforts failed

"If one of these little fuckers tries to climb up my leg I will scream so bloody loud."

I tipped my pack of biscuits onto the grass and made a quick escape while the coatis fought over the last of my Ritz crackers.

Day two at the falls was to be a combination of a quick trip into Brazil to see what that side of the river had to offer and then an afternoon in Paraguay at Cuidad del Este. Neither of us expected too much from this border town but would result in another stamp in our passports and another country visited. We got back to the Bambu Mini in time to make plans and then set out to find a local churrascuria. We did feel I little guilty as most of the hostel residents were living far more frugally but we weren't guilty enough not to go.

We ended up at the Churrascuria el Gaucho and what a feast we had. The system was simple. We were given a round disc which was red on one side and green on the other. Waiters walked around the restaurant carrying swords laden with various meats. When a green disc showed meat was sliced onto our plates. I tried to eat my body weight in meat and failed, but only just.

We caught the local bus to the Brazilian border and after the usual red tape, crossed into Brazil and caught a second bus to the falls. It seemed that the main difference between the two sides was the type of view you got. From Brazil the whole panorama of the falls was visible where as in Argentina we tended to see only parts of the falls. In Brazil we were able to walk under the falls along drenched walkways. Andrea and I stood in amazement and looked across falls, it seemed as if it was the entrance to Dante's inferno. We had never seen anything like it before. The water seemed to boil as it crashed into the rocks below and spray rose like steam. Rainbows appeared and arched across the water as if drawn by some heavenly artist. This place is amazing and I felt as if I just wanted to sit and stare at it for ever.

"What must it have been like for the Spaniards when they first came across this place?" Andrea asked.

"I've got no idea, but if they were floated over the falls on crosses, like in the film The Mission they certainly got a front seat view."

We decided not to ride the jet boats because of the cost and we had already experienced the thrill ride in New Zealand. Mind you, we stood close by for near thirty minutes discussing whether we should or not. Despite being away together for so long we were not much better at making decisions than we had been the day we left the UK. In the end it was me who decided.

"Bugger this Andrea I am not standing here all day trying to decide. Let's go."

"Jim maybe we should. After all we will never be here again."

"That's what I said half an hour ago when you said it cost too much."

In a little huff I set off back up the path for one last panoramic view of one of nature's truly great creations.

We caught another local bus to the Friendship Bridge and walked across into Paraguay. It seems so odd thinking back, "Yeh we just walked across the bridge from Brazil into Paraguay." Two pensioners don't do this sort of stuff, but here we were. We had become very independent and our basic fears of travelling were long behind us. But we of course still took very sensible precautions every day.

We checked to make certain that our valuables were locked in our hotel or room safe. We took as little as possible with us for the day and what we did take was not ostentatiously on show. While taking photos I watched carefully to make sure no grab and run thieves were approaching Andrea. We also kept our cash in money belts and made certain we understood the exchange rates before buying anything.

The stories we had read about the Friendship Bridge suggested that it had probably been very inappropriately named but on a bright sunny afternoon it didn't seem so bad. There we people carrying what appeared to be all of their worldly possessions crossing in both directions. Others were selling snacks and soft drinks or handing out business cards for restaurants, shops and hostels. Andrea and I were so tanned and we spoke enough Spanish to avoid looking like American tourists and so we were ignored by almost everyone. It did appear that Americans were their own worst enemies. Speaking in loud voices, dressing to kill and carrying cameras as large as their arms whilst wearing gold watches and neck chains. They might as well have had a sign around their necks saying "I'm rich rob me!"

We were disappointed to find that we could easily slip into Paraguay without getting our passports stamped but we opted to join the queue and officially enter the country. The boarder guard was not keen to waste ink when he discovered we were only popping in to visit. Andrea laid on the charm and in the end he gave us both a stamp making it 14 and counting for the trip. Actually, it was more than 14 but I was not counting any one country more than once. We had been to Singapore at least three time to get connecting flights and each time we had had to clear customs.

Well we had not been in Cuidad del Este too long before we realised it was not a great place. The city was previously named Puerto Stroessner after the man who was Paraguay's military leader until 1989. It is a modern city with a slightly wild west feel to it. You can buy literally anything here and most of the sellers seem to be of Asian origin. It was hectic and felt like a border town. Andrea and I enjoyed the buzz but were a little intimidated at least for the first hour or so.

We were even more out of our comfort zone when we sat in a café for a bit of lunch and the guy next to us was eating guinea pig or hamster or rat or something. It would not have been so bad but the poor critter still had a head and we could see its big front teeth smiling at us from the plate. It certainly made our empanada's look a little tame.

As the afternoon wore on and the continued pressure to buy a fake Rolex or Cartier watch or Chanel perfume became too great we set off back to the Bambu. I had read that it was possible to get across the Parana River on a local ferry so that's what we did. A taxi ride took us to the river at the Three Frontiers and after a short wait we boarded what looked like a large wooden raft. The raft was attached to a rope that stretched across the river. I think we both felt a little like Indiana Jones.

All of our fellow travellers were local and all were carrying what we assumed to be contraband. A scrawny little man with only one tooth tried to sell us what we thought were drugs but when he saw the shock on our faces he explained that it was Mate, a local herbal drink. We had heard of this and a smile broke the ice. He told us that few foreigners crossed this way, but it was cheap and a nice part of the adventure. We arrived back at the Bambu unscathed but exhausted.

Bed 50. Reminiscing in Montevideo.

Our flight back to England was getting ever closer so on our return to Buenos Aires we immediately booked a crossing on the Buquebus to Montevideo. The journey across the River Plate was fast but the bus journey down to Montevideo took around two and a half hours. We were so excited to be back in Uruguay and about seeing the places and people we had grown so fond of back in the 1980's. Would the city have changed? Would we still be able to find our way around? Would we see any old faces? Well we were soon to find out.

I had booked us into a hotel in Pocitos one of the areas of the city that nestles close to the river. The river is so wide at this point that to it looks like you are by the sea. The only difference is that only the most biased Montevidian would say the water looks inviting. We had lived in an apartment in Pocitos whilst living in Montevideo so it seemed appropriate that we stayed in the same area. The Palladium Business Hotel was modern and lacked a homely feel but it was perfect for what we needed. It served an excellent breakfast had comfortable beds and a lovely roof-top pool. It was also within easy walking distance of lots of the things we wanted to see.

It was late when we arrived at the hotel and after a quick chivito in a local bar we hit the sack. A chivito is a pimped up burger and far more delicious. The bun is the same more or less but that is about where it stops. A good chivito will have a small steak and as many different accompaniments as you wish to order. I went for cheese, salad and a fried egg, while Andrea had avocado and the obligatory egg. Locals say if the yolk of the egg drips down your chin it's a good chivito. Well mine ended up on the table, my shirt and my shorts, so it must have been excellent.

Our first full day in Montevideo for nearly thirty years was a magnificent trip down memory lane. We walked. Oh my God, did we walk. Andrea, as always, had her phone app on and at the end of the day it turned out we had tramped over fifteen kilometres around the city. On the face of it this sounds hideous but when I break the day down into lunch, snacks, beer and supper it turns out we actually took three or four shortish strolls. I much prefer to look at it this way.

We set off along the beach road more commonly known as the Rambla. With the sun shining the River Plate was almost blue. It didn't get close enough to check for floating poo but my guess is it would still not have qualified for a British Blue flag, these are only awarded to beaches that reach the highest standard of cleanliness. New apartment blocks lined the beach, and replaced the old buildings we remembered. They were all modern constructions with loads of glass. They reflected the sun and gave the beach an even more welcoming appearance.

Even at 9pm the beach was busy with sun seekers. They did not seem to be as obsessed as the Australians with finding shade I suspect that warnings about skin cancer are less thorough here. Older folk arrived at the beach with tiny little fold-up chairs that were no bigger than our primary school chairs. With great care they set them in exactly the correct position to get as much sun as possible. There were games of beach volleyball going on all along the beach which had always been the case but the addition of a purpose built beach soccer arena with fixtures scheduled for most of the day was new.

We reached Calle Manuel Pagola, the street where we had lived, and decided to pay a visit to our old block number 2136. It was still there, as was the small store a few doors away, that sold just about everything. The buildings that had been on either side had been knocked down and replaced by new blocks and we both felt pangs of nostalgia as we stood in the street looking up at the balcony of our 6th floor apartment. This, after all, had been the flat where India was conceived and where we had first brought her home after her birth in the British Hospital. It was where she had slept in a drawer during her first few weeks of life and where most evenings I had walked up and down in balmy November air trying unsuccessfully to get her to sleep. It was nice remembering these days especially as she was now all grown up and living half a world away.

We walked on pavements that clearly had not been repaired much since the late 1980's. It was remarkable that we survived without breaking an ankle or disappearing in a knee deep into a hole. For some reason most of the pavements in Montevideo are tree-lined. This looks lovely and gives the city a calm almost colonial air but it leads to the pavements becoming very uneven. The tree roots push up through the pavements and create humps, hollows and holes.

Many pedestrians have tripped, stubbed their flip-flop shod toes or stumbled like a Glasgow drunk on a Saturday night as a result of Montevideo pavements. I was no exception and made at least three attempts to dive nose first onto the floor, twice saving myself by hanging onto Andrea and once by hanging onto a rather shocked lady coming home with her shopping.

We watched the changing of the guard in Plaza Independencia and walked around the tomb of General Artigas. His tomb in the centre of the Plaza is impressive, South Americans have made honouring their heroes into an art form, and the cool of the underground memorial made a pleasant break from walking in the scorching sun.

From here we ventured into the Old Town with it street stalls, artists and knick-knack shops. The Cuidad Vieja is bohemian, the architecture is colonial and the shop fronts would not look out of place in the older parts of London or Paris. Men in sharp suits and ladies dressing like twenty-five year olds with the faces of sixty-yea-olds stroll casually around plazas and pedestrian streets. The dress sense of wealthy Uruguayans, although perhaps a little out of time, is classy. We sat on a bench and watched as if we were at 1970's catwalk show. Leather trousers, slick backed hair, fur coats in summer, linen jackets thrown over shoulders, long cigarette holders, peroxide blonde hair. We could have been on a set for the Godfather.

People watching, however, was not our ultimate aim. We were heading for the Port Market and as we approached we were drawn at ever increasing speed by the smell of beef roasting on open fires. By the time we reached the market, housed in an old railway station building, I was salivating like one of Pavlov's canine friends.

The Mercado del Puerto is the place to have lunch in Montevideo if you are visiting and fancy a great steak. We fitted into both categories and so felt totally justified in being there. There does seem to be one or two stories about the original purpose of the building. Some say it was built to house a market to sell goods brought from the sea. Others that it was made from materials destined for Bolivia where it was indeed due to be a railway station, but when payment was not forthcoming the British simply erected the structure in Montevideo instead.

My favourite story is that it was built as a railway station to distribute goods across Uruguay after they had been unloaded from the trading ships. The owner of the railway and the station owner fell out so the railway line missed the station, leaving the city with a majestic railway building and no trains.

Andrea and I didn't care too much which story was true we just wanted to eat meat. We marched past the jugglers, singers, human statues and the like performing outside the building. We didn't even pause at the stalls selling artworks, souvenirs, ceramic penguins and stuffed llamas. We positively dashed past the mime artists who fleetingly reminded me of the Old Time Music Hall programmes I saw on TV at home when I was a kid. We were there and what a sight greeted us.

The massive building with its high steel and iron ceiling had changed little in thirty years. There was still Roldo's medio-medio stand selling a drink that had no real place at lunchtime. It was far too drinkable and far too dangerous, a mix of white wine and fizz that slipped down like fizzy pop and left you almost unable to walk after a few glasses.

There was still a selection of eateries each with a glowing parillada laden with different cuts of meat, sizzling chorizos, chickens and strange bits of animals that didn't really look like anything we would eat at home. Each of the individual food places had a central cooking fire with at least one parillista working skilfully away. The cuts of meat were moved onto the lower parts of the sloping metal cooking trays if they needed a fierce heat or towards the top of the slope if they were just being warmed. The smells were amazing and it took all of our will power not to sit down at the first stand and order immediately.

Eventually we decided to eat at the Estancia Del Puerto and whether we got our choice right or not is irrelevant as the meat was delicious. Andrea chose a cut called baby beef, and this clearly did not refer to its size, I went for my old favourite filet de lomo. Both steaks were sizeable and cost less than equivalent of £12. They were served with chips and we ordered a bottle of medio-medio from Roldo's.

It is common sense to say that flying to Uruguay or Argentina just to east steak would be eccentric in the extreme. I do believe that at some time in your life if you have the time and the money it is something that everyone should do. I don't know if its happy cows, the wood they use on the fire, the skill of the parillistas or the way the meat is hung but oh the end result is simply wonderful. The Port Market is probably a place that is best avoided by vegetarians, and a translation of the menu is best avoided by fussy eaters. We did not order any of the local delicacies but noted that on most menus you could find choto, which is bull's penis, mollejas or sweet breads and chinchulines made from the small intestines. A local joke is that choto, when left alone will feed one, but when rubbed will feed a family of four.

Most of the rest of our time in Montevideo was spent quite unashamedly reminiscing and visiting old haunts. Actually, there is not a great deal to do in the city. Quiet, safe and slow paced place it makes for easy living and a gentle life. Many of the old things that we remembered had gone. There were no trams plying their trade around the city centre. The rails on which they used to run were still in place in many areas but the rattling trams had been consigned to history. Lots of the corner restaurants and cafes seemed to have given way to apartment blocks or small shops. These eateries had given Montevideo a culturally distinct feel and we really missed them. Worse than that was the fact that McDonalds seemed to have invaded the city. I hate this American fast food giant and have not eaten in one for over thirty years and I was certainly not going to start now.

All of this meant that Montevideo was growing up. The sleepy backwater of the 1980s had grown into a vibrant and modern city. It was a leader in South American business life and capitol of the Mercosur trade area. New buildings were springing up everywhere replacing the colonial houses of a bygone era.

One thing had not changed and that was the fact that almost everyone still wandered around carrying a thermos flask and a small ornate cup in to which was stuck a metal straw. No matter where you went in the city the tradition of drinking maté was alive and kicking. The younger generation who chose a McDonalds burger over a chivito or a Mcflurry over a gelato still drank maté. We had tried drinking it but it is quite simply disgusting or to put it politely it was not to our taste. The small gourd or drinking cup is filled with yerba mate, a bitter caffeine rich herb soaked in water from the thermos flask. A straw or bombilla is inserted into the mixture and it is sucked up.

The drinking of maté in moving vehicles is banned as several people have lost their lives when an emergency stop or small shunt has caused the bombilla to be driven through the roof of their mouths into the brains. In parks, offices, shops and just about everywhere else it's not banned and everyone does it. It is a social drink and couples can often be seen sharing a cup, as can families. Caring parents even pile sugar into the herbal mixture to encourage the next generation to take up the habit.

Andrea and I visited the Hospital Britanico where India was born and it too was barely recognisable. The old buildings had been replaced by a modern sterile hospital that bore no resemblance to the majestic gothic building where our first born had entered the world. The façade had been retained so we could at least take the obligatory photo of something that we did remember.

On our last day we took the D1 bus from Pocitos to the suburb of Carrasco to see the British School. I had been based there as the director of sport and rugby coach and had some wonderful memories of the place. We walked up Avenue Arocena, past the Montevideo Lawn Tennis Club and on to the school. So much of Montevideo owed a debt to us British. The tennis club would not have gone amiss anywhere in middle England especially as most of the cars in the car park were BMW's or Mercedes. We eventually reached the school and from the outside it looked the same. Once we got inside it was very clear that it had kept pace with the times and was now a well-equipped modern school.

Incredibly the secretary in reception recognised us immediately and welcomed us back. Only one teacher remained form our time at the school and fortunately he was available to show us around. Andrew a somewhat dour Scot, had married a local girl and never left. Indeed, he was now on his second local wife but seemed happy and content with his lot. His only real bother was the lack of a suitable pension plan and the knowledge that he would have to remain at the chalk face for the foreseeable future.

We saw the new theatre, and the excellent sports hall and listened to tales of the comings and goings of ex pat staff over the intervening years. Andrew was an excellent host and the time spent with him was a delight. He also knew that the old boy's rugby team was playing at home the following day and as I had coached them for a couple of years Andrea knew at once that tomorrows itinerary would include an afternoon on the side of a rugby pitch.

Actually the rugby turned out perfect for both of us. When we arrived at the Old Boys Club we were welcomed like long lost friends. Word had spread that we were back in town.

We had a lovely lunch courtesy of the Club and the sun shone throughout the match. I met so many of my former charges all of whom had retired from playing but had maintained a real interest in the sport and in the Old Boys in particular. Three or four of the lads had left school and gone on to represent Uruguay in internationals and indeed Rugby World Cups. Juan Carlos Bado and Alfonso Cardoso were both at the game and it was great to hear how fondly they remembered school rugby and how well they had done on the international stage. The Old Boys won, which of course made the afternoon even better, and the bar area was buzzing when Andrea and I slipped away in the early evening. As we left the clubhouse we heard a shout of "Sir", still an odd experience when shouted by a forty-year-old.

"You cannot catch a bus home. Let me drive you." Felipe bounced out into the car park and insisted on driving us back to our Hotel. As we drove he proudly told his young son that I had been his rugby coach and Andrea his English teacher. We returned the favour by saying what a good player (totally true) and what a hard-working student (totally untrue) his father had been.

Leaving Montevideo was hard and we both would have loved to spend another week or so catching up with friends. Conversation about the changes to the city filled much of our remaining time and although neither of us particularly like the modernisation we were delighted that Uruguay was keeping pace with a changing continent. So many people in the UK form an opinion about Uruguay based on football and footballer's behaviour. Sadly, this generally leads to a negative opinion. Well we loved the place in the 1980's and we still loved it now.

Bed 51. Don't cry for me.

The last leg of our trip around the world was spent in the capitol of Argentine. We retraced our outward journey by Buquebus and arrived in Buenos Aires mid-afternoon. I had booked a city centre apartment for the last week and after avoiding the rip-off taxi drivers at the port we caught a street taxi from half a block away and saved about £15. It was on occasions like this that I was so glad I had brushed up on my Spanish before leaving the UK.

Our apartment was almost perfect. It was very central, one block from the main drag of Buenos Aires, a strangely named street, the 9th of July. It was close to the shopping and entertainment streets, but also far enough away to be quiet at night. Breakfast was served each morning by room service despite the fact that the room had a fully functioning kitchen. We had a small balcony from where we could watch the city go by and more importantly watch the three tortoises that lived on a balcony opposite go about their daily if somewhat slow routines. On the roof there was a small pool that was so welcome as temperatures never dropped below the mid-eighties. All in all, an ideal place to spend our final few days in South America.

I had promised Andrea that when we finally ended up in Buenos Aires she could buy some more bulky items as we would no longer have to haul them around the world. After all we were now only one flight from home. She had done her homework and knew where we had to go, what she wanted to buy and how much she was prepared to pay for it. Top of her wish list was a leather flying jacket which according to Andrea were less than half the price of one in London and almost certainly better quality. I was in no position to disagree, not being hugely well informed about ladies' fashions or clothes in general.

Shopping however was not the most pressing matter on our mind and day one in Buenos Aires was spent sorting things out at home. Luckily the time difference worked in our favour and we could start contacting people early the morning in the UK which was three hours ahead of Argentina.

We had already given our tenants notice to quit and a quick e-mail to the letting agents confirmed that this process had gone ahead without problems. The Weald Letting Agents did say that they had had to employ a firm of high quality cleaners to return our house to its former glory. Thank goodness this was at the expense of the tenants not us. Andrea immediately panicked on receiving this news where as I assumed that letting agents would see that everything was OK.

Andrea made appointments to meet any number of trades persons during our first week back home. She had decided that we wouldn't move directly into the house rather we would use a couple of weeks to get it just so. I was tasked with finding somewhere to stay on our return. Luckily one of my teaching mates was spending a couple of weeks in France with his family and was happy to have us house and pet sit.

So over the course of the day Angela exchanged e-mails with, carpet fitters, decorators, roofers, kitchen fitters, and the removal company. By mid-afternoon I was exhausted from just being with her, so goodness knows how she felt. At my suggestion we wandered out to have a té completa (tea complete) a wonderful Buenos Aires tradition. We found a traditional tea-house very close to our apartment. It reminded me of the Lyons Corner house that I had visited many years ago with my mum and dad on a trip to London. It had high vaulted ceilings with hanging lights, the wall paper was heavy and a little dark still bearing the nicotine stains from the era when smoking was not only permitted but was all the rage. The tables were polished wood and the chairs high backed and regal, no cheap plastic in there.

Our waiter was called Diego and he looked resplendent in his highly polished shoes black trousers and white shirt. The shirt was partly obscured by a smart red waistcoat. Diego's hair was slicked back in typical Latin fashion. He could easily have passed for a Hollywood extra or perhaps a member of the Mafia. Diego was probably in his mid-thirties and clearly felt privileged to work in the Teahouse. He took great pride in what he did and although he spoke little English he tried very hard to use the few words he did know and was very complimentary about our attempts at speaking Spanish.

We ordered a té completa each and when they arrived immediately wished we had ordered one between us. We were each served a three tier cake stand. On the top tier were dainty little one-bite morsels, each with dulce de leche as a major component. We thought of Sophie, our youngest, who despite being in her twenties still had her childhood sweet tooth. The second tier had finger sandwiches, and mini croissants with cheese and ham. While the lower tier was laden toasted sandwiches, small slices of pizza and a slice of pascualina which is a local spinach pie with hard boiled eggs in the mix. This beautifully presented feast was more than ample but more was to come. We also received a wooden platter of cold meats and cheeses along with olives and green leaves. This came with bread and crackers.

Andrea and I made a real effort to plough through the lot but came up a long way short. I asked Diego if we could take the rest in a "doggy bag." When he returned to the table the food had been painstaking placed into a plastic container in such a fashion that it actually looked like a sort of foody gift box.

As we strolled back to the apartment in the warm evening air I said to Andrea that since we didn't have a fridge in the room and all of the food was perishable we were faced with prospect of a second helping later in the evening. We both instinctively knew this was not an option. Andrea suggested giving the food to a young vagrant we had seen sitting on a bench outside the Theatro Colon.

It was a great idea and we set off to see if the young man was still around. He had not moved and from a distance we could see that he was curled up on the bench half asleep, half-awake. Waiting for goodness knows what. As we approached he saw us and sat up clearly assuming that our purposeful walk meant that he was to be moved on or subject to ridicule or harsh words. We smiled and offered him our bounty. I tried explaining that it was fresh and simply too much for us to eat. He cut in in good English and thanked us profusely. He embarrassingly held out a grubby hand for me to shake and then retracted it when he saw how dirty it was. We held out our hands, ignoring the dirt, and he shook them with gusto. As we walked away he said

"I though the English hated Argentines?"

"Not all of us," I replied "We leave that to the politicians. Good luck my friend."

We waved and wandered off home. It is a cliché, but sometimes simple acts of kindness make the giver feel almost better than the receiver, and we felt that this could have been one of those occasions.

We still had a lot to cram into the week so despite the temperatures remaining in the high eighties our time by the roof top pool was limited to a couple of hours in the morning and then an hour or so in the late afternoon. The rest of the time was spent in earnest endeavour.

The next task was to find and capture a flying jacket for Andrea. The quality of leather goods in Buenos Aires is excellent and the prices are generally below half of what one could pay at home. I have no idea if either of these statements is true but it was on that premise that Andrea sold the shopping trip to me. She also insisted that it would not be a quick process and therefore the morning relax by the pool would have to be forgone for one day.

We set off to the main shopping area, the streets of Lavalle and Florida. These streets, although not as plush as our own Oxford or Bond Streets are certainly vibrant and act as the magnetic centre of the city.

As a man who hates shopping, I have never been able to quite fathom how a woman's shopping mind works. If I want a pair of shoes I go to a shoe shop, find a pair that fits, and buy them. If I actually like them that is a real bonus. The whole operation usually takes me less than an hour and that includes parking the car and a coffee in Café Nero. Women in general, and Andrea in particular seem to get as much of a thrill from hunting down their prey as they do from actually purchasing it. Then after purchasing something, Andrea usually brow beats herself for hours as to whether it was the correct choice.

The first leather store, Pacifico Cueros, was at the top of Lavalle where it joined the 9th of July. This was only a couple of hundred yards from where we were staying. I got a warm feeling inside. Maybe, just maybe this wouldn't be as bad as I feared. There were more styles, sizes and colours of jackets, coats and bags than I had ever seen in one place. There were also three flying jackets that immediately caught Andrea's eye. One seemed to fulfil every requirement she desired. It was well made, it fitted and she really liked it. I perked up from my chair in the corner of the store and I even got my wallet out. It was to cost £200 or £180 if we paid in cash. No problems I had the cash in my money belt, it was still only 9.30am and the deal was done.

Andrea turned to the shop assistant and said "That's lovely. Can you put it aside for me until this afternoon as are just going to have a look around?"

Her words were like a dagger to my heart. Clearly it was not sufficient to find the perfect article, now we had to wander the streets of Buenos Aires looking at every other flying jacket simply to confirm that there were no other even more perfect ones.

So the sojourn began, with us looking at least half a dozen more stores in Lavalle and another half dozen more in Florida. Just when I thought it could get no worse, the last shopkeeper in Florida suggested we try our luck in a couple of other streets. It was early afternoon when Andrea decided to call off the search and do a bit of sightseeing. Her explanation was clear to her but made no sense to me.

"I need time to decide and then we can buy the first jacket later today"

I replied

"Since we have to walk back across Lavalle to get to the Casa Rosada we could buy it now, drop it off at the apartment and stop bloody well thinking about it."

Andrea said she needed time to think about it and with this she set of towards the Casa Rosada. Not at quite her shopping walk pace but nonetheless it was still a good lick. The matter seemed, for the time being at least, closed.

We walked the relatively short distance to the Plaza de Maya to see the Casa Rosada. It is not a great building. In fact, to me it looked like a large pink mansion rather than a grand seat of governance. We stood outside, under the glare of fierce looking soldiers, and looked up to the balcony where Eva Peron had addressed the people back in 1951. I could not get the image of Madonna standing on the balcony out of my mind and "don't cry for me Argentina" was playing in my head, but I had read enough to understand what Evita had meant to her people. She had been a heroine to the poor and was still held in high esteem by the workers of Argentina.

We walked across the Plaza somewhat sheepishly as around the edge there were posters and placards relating to the Falklands conflict. We had no guilt to bear for this event but as Brits in Argentina we thought it better to avoid any unnecessary unpleasantness. The veterans of the Malvinas War, as it is known in these parts, were protesting about something but we were not entirely sure what.

There were no Mothers of the disappeared marching around the Plaza as it was not a Thursday. Their long and silent vigil which began back in the early 1980's still continues today but only once a week. These women march to remember the 30,000 who arrested, tortured and ultimately murdered during the "dirty war" between 1976 and 1983.

I recalled an evening I had spent in the River Plate stadium back in 1988 watching Sting perform. He had dimmed the lights in the stadium and sung "They dance alone" while the mothers had walked around the stage, and the crowd in their thousands held lighters up to the sky. It was as if each light represented one of their missing loved ones. At the time, it was the most moving thing I had ever witnessed.

From the Plaza de Mayo we ventured across the city heading for the heart of the argentine Tango, in the Plaza Dorrego in San Telmo. This small district is only a few blocks from Plaza de Mayo but a million miles away in atmosphere. No political protests, no memories of the Falklands or the Peronists just slinky men and women dancing the tango. As the lunch rush was over, we managed to get seats at a table on the main square. We ordered our customary beers and a couple of local snacks and sat down to watch.

The male dancer was not young but my goodness he was sharp. Dressed in a light blue suit with a trilby style hat perched on his head, he was not what I imagined a tango dancer to look like. Somehow I thought of a slim Dracula type dressed in black with slicked back hair. His partner was considerably younger and looked as if she lived on cigarettes and gin. She wore a bright red figure hugging dress with a slit up the side that almost reached her arm pits. Her elegant legs showed clearly as she snaked around her partner's body to the evocative tango beat. Across the Plaza a second couple strutted their stuff, clinging to each to her as if expecting some imminent disaster to strike.

We sat for the best part of an hour and watched the dancers perform. We sipped our Quilmes beer and nibbled at the complimentary bowl of unshelled peanuts. By the time we set off back to our apartment it was early evening and we were thoroughly beginning to flag. It took a good forty-five minutes to walk back. As I collapsed on the bed and debated with myself whether I would have the energy to go out and eat later I heard a very quiet request emanating from the other side of the room.

"Do you think we could pop out and buy the flying jacket? Andrea said. "It's just if we leave it until tomorrow they might have sold it. I do love it will be heartbroken if it's gone."

I pretended to be asleep in the hope that Andrea might be afraid to awaken me after such a long day. No such bloody luck!

"Jim did you hear me. Can we go back and buy the jacket?"

It was pointless to resist, so off we trudged once again, back to Lavalle. As we neared Pacifico Cueros the tension mounted, and Andrea's scatter gun questioning began in earnest.

"What if they have sold it?"

"That would serve you right!"

"What if I don't like it anymore?"

"Why the bloody hell would your tastes have changed just because we have been on a walk all bloody day"

"Have you got the cash?"

"Yes of course. You don't think I want to walk back again do you?"

"What if they have shut?"

"They don't shut. It's the capitol city they are open all hours."

Not only was I physically exhausted when we reached the store, but my mind was whirling like a dervish. Thank goodness the shop was open, they still had the jacket, Andrea did still like it and I paid for it. She is now the very proud owner of a magnificent flying jacket, even though it's far too hot to wear it in an Argentine summer.

Buenos Aires is laid out like an American city, on a grid system so finding our way around was straightforward. Having seen the balcony where Eva Peron gave her famous address it seemed fitting that we should visit Recoleta and see her final resting place. Andrea and I had absolutely no idea if her politics were sound or indeed if her husbands were sound but the haunting music of the Lloyd Webber-Tim Rice musical had imprinted the memory of Evita in the hearts of our generation.

We walked to the district of Recoleta and found the cemetery without too much trouble. To be fair, you would need to be pretty ignorant not to find it, plus everyone in the area knows where it is so directions are easy to solicit. Once inside finding the actual tomb was a little more difficult even though there was a good map available.

Even in death Eva Peron had not been able to rest in peace as her embalmed corpse was stolen in 1955, by the military, and removed from the country. Eventually the Vatican became involved and her body was buried in a cemetery in Milan under a false name. Her body was not returned to Buenos Aires until 1976 when it was finally laid to rest in the family tomb in the cemetery in Recoleta. It is said her body now lays under a meter of concrete to make it impossible for it to be easily removed from the city a second time.

The black tomb is also home to members of the Duarte family. Several plaques on the tomb show images of Evita and words of love. The day Andrea and I visited, two elderly women dressed in black from head to foot, sat by the tomb, with tears streaming down their cheeks. They placed flowers, prayed and then moved away. Eva Peron is still held in great esteem by many. Tourists, like ourselves, simply want photos and to be able to claim they've visited the tomb. Yet no-one on this day, spoke in a loud voice or joked. Even the Chinese took solemn photos without making the usual V sign. There was a sombre feeling of remembrance even though few of us really remembered.

Our next stop was the Parillada Pena a local restaurant mentioned in almost every food guide book to the city. The general opinion was that it was a haunt for locals and the staff didn't speak English. It came so highly recommended that we simply could not miss it.

It turned out to be a relatively small restaurant with pretty basic décor. It reminded me more of a transport café rather than a city central eating place. The place was almost full with a mix of businessmen, fathers and sons and blue collar workers. Andrea was the only woman in the place. Our waiter Alverez appeared to be rather surly, but turned out to be a diamond.

"Queramos dos filet de lomo per favour."
"No nesicitan dos, unico es suficiente."

Alvarez more or less told us what to order. We didn't need two steaks rather one would be enough. He said the chips were good but the steak was better with mashed potato. He brought us a half bottle of local Malbec to accompany meal and we just sat back and waited.

The steak arrived with the mash and two fried eggs. I was already a fan. I am happy to record in print that the meat was among the best I have ever eaten in my life. It was tender, juicy and the char on the outside gave it a taste to die for. Alvarez could see from my face that I was really enjoying it.

"Ees good no!" he said.
"Ees excellente gracias." I replied.

What a magnificent lunch.

New York has Central Park and London has Hyde Park these oases in the city centre give wildlife and people a chance to escape the furious pace of the cities. In Buenos Aires there is an equally important oasis down near the port. The Constanera Sur Nature Reserve provides a safe haven for birds, mammals and Portenos (local people). At pretty much any time of the day people can be found, jogging, cycling and strolling around the lakes in the reserve. I went there for one last birding session before returning home. I had set myself a nominal target of 400 different species for the trip along with 100 life ticks.

I was already well over the hundred for lifers but was just shy of my other target with 392 species. As soon as we reached the lakes. I realised that finding eight more birds was going to be a doddle. The place simply thronged with life. I had two life ticks in the first minute. Rufescent Tiger Heron and Limpkin. By the time we had finished our three hour walk I was up to 410 and of the eighteen new ones seven were life ticks.

We spent our last few hours in BA's strolling around the shopping areas and we ate one last steak. I was sad that our adventure had drawn to a close but I knew that Andrea was just itching to get on the plane and return home. We had seen and done so much in our time away and grown to understand each other so much more. It remained to be seen if this new-found tolerance would continue back home but we both hoped it would.

Bed 52. back our own bed

The British Airways jet soared out of Eziza airport across the South Atlantic towards London Heathrow. For the first part of the homeward journey we chatted about the amazing time that we had spent travelling around the world. It was quite difficult to put into words what we had done. Our trip had not been arduous but it had taken us out of our comfort zone. We had learned about different cultures, eaten different food and seen so much. We were proud of ourselves.

We asked other the obvious questions. Which place was best? Where would we like to go again? Which place did we not like? And so on. These discussions passed the time on the flight and before too long night was upon us and Andrea slept while I fidgeted restlessly in my seat for twelve hours.

As luck would have it Sophie was returning to the UK from a trip to the USA and was due to land at Heathrow about an hour after us. She had parked at the Airport and planned to drive us home and spend a couple of days with us before returning to work at hospital. Everything went according to plan and by lunchtime we were settled in our rented summer house in the little village of Sandhurst. The next morning, we were up early and Sophie drove us to collect our car from a friend's house. The short journey to our house, now tenant free took about five minutes but it felt like hours. We parked the cars and strolled up the drive to open the front door and begin the rest of our lives.

I know that I will not be able to settle for a traditional retirement. I hate gardening, have no real interest in domestic things and will find it hard to cope with sitting around. Thankfully, as I write, the cricket season is upon me and the golf course is drying out. Summer I am sure, will be filled with activities to keep me occupied.

I have learned enough to know that another long trip will never be accepted by Andrea but her love of Vietnam and Indonesia may be a starting point for another visit to South East Asia. I have also learned enough to know that to even contemplate bringing up this idea before the house is in a fit shape for Andrea to call home would be idiotic.

Our months on the road taught us a great deal about each other and we have become so much better at relying on one and other and indeed trusting each other's decision-making. We were in very close contact for more than seven months something that during thirty years of marriage we had not done before. Work and bringing up our girls had seen us live fairly separate lives. Travelling however forced us to look after each other. Being at home retired together will present a different set of issues, but I feel we should be better placed to handle them.

Printed in Great Britain
by Amazon